A BOLD MOVE

"We'll ride out now," said The Duster.

"We'll do what?" I cried at him, for the noise of the fire covered our voices.

"Well try to lose ourselves in an excess of light," he said. "They'll spend half a minute admiring the greatness of their work."

Then I looked closely at them and saw, as a matter fact, that all six men in the posse were turned toward the fire, shading their eyes against it, and look-ing up to see the height to which the heads of the flame were tossing.

The Duster, without stopping to argue with us, rode straight out from the marsh and into the open, where the sight of that fire swept us.

Every step that we took I could feel the bullets searching my flesh. The light went through me. It seemed to me that I never had seen horses walk so slowly....

Other *Leisure* books by Max Brand ®:

MAX BRAND®

TWISTED BARS

LEISURE BOOKS NEW YORK CITY

A LEISURE BOOK®

July 2007

Published by special arrangement with Golden West Literary Agency.

Dorchester Publishing Co., Inc.
200 Madison Avenue
New York, NY 10016

ISBN-10: 0-8439-5871-5
ISBN-13: 978-0-8439-5871-3

Visit us on the web at www.dorchesterpub.com.

TWISTED
BARS

TABLE OF CONTENTS

Editor's Note

Throughout his writing career Frederick Faust featured series characters in his contributions to Street & Smith's *Western Story Magazine*. Among his creations are Bull Hunter, Ronicky Doone, James Geraldi, Chip, Speedy, and Reata. In the November 2, 1929 issue of *Western Story*, he introduced another series character: The Duster, nickname of John Penny Thurlow, in "The Duster." Two additional Duster stories appeared that month in the magazine: "Twisted Bars" on November 16 and "The Duster Returns" on November 30. Like Faust's other series characters, The Duster was a young, cunning, and brash outlaw who could outwit any adversary. In this trio of stories, The Duster settles in the Western town of Christmas where he elicits both admiration and fear among the inhabitants. The stories were published under Faust's Max Brand byline and appear here for the first time in paperback with their original texts fully restored.

The Duster

I

When I heard that The Duster had come out of the
mountains, I was working for the Leeman ranch up
in the Kerry Hills, and Bud Towers was with me eating lunch in the cook house when Old Man Weldy
came in and got a handout. He told us about The
Duster coming out into the open, and we all wondered a good deal what mischief he could be up to
now. The odd thing was that The Duster wasn't in
the saddle; he was driving a buggy with a span!
That was what made us all sit up and take notice. We
accused Weldy of lying to us, but he swore that he
had talked to Chick Monroe, and Chick had seen
the outfit with his own eyes, and that it was one of
the slickest turnouts he ever had seen.

Of course, we wondered what could be eating The
Duster to make him take to a buggy. Weldy thought it
was just because he'd found it too easy to get out of
trouble so long as he had a fast horse between his
knees; he said he thought The Duster wanted to liven
things up a little and hand a head start to the other

fellow. But Towers and I both agreed either that The Duster was finally so broken up with bullets that he couldn't sit a saddle any longer, or else that he had gone crazy, for there were 500 men in the country who were so anxious to feed him lead that, if they couldn't do it one by one, they'd gather in gangs to fix him.

Finally I said to Weldy: "But it can't be right. I know Chick, and he was sure stringing you."

"Chick was so particular," vowed Weldy, "that he described everything exact, right down to the horses. They're a pair of bays. The off one has three white stockings, and the near one wears a white star, and has one white stocking, and an old OH brand on her shoulder."

That got me onto my feet. "That's Dolly!" I said.

"Who is Dolly?" asked Towers.

"The best cutting mare that ever stepped," I told him, and what I said was true. "That's what became of her, is it? If The Duster has her, he's going to give her up."

"Are you going to take her away from The Duster?" they asked me, grinning at one another.

But I left them without finishing my second cup of coffee, and rode straight in to the ranch house, where I saw Leeman, and told him where I was going and why. Leeman was as tough an old codger as you ever saw, but I must say he was white to me. He pointed out that I had been with him only a year, but that he'd made a foreman of me and would put me on ahead fast.

"Besides," he said, "a man of your age oughta be ashamed of carrying on with gunmen and worthless crooks like The Duster, no matter whether he's got a hoss of yours or not."

"Leeman," I said, "that mare comes when I call

her, lies down and stands up, can turn on a dime, and dodge a bullet. She can . . ."

"Talk French?" Leeman said. "Go on and get out of here, if that's the way you feel about her, and, when you get tired chasing that white streak across the hills, you come right on back here and I'll boost you ten."

I thanked him mighty sincere. Coming on the way I was, nigher to fifty than to a good time, it was pretty important to get well placed, and it isn't every boss that boosts you ten whole dollars a month. It isn't every boss that boosts you at all, but mostly they pile on more work, and give you all your raise in the title, as if that word foreman could be turned into bread and meat, whiskey and bullets.

I had a good tough roan gelding, a wild-caught mustang with the heart of a rattlesnake and the strength of blasting powder. That brute jolted and jarred and hammered me all the way down from the Kerry Hills until I got to Christmas, but he made good time, although I was watching the scenery through a haze most of the time and finally reached the town clean punch-drunk.

I had figured that The Duster would take in Christmas when he left the mountains, the main reason being that he had spread himself like hot butter over most of the rest of the landscape around our neck of the woods, but he never had called on Christmas. That was a fine town, too, and the sort of a place that would be sure to make the mouth of The Duster water. I mean it had a good bank with a safe that wasn't too new, and it had a couple of pawnshops that dazzled you going by, they were so loaded up in the windows with stick pins and such that unlucky cowpunchers had had to leave behind them. It had a lot of other opportunities, like the till of the Mason & Baxter store. Or if everything else failed, The Duster would be able to pick up a pretty rich poker game at the hotel. For there still were some people who would play with The Duster; professionals, all of them, who did it partly to learn, and partly from pride that kept them from refusing.

I had figured, on account of all these things, that The Duster would be coming over Christmas way, and maybe the reason he was driving a span, instead of riding, was that he wanted more than saddlebags for carrying away the loot.

The first thing I did was to walk into Dick Kenyon's saloon to gather the news. Dick was sure glad to see me. We had done the Klondike together years back, so you can imagine how it was when two old sourdoughs like us got together. He set up a drink and called to his youngest boy to go out and take the horse to the barn.

"You better gather that pony up in a mosquito net before you take him anywhere," I said, "or he'll sure bite you."

"Aw, that's all right," said the boy, as fresh as paint. "I don't think that he'll like the taste."

He went out and started wrangling the pony while I talked to his dad. Dick had a lot to tell me about his family and old friends, but finally he got down to what I wanted to know—The Duster. He told me it was an actual fact—The Duster had been seen by a dozen people at different places, apparently drifting in the general direction of Christmas or thereabouts. He had a grand turnout, with big rubber tires on the wheels, and rubber-mounted harness set off with silver points, and a slick span of horses.

"That's just it," I said. "He's gotta pull that buggy with one horse after I get through with him."

"Are you going to tackle The Duster?" asked Dick, laughing a little.

"I am," I said, and walked out of the saloon, pretty hot because he wouldn't believe me. But I could believe myself.

I don't think it was all on account of Dolly, although she was the most quick and honest-minded horse that I ever saw, but, just on general principles, I was getting too old to put up with robberies. I was getting nervous and mean, I suppose. And I had told two people what I intended to do, so that I couldn't turn around and go back in my tracks. On the other hand, I certainly expected a little more time than I had before running into him.

I had just met Pudge Larkin who owned the bank, or a large part of it, and was president as well. Pudge was the man who gave the place the name of Christmas before even there was a town in the valley. It was so green to his eye when he came through from a desert freighting trip that he gave it that name of Christmas that had stuck to it to this day. Pudge seemed pretty glad to see me; we had done some freighting together before he got rich. And just as I left him, a man came scooting up and said to Pudge: "The Duster is here!"

"The dickens he is! Not in broad daylight! He wouldn't dare!" Pudge exclaimed.

"I seen him with my own eyes," said the other fellow, "and I wouldn't believe it, otherwise, but that I'd seen him. He'll come around this corner inside of half a minute."

That was exactly what he did.

Pudge Larkin asked me to go with him to the

bank and help him stand guard; he said his Sunday watchman wasn't worth a whoop. But I stayed where I was and watched Pudge run off up the street at last, reeling a little from side to side, he'd grown so fat.

My mind was as fixed as fate to step out and stop The Duster, when he came along in the buggy, and claim my stolen horse from him, and, if you think that's pretty desperate, you have to remember that life hadn't been so sweet to me that I hated to give up the taste of the last part of it.

The rumor had flown ahead of The Duster far enough to bring people to windows and doors with a rush. You could hear screens jingling and slamming all around, but I noticed that there were mighty few men lingering around the walks. You couldn't tell what The Duster would do, as a matter of fact. He might even drive down that street and shoot someone in cold blood. He had the nerve for it and self-confidence, and, after having been tried and acquitted five times for robbery and murder, it would have been a wonder if he had not believed in himself.

Where I was standing, I had a good slant up to the corner of the street and across through some vacant lots to the other side of the valley, where the cattle were grazing—all big red Durhams, so fat they fair shone, even at that distance. And now, around the corner and across my view of the other hillside, as you might say, came The Duster.

But when I saw him, no matter how I had heard him described in his new outfit, I couldn't believe my eyes. There was the span of bays to begin with, and the near horse was my own good mare, Dolly, just as I had suspected. However, I didn't step out and stop The Duster. I simply couldn't. My head was too full of what I was seeing.

In the first place, you would have to get into your mind the picture that we usually saw when The Duster went by—that is to say, a handsome young buck togged out in enough color to paint a rainbow clean across the sky, with pearl-handled revolvers showing in the saddle holsters, and a lot of silver and gold work on the saddle and the bridle. His horse was always shod with fire and went on its hind legs by preference, but now all that was changed.

The bays trotted along like Sunday school, so smooth and quiet, and there was a fine rubber-tired rig behind them, bright as water in its new paint, and in the seat there was The Duster all togged up in black clothes, with a white cloth twisted around his neck, so that he looked like a picture of 1840, sort of. And he had yellow chamois gloves on his hands, even on his gun hand! Although I could notice even in a passing glance that the leather of those gloves was hardly thicker than a weevil's skin.

This sight of The Duster fairly staggered me, but that was nothing compared to what I felt when he raised a hand to me and nodded and said: "Good morning, Mister Wye." Which was the first time in fifteen years that I had been called anything but Baldy.

II

That Sunday morning, the town of Christmas had nothing to do except to plait new horsehair bridles, or scrape the sweat-salt off of saddles, or think up new lies for old neighbors, and a few of them went to church. So the town of Christmas, being at leisure, was able to follow The Duster, partly with its eyes and partly by report, and to trace him straight up to the one church in the town. There wasn't much need for that church on Sundays as a matter of fact, because hardly anybody went there. But it was very handy to have a preacher around for weddings and christenings and burials. Besides, the Reverend Kenneth Lamont could make speeches for any old occasion, from a housewarming to the Fourth of July. All he needed was a warning the night before, so that he could pick out a couple of good texts, and then he would sail in and make you the finest sort of a speech just offhand. Words flowed out of that preacher as easy as beer out of a beer keg once the bung is knocked out of it. Besides that, he had a good little herd of cattle worked up, and almost any day you could see one of his tow-headed kids riding barebacked and bare-legged through the town. Their father was pretty hard-boiled, and his kids used to lick everything on two legs that walked the streets of Christmas.

That will give you an idea of the sort of a church that the Reverend Kenneth Lamont ran. It stood on the top of a bald little hill at the east end of the town, and it was a scalped-looking shack itself. It had been built by free labor out of free lumber, and it looked the part. There were about 100 knots as big as your fist that had been knocked in by the kids or by time and weathering, and every one of those holes looked right through the thin sides of that house. When you went inside, which I never had done before that day, you could see the sunlight blinking on both hands.

There were a lot of other people in Christmas who made their first trip to the church that morning along with me, and the reason was that The Duster had gone up there to the top of the hill and hitched his span in the horse shed near the church.

It was just before the service time, and the minister was inside, whanging and banging away at the bell. That hill was so high above the rest of the town that, when the bell rang, according to how the wind was, sometimes it sounded like a mighty fire alarm, and sometimes it was like the honking of a great flock of geese far up in the sky.

When Reverend Kenneth Lamont came out of the church, he saw there was a man hanging around the little graveyard that stood on the south face of the hill, so it could get all the sun. The rain came smashing and crashing there in the winter and washed out gullies between the headstones and undermined some of the stones themselves. Nothing seemed to grow easy and natural in that yard except thistles and cactus, but they did pretty well, and you could always be sure of stepping on some sort of a sticker the minute that you stepped inside the wall of that consecrated ground.

The preacher, when he saw the stranger, went up and hailed him.

"Are you lookin' for a friend?" he said.

"Yes," said the stranger, "I'm looking out a place for him."

"There's a good south corner down there, where grass would grow in a decent summer," said the minister, "and I could maybe fix it for you at a cut rate."

"Business been sort of dull?" said the other.

The minister, when he heard this, stepped around the corner of the stranger and looked him in the face. "The Duster!" he said.

"The same," said The Duster. "How do you do, Mister Lamont?"

"Poor," the minister replied. "I'm doing sort of poorly, because the time has come when nobody much comes to the church except the yeggs and gamblers and confidence men and bank robbers, and such."

"Well, that ought to make excitement," said The Duster. "They ought to bring a few reporters up here, besides. But speaking about that corner lot, I'd like to see it."

Lamont took him down, and they looked at the lot. The shadow of the south wall kept it from a good deal of the sun, so that, as the minister said, some grass could grow here and keep green most of the year round.

That seemed to look good to The Duster, although he pointed out that the view was none too good.

The minister said: "The man that lives there will either be lookin' straight down or straight up, and he won't care about the side views all around."

The Duster admitted that this was right. Then he said that he would buy the plot right off, and asked for a price.

"Who is it for?" the minister asked, "or have you just made a reservation like a good businessman and expect to fill it later?"

"He's already dead," said The Duster.

"And he wanted to lie here?"

"I wouldn't say that. But I figured that this would be a cheap place to put him away."

"My prices," said Lamont, "depend on the customer. There's the stone of Missus Greenway that died last month. She got that spot for nothing at all. And there's Tom Loftus's place over yonder. Well, Tom had to pay seventy-five dollars for a place to lie down and rest."

"It's too much," The Duster said.

"I'll make it seventy flat to you, my friend," said the minister, "if it's the right sort of a man that you want to bring in here."

The Duster laughed a little. "I'll answer for him," he explained, "that he's been all his life one of the best pals and the straightest shooter that I ever saw."

"In that case, we'll be glad to have him. What's his name?"

"Hector Manness," The Duster answered.

"Hey!" the minister blurted. "Manness?"

"Yes."

"The worst scoundrel in seven states!" yelled Lamont. "And a traitor to his friends! How can you call him a straight shooter?"

"Would you like to have taken a chance in front of his gun?" The Duster asked.

"That has nothing to do with the case."

"What difference does it make, though? I'm willing to buy the ground for Hec to sleep in. That ought to end your trouble."

"Did you ever go to a hotel where the rooms were

full?" said the minister. "And were you ever refused while the clerk was still handing out rooms to
others?"

"Yes, I've had that happen to me."

"What did you do then?"

"Well, to make a long story short, I slept in that
hotel, all right."

"And so you'll have your friend sleep in this
graveyard where he isn't wanted?"

"I don't threaten," said The Duster, which was true.

"Don't you? You don't waste time in talk. You just
act, I suppose?"

"You're peevish today," The Duster observed.
"And you won't listen to reason."

"When I hear it, I will," the minister said. "Is it
reason to ask the widows and children and all the
mourners of dead men to take in a murderer to sleep
among them and be buried by the same hands and
voice?"

"The wolf ate chalk," The Duster said, "to change
his voice."

"I don't foller that."

"You will, later on. In the meantime, I have reason
for wanting to bury him here that you would never
guess."

"Perhaps I wouldn't. But I don't want to guess. I
want to simply tell you the facts about where you
stand."

"You're hard," said The Duster.

"But truthful. For eight years I've heard a great
deal about The Duster and his works. I saw you for
the first time five years ago on the Ohio Eastern,
when you held it up."

"I was acquitted of that, however."

"I didn't acquit you," the minister said. "And if I

had had my way, I would have seen you strung up to the highest cottonwood tree around the town."

"You're talking about me, and I'm talking about my partner."

"The money to buy the ground would be tainted."

"This is the price of his horse, that I'm offering to you. He owned his horse."

"I suppose he may have. It isn't merely a matter of tainted money, though . . . it has to do with a corrupt soul asking to come and lie among Christians."

"Heaven forgive you!" The Duster said. "I've had my life saved by poor Hector Manness."

"Are you sure that he was a good man?"

"He was. He never would cheat you at cards out of more than fifty dollars at a time. That was how poor a businessman he was, my friend."

"You can say what you want," remarked the minister. "But if he had been the hardest-headed businessman in the world, he could not be buried here under any circumstances."

"You hit me pretty hard," The Duster said. "I'm begging you to let me bury my poor dead friend in your churchyard."

"I hear you beg, and I laugh," the minister said. "I keep that yard for the honest men and women of this town, and they're not to blush when they see the name of Manness on a headstone." As he said this, he turned on his heel and walked off to the church door.

III

You may gather by this that Lamont was a stern man—and that he was. He came from a hard-headed, hard-handed Highland clan and he knew his own way no matter where he was.

But by this time the congregation was gathering, and it was the biggest that the Presbyterian church on the hill ever had known, including any Christmas or wedding. The whole town was up there. You could even see the little boys trudging along. They had washed their faces as far back as the cheek bones and some of them looked like faces peeking through a hole, but they were all eager to get into that church. Not that they cared a rap about the church or the minister—as a minister—but because they wanted to see the great Duster.

He was a sight to see, all right, as he sat in the back of the church. He looked a little older and calmer than ever, and the minister was in a terrible heat, so that it made you hot even to look at him. Before the crowd came, The Duster had walked up to him and said: "Let's cut this all short, Lamont. I've got to bury the ashes of my friend in that yard, because he begged me to do it when he died."

"I knew Hector Manness for forty years, man and child," said Lamont. "I never knew him to think a good thought or do a good deed, and the request he made of you was no better than the rest of his ways."

You see, Lamont felt that that church and churchyard were the antechamber of heaven itself, which he had to keep clean. He swept the church himself, and washed the windows. He weeded the church-yard, fought the cactus off the graves, and carried on the whole battle by himself, but this was not the sort of a life to make him charitable to professional gamblers, gunmen, man-killers, and sneaks. All Christmas knew how Lamont had spotted Dick Kirby in the church, dead drunk, and thrown him out through the front door. I suppose he wanted to do the same thing with The Duster, but even Lamont was not quite man enough to tackle such a job as that.

When he had made this retort to The Duster, the latter said to him: "Look here, man. You live on short rations. You have a lot of children. How far would five hundred dollars go with you?"

"So far," said the minister, "that it would take me and all my family nearly to the gates of perdition!"

You see how quickly he had taken up the challenge of a bribe, so that there was no chance for The Duster to carry on with his argument and his persuasion.

Matters had gone along like this when the crowd began to arrive and to drift in, eager to see The Duster. And they saw him plainly enough. He had a seat right in the rear corner of the church—I suppose because he wanted his back guarded—and, while he was there, everyone could turn around and take a look at him, sooner or later. The little children whirled right around in their places and gaped and rolled their eyes, in spite of the way their mothers poked at them, but the mothers were there for the same reason and got in their own curious glances from time to time. The men would not be undigni-fied, but they would cough behind their hands, and, pretending to turn to speak to a friend, they would get a whack at The Duster in the midst of it all, and note down the looks of the man who had killed Tex Wycombe, Harry Bister, Lew Morris, and Charlie Young, and run Dick Packard right off the face of the earth. I mean Packard ran to Mexico and never came back.

We all knew that The Duster had done a good many more things than these, but no one knew the whole list of the men he had dropped, or nicked, or laid away for repairs of some sort. We were only sure that he had met these famous gunmen and beaten them all, and I suppose there was not a boy in that church—or hardly a man—who would not rather have had the long and terrible record of The Duster than to be the President of the United States. And so would I.

There was nothing extraordinary about The Duster. He was average size, maybe twenty-five or twenty-seven years old, good-looking in an indistin-guishable sort of way, and rather with the look of a dude about him, especially in these dark, fine clothes that he had on. He had one thing to set him off and that was the strong blue of his eyes, which you would see once and never forget again so long as you lived.

The girls were the ones most apt to notice The Duster, even though he was so quiet. But back there by the wall he sat looking straight before him, or, if an eye crossed him, he was apt to meet it with a faint sort of pathetic smile.

I watched him, I think, a little more carefully than any of the others did, and I was sure that he was working his wits all the time, because it seemed to me that there was just a shade of mist over his eyes, such as thought will put there with the best of men.

I watched him carefully, because I had made up my mind. Having announced my intention a long time before of reclaiming my horse from the gunman, I intended to challenge his right to it immediately after church. In other words, I had maybe an hour of life left in me. And there's nothing like that feeling of the last hour to sharpen your eyes.

This affair of mine had me so excited that I don't remember the ceremony very well, except that there was some praying out loud and some organ music and singing, particularly of a pretty, sandy-haired girl with a pair of soft gray eyes, like bits of blue-gray flannel. She was so sweet and innocent and young that you could look slam at her, exactly as though she were a child, and she would look back at you and give you a bit of a smile in the middle of her singing.

I hooked an elbow into the ribs of the man next to me and he said that was Marguerite Lamont, the daughter of the minister. She was about all the music in the church, and she was enough to be a credit to a good deal larger place than Christmas.

Then along came the sermon, and the minister rolled his eyes a couple of times, got redder and hotter, until it looked as though he had just dipped his face in a basin of water, and then he began in a voice that you could hear through the trembling walls of that shack clear down to the grocery store.

Gosh, what a gasp of whispering went through that church when Lamont finished bellowing his text. He gripped the edges of his little pine reading stand and glared over the rim of his big Bible straight down at The Duster, and everybody had to turn around and stare, so that it made me think of a funnel of curiosity, and hatred, and fury, all poured down into the face of The Duster.

But he merely met all those eyes with his faint smile as though he was troubled by some sort of inside sorrow. His black coat made his face seem pale; he sat up stiff and straight; I never saw a human more perfectly controlled.

He needed more and more of that same control, however, for now the minister was fairly started, and all he did was to make hay out of The Duster. Then he burned the hay. There ought to have been nothing but cinders and a whiff of ash left of the great Duster, I can tell you. For Lamont began at the beginning, drawing a mighty clear picture of the poor and honest workers, piling and putting away a few savings for the sake of their children rather than for themselves, and then he drew a still more vivid picture of the sneaking robber who entered the bank where those savings were kept, and took them away, so that all the honesty of the victims and all their labor went for nothing. They were cast away—they were withered. And how Lamont turned in and withered the robber for that!

It was as good a sermon as I ever heard preached. The best thing about it was that it was turned out improvised, like that, and we all could see the point of it, sitting back there in the shadow of the corner, looking pale and serious.

I think that some of the people half expected that The Duster would pull guns and start blowing daylight into all of us, but I knew him better than that. As I watched him and thought about him, I couldn't help wondering how it was that a single man should be able to inspire so much fear in a whole crowd. If he had pulled out a gun, I'll wager that the entire crowd would have started running like sheep. One frightened mother, as the sermon went along, actually got up and herded her three children out of the church, before the lightning should strike.

But The Duster made no move and gave no sign of trouble coming, and presently the sermon ended. At the last words of it, The Duster stood up in his place, and the whole of that packed-in congregation shrank a bit away from him. I know, because I did part of the shrinking, although I was a good distance away.

But all The Duster did was to say in the most quiet voice in the world: "Do you know me well enough to talk about me as fully as this?"

"I know you," said Lamont, always ready to fight. "I know you as well as I know smoke and fire."

"Do you so much as know my name?" The Duster said.

Very neat and pointed, that was. No, the minister did not know the name, and neither did I.

The Duster said: "I am John Penny Thurlow." After he said that, he turned and walked out of the church.

I can't tell why this made such a great impression upon all of us. Perhaps it was because Lamont himself couldn't fish out some last stinging remark with which to chuck The Duster out of his church. The crook walked off with the honors of the day, it seemed. Not that having two names made him two men, but that his final retort seemed to parry everything that the minister had said. There was a certain amount of dignity about it, too. Because every soul there realized by something in the voice and the manner of The Duster that this name he gave to them was the truth.

It fairly choked Lamont. I thought that the man would die as he hung onto the sides of his reading stand and glowered down at his congregation, and at the door out of which The Duster had just stepped.

I didn't wait for Lamont to catch his breath, but I went out to see The Duster face to face and get back my Dolly mare, or die trying. Besides, although I was a slower man than The Duster and he was bound to sink a bullet into me first, one shot doesn't always kill. And certainly before he fired twice, I would have lead in him.

IV

That was the way I felt when I went up to The Duster in the shed outside the church. He had on his thin chamois gloves again, and he was untying the lead ropes of the span. Mighty neat and fast and slick they looked, and the buggy, since he had given it a wipe, looked as if it were made of glass. That was the way with The Duster: whatever he did was done better than other men could do it, and whatever he had seemed better than all other men's possessions. Those lead ropes, for instance, were good smooth cotton rope, and the top of the neck stall was flattened out, so that there would be no harm done if a horse began to back and plunge while tied. I never had seen an arrangement like that before, and it made me feel pretty inferior to The Duster to begin with.

When he saw me sauntering up, he gave me a salute and a smile, and then he came back and shook hands with me while he gathered the reins and made ready to step into the buggy.

It was Mr. Wye again, as he spoke.

"You must've pretty nigh forgot me, Duster," I told him. "Why the mister?"

"Because I'm tired of nicknames . . . like my own," he said. He waited, holding the reins and looking me in the eye. The glance of some men weighs you down like lead. The Duster was one such.

"Well," I said, "I've got some bad news for you. That near mare you're driving belongs to me."

The Duster glanced at Dolly and then back at me. "Well," he said, "I'm sorry to hear that, but I won't ask for much proof."

I was surprised to hear him say that, and I was terribly happy, too. I went a bit closer and spoke her name. The way she jumped and turned would have done you good to see. Of course she knew me, and she showed it so well that nobody could have doubted.

"I paid four hundred dollars for that mare," said The Duster, biting his lip a little.

I watched him like a hawk, of course. It was true that he seemed on his good behavior, but I wouldn't go by the appearances alone. Every second, I was expecting that hand of his to move like the flick of a snapper on a whip. But it did not move. He was as calm and as slow as could be, but when he named what the mare had cost, I knew he was telling me the truth.

"The fellow who sold that mare to you was a fool, then," I said. "Because she's worth a cold thousand of any man's money, and if you don't believe me, ask any of them that have seen her cutting."

"She's a cutting horse, all right," said The Duster. "I've had a saddle on her, and she nearly twisted herself out from under me the first morning. This mare belongs to you, you say?"

"Have you got a regular bill of sale for her, and all that?"

He shook his head. "The fellow was a thief," he

said, "but usually he works the northern range and sells on the south, so that it's pretty safe to buy from him. However . . . you shall have your Dolly back again, Baldy."

I was glad to hear the nickname from him, but still I was a good deal upset. Men don't give up horses like Dolly without a twinge.

"Come home with me, Baldy," said The Duster, "and then I'll give you the mare."

"That depends on where home is," I told him frankly. For I was expecting some trick from him.

"I've got a shack on the edge of town," he said.

It ended with me getting into the rig with him and driving off through the crowd of people who still were streaming out of the church. Just as the team was breaking into a trot, The Duster pulled them up again. He had stopped beside Marguerite Lamont, and, as she turned her gentle, frightened face toward him, he lifted his hat to her gravely and with dignity.

"Your father seems pretty badly upset about me," he said. "Do you think he'd let me come to see him at his house?"

She had to wait a minute to draw breath. Then: "Of course he would want to see you, Mister Thurlow."

"Thanks. I won't fail to come around." He put on his hat again, and the weight of his glance still was lingering on her face, so, with a little smile, he started the team on once more.

There couldn't have been a more proper way for him to act, but all the while I was worried a lot. I didn't know why. I had the feeling that there was something back in the mind of the gunman, and I hoped that nothing would drop on me—nor on young Marguerite Lamont.

The place that he had was out on the edge of the

town, looking down into the valley and across toward the hills beyond. It didn't amount to much. All the house there was huddled under the arms of a great big oak tree; there was a little barn—a shed, rather—behind the house, along with a couple of acres of corral and pasture surrounded by ragged fencing. The Ridley family had grown up here, and that family could have wrecked a jail as they grew. They would have broken iron, and they frayed the little house, all right. The windmill looked as though it was going to fall down, and the fences had rickets, and the barn stood there with a broken back.

It was a ramshackle place, but it was usable, though I wondered why The Duster wanted a place where his hundred enemies could all come out and find shelter among the trees while they stalked him. However, the trees were the best part of it, in a way. They gave you good shade, and still it was easy to look through openings in them and see the valley on the other side. Farther off, under the same kind of trees, the cattle gathered thick in the heat of the day, flinging their tails and heads all the while to keep the flies off. Everything had a good, lazy, comfortable look, and, for my part, I don't like a dressed-up house and garden. I like clothes you can sit on the ground with, if you want, and all I ask is chairs that don't creak and that don't bust when you tilt them back.

I looked over the shack and the grounds a little with The Duster, because he asked me to go around with him. I told him that it looked pretty all right to me, but not the sort of a place that I would expect him to pick out.

"Why not?" he asked.

"Because you've got enough money to swell around, if you want to."

Nobody ever could be as frank as The Duster, when he wanted to. He felt frank today, and he added: "I couldn't enjoy swelling around in front of a whole town. Everybody that saw me go by would wonder where I stole the money for my house, or my diamond pin. But you like the place well enough for yourself?"

"Yes, it looks right to me."

"Then I'll tell you what you do. You go and drive down to your hotel, pick up your stuff there, and come back here."

I shook my head. "I can't do it."

"You've got to."

"I came here to get this mare. I've got her, and now I'm going back to my own part of the range."

"I thought you knew the whole range?" he said.

"I've rode a part of it," I said. "But I need to get back on the job. I'm not a rich man like you, Duster."

"You're staying here," said The Duster. "Listen to me. I've argued with another man already today, and I'm not going to start arguing again with you. I'll pay you anything you want. You name the price."

"What sort of a job? What doing?"

"Just staying here with me."

"Nothing to do?"

"You can cook, can't you? And you can handle a pair of horses that I'll have?"

"I can do those things. You can guess the kind of cooking that I do."

"I can eat raw, so you're cooking won't bother me. You'll stay?"

"I don't understand this," I came out at him frankly. "We've never known each other well . . . we've never been friends . . . and, besides, it's not likely that you'd enjoy my lingo for very long. I don't follow your drift, Duster."

"It may be that you'll sometimes see strangers loafing around among these trees with guns in their hands. You'd be a scarecrow to keep off birds of that kind," he said. "But most of all, I want you here to give me a good name."

"A what?"

"People know that you're honest, Baldy. No matter who you're with, the people know that you're honest, and it will do me a lot of good to have you along. I'll pay you ten dollars a day."

Big pay any time on the range, but, in those days, it was like rolling in gold. I stared at him until my eyes swelled, but he meant what he said. This made me scratch my head. No matter what sort of a fellow The Duster was, or how mysterious, ten dollars was ten dollars. However, I finally said: "This sounds very well. It's a comfortable sort of a thing to hear that you want me because I'm honest. But I can tell you this . . . I won't take this job unless I know why you're in Christmas."

"What difference does that make?"

"Maybe none at all. But I'm curious."

"You ask a good deal," said The Duster. "You'd better take your mare and go."

He turned on his heel and walked into the house, and I can tell you that this was a good deal of a chill to me. However, I did what he said, but, just as I got the harness off of Dolly, he called to me, and I saw him leaning in the door of the house with one foot crossed over the other.

"Come here, Baldy," he said.

I went up to him and saw he was as grave as ever, although there was a hint of a smile in his eyes.

"You insist on knowing my private business?"

"Yes, if I take the job."

"Well, then, I'll tell you why I'm in Christmas. Go get your things. I'll tell you this evening, because I couldn't put that story into less than an hour's talk."

V

It would take too long to put that story into his own words, the way he told it to me that evening. We sat around in the open under the trees, after finishing supper, and my new boss told me a lot of things about Hector Manness, first of all—about the character of Manness, I mean.

I had seen that fellow myself and always wrote him down a hound and a skunk, with just the courage of a rat that will fight in a corner and poison you when it bites. Manness always would rather run than fight, though they say that before the end of him, he had finished off eleven men. But this was not credited by The Duster, who swore that most lists of a killer's victims were fattened up a good deal, and that Manness had counted for five men, and not a soul more. Five was enough, however, for a ratty cur like Manness.

But it seemed that Manness was something more than a cur, too. That is to say, The Duster swore by him as the best of friends. They had done a hundred jobs together. They had cracked safes, ridden the road, played crooked cards, and, in all the things they had tried in partnership, Manness never had failed to be perfectly square. His crookedness with everyone else may have pleased The Duster all the more. At any rate, he stuck by Manness, and Manness stuck by him, so that they were often together when they had big deals on.

The end of this partnership had come about three months before this time. I'll sketch in what had happened just before. They had framed a good job against an Idaho bank, and it would have worked perfectly if their inside man had not wanted a bigger split. They wouldn't give it, and so he told his employers, and the two of them stepped straight into a trap. They got out, however. They did some shooting to clear their way outside, where they snatched a pair of horses and rode into the hills.

They were followed, of course, but they were making pretty good time when a bullet from the rear struck the horse of The Duster. Not a fatal wound, but the loss of blood was taking the sap out of it fast. When this happened, Manness pulled up and helped fight off the first part of the posse, then in the dark they gave the whole gang the slip, and, going to a ranch, they "borrowed" a pair of fresh horses. They were followed again the next day, and that day a long-range rifle shot struck Manness.

Even then he played the man and said nothing about his wound until they were safely away from the pursuers. Then he was too far gone to be saved. The Duster did what he could, but the life of Manness dwindled and flickered like candle flame in a breeze, and he knew that his partner was close to the end.

"You know, this fellow was a skinny little runt," said The Duster. "He looked dried out, no juice left, nothing but fur and meanness, like a lynx. When he knew that he was going to die, he took a stiff shot of whiskey, lighted a cigarette, and simply waited for the finish. I thought that he was thinking over something to say, but he wasn't. He was simply lying there, looking death in the face and trying to scare it away, you might suppose.

"I sat down beside him. 'Is there anything you want?' I asked him.

" 'A grave,' he said.

"I thought he was joking, naturally.

" 'You'll have a grave fast enough,' I told him.

" 'I mean a real grave in a graveyard,' he said.

" 'Old son,' I said, 'we're a hundred miles from that sort of a thing.'

" 'Christmas,' Manness said, 'is where I'd like to sleep the rest of my life. Life?'

"He put in that last word with a little chuckle. I never thought that he believed in anything, but I was wrong. He believed in life after death. And gradually I got out of him that all his latter days he had always hoped that his burial ground would be the churchyard in Christmas. When I learned that, I told him that I'd see that his ashes, anyway, were buried in Christmas. He laughed in my face, though it nearly snuffed him out to laugh like that.

" 'That minister, Lamont, knows all about me,' he said, 'and he'll never let me be buried there.'

" 'He'll never have to know that it's you,' I said. There poor Manness grew peevish. 'What good would it do me to lie there and have nobody know that I was around? I want to have the smart fellows inside the law come along and say . . . there's Manness, the robber. His grave looks as happy as the next one!' "

I could understand what he meant, though it seemed a funny way of looking at the matter.

" 'If that's what you want, I'll give you my word of honor to put you in Christmas graveyard,' I said.

" 'You can't,' he answered. 'You don't know Lamont.'

" 'He can be scared,' I said.

" 'Not by a herd of buffalo!' he said.

" 'He can be flattered.'

" 'I've never seen anybody succeed.'

" 'He can be bought, then!'

" 'Not even if you could promise him the gift of life.'

" 'I don't believe he's half as hard as you make out,' I told Manness, but he swore that the minister was like a fellow in armor.

"Well, Baldy, to make a short story out of it, the death pain began to hit Manness, and I held onto him while he struggled and shouted, because his nerve gave way a good deal toward the end. His mind went bad, too, and he told me that he was certainly going to wind up in fire unless I could promise him that he would sleep in the Christmas graveyard. What could I do? I simply told him that I would certainly bury him in the Christmas graveyard and put up a monument over the spot where his ashes were planted.

"Now, the minute that I said that, Manness seemed to stop feeling the pain. He lay looking up at the sky like a child listening for a voice, and smiling. He kept hold of one of my hands and a couple of times he said . . . 'My boots are off, Duster.'

"You see he had a horror of dying with them on, the way that most of the gunmen do. It was the prayer of poor old Manness, I think you might say. 'My boots are off!' . . . like that . . . sort of laughing in the depths of his throat.

"Then, just before he died, Baldy, he said something to me. . . ." As he got this far in the story, The Duster slowed up and looked me in the face.

"You're an honest man, Baldy," he said, "and so I can tell you this. Just before the end, Manness gave my hand an extra hard squeeze. I saw that his lips were stirring a bit, and, when I leaned over him close, I heard him say . . .'God bless you, Duster. You make me sure of heaven!' That same instant he died, smiling and happy, if ever I saw happiness."

Here The Duster stopped again and began to walk up and down as though the memory of that death scene stirred him up a good deal. But still I couldn't be at all sure, for he was able to play any part he chose just like an actor on a stage, except that The Duster never had to rehearse. So I watched him carefully, to see if he would flick an eye in my direction, at any time, to discover how his play was affecting me. Yet I wasn't able to detect any flaw in the naturalness of that acting.

Presently The Duster stopped his pacing and said to me: "I've told you the story of how Manness died, and how I came to promise him a place in the Christmas churchyard."

"Why should he pick out that place?" I asked.

"Because it looks down over the river, I suppose," said The Duster.

I could see something in that, because down at the bottom of the hill the yard looked onto the run of Christmas River, morning and evening and night. If you looked at it long enough, it seemed to be moving with every image that fell into it—the hills, the cattle, the trees, the blue head of the sky, the little white puffs of clouds curling at the edges like smoke. Until pretty soon you felt that you were in movement with the stream, and that it was carrying you along under new skies, and all that sort of thing, but keeping you and the hills and the trees and the rest of Christmas all together. I saw that picture, and suddenly I knew that it must have run into the mind of poor dead Hector Manness, so that really he felt in his heart that no matter what his life had been, in his death he could find the gate to heaven if he were put into the graveyard there on the hill. A crazy man's idea, you may think, but I've known people to risk their lives for the sake of rescuing a lucky pin, or some such foolery. At any rate, all at once I was able to understand almost perfectly just how Manness had felt, and I told The Duster so.

He nodded at me and seemed satisfied. "I knew that you had a brain, old fellow," he said, "and this is another proof of it."

I couldn't tell whether he was laughing at me or really patting me on the back. That was often the way with him. If he praised you, he seemed to be laughing at you, too, and, if he laughed at you, he seemed to be praising you. If he got angry, you felt that behind the anger there really might be a great regard for you, and, if he showed the least touch of affection, you kept wondering how much he scorned and despised you. That is to say, you figured out all of these states of mind, until he hypnotized you.

Now he said to me: "I built a funeral pyre for Manness. His horse had gone dead lame. I killed the horse and I piled the wood around him and set the saddle and bridle and rifle and gun and knife and bedroll and slicker and the whole pack of Hector's stuff on the top of the big pile of wood. I worked hard for a whole day heaping up the brush. At last I carried Manness to the top. His eyes were open. He lay and looked at the sky while the flames whistled and roared around him. Then that fire burned out and I took up the ashes of Manness and carried them away with me, and there they are."

With that, he pointed to a little square casket that stood on the table close to the fireplace.

I wish I never had laid eyes on it.

VI

The point of the whole of his visit to Christmas, you can see, was to force the burial of Manness in the Christmas churchyard. He already had tried several tacks with the minister, and he had been baffled each time. Besides, in the conclusion, he had simply upset Lamont and roused the Scotch fury against himself.

He had promised to call on Lamont, and, right after supper that evening, he asked me to harness the horses.

I did that, and rubbed the dust off the buggy, but when I came around and stood at the head of the team, he told me that I had to go with him.

"I want everybody in Christmas to see me parading around with honest old Baldy," he said.

I explained that I wasn't as old as I looked, but he only laughed and wouldn't answer. However, there I was spinning through the alleys and up the main street of Christmas, and looking down at the wrinkling hips of the horses as they stepped out, because Duster let them fly. He had them stretching all the way, but he had them firmly and quietly in his hand, too. He was a good driver. I never hope to see a better.

No one ever told me how Thurlow got his nickname, but I've wondered if it came out of the many times he "knocked the dust out" of other people, or because of the way he used to go foaming along with his horses.

Right through the middle of the town he still kept up the pace, turning the corners so fast that the light wheels skidded with loud tremors, or the whole rig tipped violently. I wondered if The Duster really enjoyed this sort of driving, or if he were showing off to the crowd, for people ran out into the street to see us come and to watch us going.

You couldn't tell by the face of The Duster what he felt. You couldn't tell at all. He never looked sleepy, and he never looked excited, but in the midst of this dash of his through Christmas, he said to me: "Watch that man in the red shirt we just passed on our right."

I turned and saw the man behind a pillar of the verandah in front of Morley's saloon. It seemed to me as though the man were pulling a gun, but, when I swung about and stared at him, he slunk off through the swinging doors of Morley's place.

"He looked like trouble," I told The Duster, "but he changed his mind."

"Well," said The Duster, "I'm not going fast enough to beat a bullet, but I may be traveling fast enough to spoil somebody's aim."

That really put the whole thing in a nutshell. Every instant that he was in Christmas, he was in danger. In increasing danger as his enemies heard where he was, and gathered to nail him. This was so clear that I couldn't believe that he would stay long in the town.

Presently he pulled up at the minister's house, which stood on the far side of the hill on which the church had been built. That little house looked like a suffering, bare man, tied in one place, because it didn't have any cellar, but stood up from the ground on four stilts. I never quite understood how the minister and his books and his two boys and his girl managed to cram themselves into the three rooms of that shack. Of course the boys didn't count much. They were a pair of fourteen-year-old twins made of leather outside and lined with steel inside. You could have chucked them over a clothesline and somehow they would have managed to have a good rest. Besides, in the warm part of the year they camped in a little tent behind the house, where they lived like a pair of Robinson Crusoes—the neighbors being the goats, if you don't mind me saying it.

What kept the minister so poor, and his kids in rags, and his beautiful girl threadbare? Charity, just charity, because that iron face of Lamont went with an open hand, and he never turned hungry people away from his door, and because he brought Christmas to a lot of homes that wouldn't have known what the name meant, except as the title of the town.

Just as we got in front of the minister's house and pulled up, there was a rattle of hoofs and one of the boys came dashing in from the pasture, bareback, on a mustang that was a cross of a wildcat and a thunderbolt.

When the boy saw us—saw The Duster, I mean—he stopped that mustang with a long skid that wound up on two hind legs while the horse punched holes in the air with its forehoofs. That maneuver would have slid nine people out of ten over the tail of the horse, but the boy didn't mind it a bit. He didn't seem to know he was on a horse, but just opened his eyes and his mouth at the great Duster.

We were getting out of the rig, in the meantime,

and The Duster said in his quiet, pleasant voice: "Aren't you Tom Lamont?"

The boy had flashed off the back of his pony by this time. The horse tried to snap his head off, but, without so much as looking aside, this kid took a twist on the jaw of the brute and made it stand quiet as a lamb.

"Yes, sir," he said. "I'm Tom Lamont. But how . . . how could you tell me from my brother, sir?"

It gave me a funny feeling to see that wild young Westerner talking good English, and polite, and throwing in his "sirs" so regularly. But that was the hand of the minister, of course. I looked aside at The Duster, wondering what he could possibly know about the boys, but he said at once: "I knew, of course, what everybody knows . . . that Tom Lamont is the great rider."

The youngster turned as pink as a girl. He was so pleased he could hardly speak. He managed to say: "I'm not much good. But I can't shoot like Billy."

"You can learn," said The Duster.

Tom swallowed twice, with his eyes like saucers. He was fairly shaking with excitement. "I could learn from you, sir," he said.

"Do you think you could?" The Duster said very gently. "Nothing would please me more than to show you whatever I know."

"Do you mean that, sir?" Tom asked.

"I mean it, every word. You can drop around at my place anytime."

That was too much for Tom. He dragged down a great breath; he had to hang onto the reins to keep himself steady, and, as The Duster walked down the path toward the door of the shack, Tom turned and stared after him. No matter what the head of the house thought of The Duster, it was pretty plain that to this lad he was a hero—a regular Alexander the Great.

Perhaps I'm judging by the light of what I knew afterward to be the fact, but even at that moment an idea knocked at my brain, so to speak, and told me that The Duster might try to use his hold on this boy against the minister. It turned my blood cold, that idea. It turns it cold still, even to think.

We were almost to the door when it was snatched open and a burst of song came thrilling at us, and with the song came Marguerite Lamont, and her gray-blue eyes all lighted, her cheeks flushed. She saw us suddenly and stopped with one foot on the ground and the other on the last step. She made a little movement aside, and, if she had been a year younger, I think she would have turned and bolted back into the house. How I wish that she had.

But now The Duster had his hat off, and was bowing to her, and was saying that he hoped it was proper for him to come at this time, and that he trusted she would use her influence with the minister to persuade him to permit The Duster to talk to him. That was the way he carried on, in a low, confidential voice, as though he were talking over a thing in which she had an interest, and as though he looked up to her for advice and guidance in this business.

I had another qualm as I saw her eyes fluttering up to the face of The Duster and back again to the toes of his boots, but I argued myself out of the idea by restating some of the facts of the case. In the first place, The Duster wasn't any beauty. Those keen, strong eyes of his were really like a pair of headlights warning any reasonable human being of danger coming. Besides, he was a known gambler, yegg, and gunman. That very day he had been denounced by Lamont himself in the church. I added up those facts, and for a sum total told myself that she must look on The Duster as a fiend.

As if women ever were logical! The nicer, the prettier, the sweeter they are, the harder they hunt for a good solid chance to throw themselves away and break their hearts.

She managed to say that she was sure her father would see him at once; she would ask. So she went inside, and we could hear the murmur and the fall of her voice. It was a low-pitched, rather throaty voice; you could listen to it with a physical pleasure, quite aside from any music in it.

A rumble answered her. That would be the minister, and a second later we heard a book slammed, the floor trampled, and Lamont came into the doorway. He did not pause there, but like a true fighting man he came straight on down the steps and into the path. His face was red with anger, as it had been in the church, and he glared at The Duster, so that I thought of an old hen ruffling feathers, waving wings, and scolding at a hawk—a hawk that said nothing, mind you, and never would, until it whistled downward to strike. A brave man and a strong man was the minister, but somehow that comparison stuck in my mind. He had better challenge Old Nick than challenge The Duster, because no good man stands a fair chance against a bad one.

"I came to ask if you are willing to talk to me," said The Duster. He had put his hat back on his head when the girl went inside, and now, as he said this, he deliberately took it off again. A mighty clever move, because it was as though he put the minister on a higher plane than himself—as a man of the church, as a wiser man. He put him, in fact, as high as a woman.

A clever move, but it didn't work with old Lamont.

VII

"Have you come here to mock and scorn?" said Lamont in a voice big enough to have scared a congregation of 10,000.

"I've come to you like a sick man to a doctor," said The Duster. "If you will. . . ."

"Sick, sick!" thundered Lamont. "But I know that there's a sickness of yours that only fire can heal, and that fire will purge at last!"

The Duster stirred a little at this, but he kept his head bowed and looked down at the feet of the preacher. Inside the doorway, where she had shrunk, I saw Marguerite standing again, and I knew that she was drinking in everything that was said, and she was marveling, I suppose, at the humility of this famous Duster, come here to swallow abuse.

"I understood," The Duster began, "that there is always time for a man to repent."

"There is always time for a man to be a hypocrite," said the minister, "for the sake of pulling the wool over the eyes of a whole congregation. There is always time for canting, ranting, treachery, and for wolves in sheep's clothing!" He advanced a little as he said this, shaking his fist in the air. "I know you, young man," he said, "and I know no good about you. Heaven forgive those who are led into sin by temptation that they cannot overcome, but you are one of the people whose eyes are open and who select the way of evil because you love evil. You have come into my church to flout me, and you have come to my home to insult me, but I fear you no more than I would fear Satan himself!"

You see that Lamont was proud, which is a dangerous way for a man to be. He had reasons for pride, too. That is to say, he was without fear, he was willing to lay down his life for the sake of the principles that he loved, and all his life he had done nothing but work for the good of others. He saw the right way so clearly that he could not believe there was any proper path in the world for a man to walk except his own way. Well, it's all very well for a man to be confident in his own strength and in his own virtue, but I don't suppose that anybody ought to ask trouble to come up and fight, because trouble is likely to do so. They say out West that there's no horse a man can't ride and no man a horse can't throw. The minute that I heard Lamont talk like this, I knew that he was in to find trouble; I only could not tell from what direction the lightning would strike.

In spite of this outbreak from Lamont, The Duster did not show the slightest temper in return. He kept the same position of humility, with his hat in his hand and his eyes usually fixed on the ground. If he had raised them, even a hot-headed man like the minister would have thought twice, I suppose.

Said the terrible Duster: "Mister Lamont, there is such a thing as Christian charity. I've come here to ask . . ."

"You've come here on a ten-thousand-dollar bet that you'll bury the ashes of Hector Manness in the holy ground on this hill, but I tell you, my man, that you can't pull the wool over my eyes. I thank the Providence who lets me see through your designs. Now, leave this house and never come back!"

"Lamont," The Duster said with wonderful solemnity, "I've come here to bury the ashes of a dead friend. I thought it was a good thing to do . . . and you've whipped me and beaten me with your words. I come crawling back to your feet and ask you to hear me. I've tried to speak to you alone, but you've forced me to humiliate myself in the presence of others . . . your daughter, your son, and my friend, here. You're a hard man, Lamont, and you're whipping my heart as I would not whip a horse."

"I listen to a liar speak," said the minister. "And I see the lie as well as hear it."

"Lamont," said The Duster, "I came here to bury my friend . . . and I also hoped that I could learn a new way of life in Christmas. Are you going to shut the door in my face and keep me back in the other way of living?"

"Bah!" snorted Lamont. "Am I the only minister in the world?"

"You're the only minister in Christmas," The Duster said, and this was so true that, in its very naked simplicity, it seemed to mean something.

Besides, I suddenly wondered if The Duster would be true to what he said. Not that I expected him really to reform, but still one never could be sure about that fellow. I would rather try to follow a teal in flight than to understand the twists and the turnings of John Penny Thurlow, as he called himself.

"I'll have no more words with you," said the minister. "I'll have no more dealings with you, and I'm best pleased if I never lay eyes on you or anything about you, except the news that you've received the reward for your evil in the end. Thurlow, leave my sight!"

The Duster heaved his shoulders once, as though the sigh came out of his heart as he listened to this. Then he said in a low voice: "Heaven forgive you, Lamont."

Of course that was too much. It showed me suddenly that all his attitude of humility had been a fake from the start and that he was only playing a part, but I wondered at such a raw fake in The Duster, who was capable of being such a clever actor that I couldn't see through him at all. Heaven forgive him. That was entirely too much, and I could have laughed at the whole scene, except that I got to figuring the thing out. What The Duster had said and the part he played had not fooled the minister, and it had not fooled me. Then whose eyes was he blinding? Why, the girl and the boy, of course!

Young Tom Lamont was standing by with tears in his eyes at the sight of the humiliation and the agony of this great man. And yonder was the girl in the door of the house. Tears in her eyes! Yes, sir, those tears were actually running down her face, the little simpleton. She had been drawn a shade closer to the door, so that I could see her clearly.

It was on the youngsters, then, that The Duster had tried to make an impression, and he certainly had succeeded, although what he had in mind I couldn't tell. When he got out his "Heaven forgive you," he turned around and put a hand on my arm and walked toward the buggy uncertainly, as though he had been staggered. He went past the boy, who stood by fumbling at his throat, pretty nearly choked with grief, I suppose, and with sympathy, and with pity for the terrible Duster, who had killed so many men, but who could be lashed to the mast and tortured by the words of an unarmed minister of the Gospel.

Well, I didn't do any pitying of The Duster. I only hoped that poor Lamont wouldn't find no ground under his feet one of these days, and I was still hoping that when he booms after me: "Baldy Wye!"

"Aye, sir," I said, turning around.

"Baldy," he said, "there's no man on this range that has a better name than Wye for honesty and straightforwardness and trustworthiness. Are you going to throw all those good qualities away for the high pay given by a ruffian and thief?"

It made me mad. Particularly because I couldn't help feeling that there was something guilty about taking $10 a day in pay, that being more than three times what I was worth to anybody. So out I roared at him: "Lamont, I don't need a preacher to be teaching me the way I want to live and what's right and wrong!"

"Ha?" the preacher shouted with anger.

"I've as good a notion of right and wrong as any minister in the world," I said.

"Hush, hush, Baldy," The Duster said, beside me. And he put a hand on my shoulder, as though he wanted to stop me from talking. The scoundrel! When he could barely fight back the smile from his lips and couldn't begin to keep his delight out of his eyes. "Hush, hush, Baldy," said The Duster, "and don't be letting me poison your life. You're free to leave me, Baldy," he added with another hypocritical sigh, "if I'm doing you a wrong, Baldy."

I wanted to punch him—if it hadn't been like hitting a bear that was set for trouble.

"The heart that holds pride holds evil!" thunders

Lamont. "Baldy Wye, be careful of what you do. No man is old enough to be absolutely sure of himself."

"Confound you!" I yelled back at him, driven pretty furious between him on the one side and my knowledge that I was helping out The Duster on the other—and not wanting to help him at all, mind you—and so I broke out like this: "Keep your tongue to yourself, you danged word-maker . . . you and all the rest of your tribe do more trouble than you do good!"

I thought that Lamont would plain explode at this. He doubled up his fists, and I think that in another minute he would have been at me. And he was able to give me a tough time of it, too.

Now, when this happened, The Duster grabbed me, and he pulled me toward the buggy and turned me around, saying in a very loud voice: "Baldy, Baldy, for heaven's sake remember that you're talking to a minister and a man of God."

Bosh! Think of him talking like that—The Duster! Of course he was delighted that the row had started. It gave him a chance to look like the mildest, most controlled man in the world, and it made Lamont and me look like a pair of fools.

In the midst of all this, Lamont got hold of himself and at least kept from saying any more to me while we climbed into the buggy.

"Baldy, will you drive?" The Duster asked.

I did it, not thinking, blindly. And, by gosh, he used that chance to press a hand across his eyes, and so go off in that way, as though he had been staggered and just about blinded by the terrible scene that he had gone through and all the words that had been thrown at him.

Then I saw that he was suffering. He was fairly quivering with pain from head to foot, and, when I looked at his face, it seemed to me that his eyes were bursting out of his head with some great emotion, and his mouth was pinched and pale with it. That I understood. It nearly killed him to sit there and keep in the laughter that was exploding in him!

VIII

Thinking about how I had been twisted around his finger and used all through this affair, and thinking also what a terrible fool I had made of myself for the benefit of The Duster, I got angrier than I ever had been in my life, and I got back to the Ridley house almost as fast as The Duster had come from it. When we arrived, I said: "I'm through. I quit right here."

"You don't mean it," said The Duster. "You wouldn't turn me down flat, Baldy?"

"I would and I do," I said. "You've got some sort of mischief working in you, and that's the end of it. Whatever your scheme is, I'm not going to help you."

"I didn't ask you to. I ask for your companionship, and that's all, and the support of your honest name, Baldy, which I promise you that I won't taint the least bit."

"Companionship!" I said.

"I'm fond of you, old-timer, and that's a fact," he said.

"They made a grand liar when they made you," I told him.

"Check," said 'The Duster, without hesitation, "but just now I'm telling the truth, partly." He put that in with a smile, and it was sort of an appeal to me, because it made a concession and admitted that he couldn't pull the wool over my eyes all the time.

"What's on your mind about the boy?" I asked him, point-blank.

"I want the kid to help by persuading his father that there's no particular sin in letting what's left of Manness sleep in the cemetery over there."

"And what about the girl?"

"I want her help even more, and for the same thing."

"D'you mean that?" I asked, trying to search his eyes. I might as well have tried to search the bottom of the ocean.

"I mean it," he said.

Well, it was evening, and that's a time when it's hard to hold a grudge out West. I could see the cattle trooping down to the river to drink. It pleased me a good deal to watch them, considering the deserts and the hard ranges I've ridden, where a cow gets a drink about once a week. I watched the green hills and the tree shadows floating down in the rosy and golden water and the meanness went out of me.

Perhaps The Duster saw this, because he went on: "I'll tell you what, Baldy. No man ever needed help more than I need it, trying to go straight."

"Bosh!" I said.

"Let me put it this way, if you won't believe the other thing," he went on. "Has Lamont really a right to keep poor Manness from sleeping where he wants to sleep?" And he pointed to the box that held the ashes.

That was a pretty convincing stroke, because every time that I looked at it, my mind went back to the picture he had drawn of the death of Manness, and that was so pathetic and so real that I could almost see the flames climbing up into the sky. It seemed to me, too, that no matter what Manness had been, there was enough in the friendship between him and The Duster to forgive a good share of his sins. Anyway, he was dead, and, if what some people thought was true, he was getting plenty for his sins in another world. I had to admit that I thought The Duster was right, and that the minister, at any rate, was the last man who ought to help punish a dead man.

"Then," said The Duster, "I want you to promise to stay by me in this job to the end."

"I do promise!" I said. It broke out of me, do you see? I didn't really want to say that, but somehow the words came.

He took me right up before I could change my mind and my words. "Thanks," said The Duster solemnly. "I don't need anything more than that from you, Baldy, because I know you've never broken your word in your life."

That wasn't quite true, but take it by and large, I suppose that I've tried to live up to my word as much as most men. And if you want the truth, I've always been as proud of being called honest as most men are proud of being called brave, or good riders, or any of those things.

"I'm to stay on until you've got the ashes buried, am I?" I said with a growl.

"That's it," answered The Duster, and, even by that dim light, I could see a twinkle in his eyes that made me pretty uneasy. However, the thing that meant more than anything else to me was that the preacher had seemed so much in the wrong.

"Well, I'll go and try to take a turn with Lamont myself," I said.

"Do that," said The Duster, dropping a hand on my shoulder.

I shrugged the hand off. "Confound you, Duster," I said, "the fact is that I about two-thirds disbelieve in everything you tell me. But the other third of you is such a dangerous and amusing rascal that I can't help sort of liking you, and that's the fact."

"Thanks," said The Duster. "I'm grateful for that, old-timer. And if you . . ." He broke off here and jumped sidewise the width of that room, where we were talking. He landed on the floor, face down, with no more sound than a cat would make in jumping off the back of a chair, and I saw the glitter of the revolver that he stretched out before him, pointing toward the door. He had moved just about as fast as I could think, and then I saw a shadow sway into the doorway. . . .

"Stand fast!" said The Duster. "Stand fast, Renney, or I'll blow your head off!"

The shadow of the door swayed back, steadied, and then seemed to lift arms above its head.

"Don't move," went on The Duster, getting up from the floor. He sneaked forward like a cat and pretty soon there he was in the door, poking his gun into the stomach of the shadow. "Light a lamp, Baldy," he called over to me.

I did that, and, when the lamp was lighted, I saw a slim, worn-looking man with his arms rigidly held above his head. He was rigid with fear, all over, and yet there was courage in that face, too. I looked at him again, and then I knew Steve Renney, as good a rider, as wise a head on the trails, and just about as fine a shot as I ever ran into in all my days. He stood there like a man made of paper, expecting to be touched with a match's flame.

"What's it all about, Steve?" I asked.

He didn't even answer me, that's how terribly hard he had concentrated on The Duster. For that matter, I really didn't need an out-and-out answer, for there was hardly a man on the range who didn't know that for five or six years, at the least, Renney had been following The Duster, off and on, and no less than four times he had supplied the evidence against The Duster at trials.

"Now, Renney," said The Duster through his teeth, purring like a cat. "You can talk, now. Say your last words, Renney."

Renney did not smile, but he said quietly: "I know you don't kill . . . when there are witnesses around, Duster. Or unless the other fellow is the attacking agent." He did smile as he finished.

I began to guess that he was not tense with fear so much as with a vast desire to make the most out of this situation.

"You've come sneaking to my door. I should have killed you then, but I was sort of minded to see your face when a gun was in your stomach, old son. I've seen it . . . and it's a picture. But what a simpleton you were, Renney, to be pulled in by the talk I was having, and by the fact that my back was turned to the door. As if I would keep my back turned on any door, Renney, so long as you and half a hundred other hired law dogs are hunting for me." He laughed.

I never heard anything like that laughter of The Duster's, it was so exultant, so beastly savage, with a snarl in it. Ordinarily he was so smooth and gentle that you could only guess at the worst of him, but now the whole picture was suggested under my eyes.

"I don't deny that I wanted to have a quiet look at you, Duster," said Renney. "But the fact is that I ain't so much fool as to come right into your doorway if I hadn't another thing on my mind."

"What's that?" asked The Duster in an impatient sort of way.

"I've been off your trail for some time, Duster," said Renney. "Except where it crossed and tangled up with that of your friend, Manness. He's my meat, now. And I've come to talk to you about him."

"Talk away," said The Duster.

"Alone, Duster."

"This is Baldy. There's nothing you can say to me that I'd keep from Baldy Wye."

The sheriff gave me a look and a nod. "Duster, the only way that I can get Manness is through you, it looks like."

"D'you aim to think that I'll help you?"

"I do. Manness tried to double-cross you only a couple of months ago. Why shouldn't you help me against him now? The first time there's a pinch, Manness will sure fix you, old son."

"Manness will never double-cross me again," said The Duster. "There he is in that box."

The sheriff blinked like an owl.

"Whatever he tried to do," went on The Duster, "he died my friend, Renney. And that's the end. My job is to get permission to bury his bones in the Christmas cemetery."

"How do I know," said Renney, "that Manness really is dead and that those bones aren't a fake?"

The Duster hesitated. "You remember there was a bullet lodged in the thigh of Manness? Then look here!"

He let the sheriff put down his hands, and, crossing to the box, he opened it. It gave me the horrors to see the casual way he did it, but Renney was mighty interested and looked in for quite a while. Then he nodded and stepped back.

"I'm glad that he's gone," he said. "Because he's cost me a good many hundreds of hours, Duster."

"You can pay more attention to me after this," replied The Duster with a sneer. "Now get out of here, Renney. And in the final count, mind you that I've had you with your back against the wall, and let you go."

Renney didn't wait for two invitations. He left at once, backing through the door, and then hurrying off into the thick of the night.

IX

When I look back, it's easy to see that The Duster had planned everything carefully from the beginning, although he contrived to make it all seem casual and by chance.

That same night, the editor of the Christmas *Appeal* came up to interview him, and The Duster did a little talking. Not much, but it was mighty clever.

He said: "Mister Heron, I know why you're here, well enough. But if you ask me about my own life, what am I to say? You don't want me to lie to you and tell you that I've been a good man all my life. And you can't very well expect me to tell you the truth about the shadowy things I've done."

That was frank, and the editor said: "Well, is it true that you're only here to bury the bones of Manness?"

"To the public that's my reason for being here. To you, I'd add something else, confidentially."

It flattered Heron to be talked to like that, because he was a pretty young man. He said at once that he would keep the thing quiet, no matter what happened.

"The fact is that I'm trying to go straight," said The Duster.

It nearly floored Heron. He begged The Duster to let him write that up, because he said it would make a story that would be copied all over the country.

"I don't want you to use it," said The Duster. "I hate a man who fails to keep his promise, and I'm not announcing any reform until I've proved that I can stick to it."

Heron shook hands with him warmly, congratulated him, and swore that The Duster could accomplish anything he set out to do. I felt exactly the same way about it, but I was only two percent sure that he really was interested in reforming himself. From the first I suspected that he was mixed up in some really big crooked scheme, although, of course, I couldn't spot its nature.

Then the editor asked him some typical newspaper questions, such as what was his best job with shooting irons, the most dangerous moment in his life, and all that sort of thing, which The Duster answered patiently, but asked Heron not to print what he said.

Heron promised, but he did not keep his promise. The next morning the paper was out with a big front-page headline about the coming of the great Duster to Christmas, and then it went on to talk about his career, not in quotes, but as though everybody already knew the things that Duster had told him the day before. They did know, in fact, most of the chief heads, but they didn't know the details that made that news story such a success.

The editor, of course, said that a mistake had been made and that, when he gave in the story to the rewrite man, he had handed him by mistake all the notes that he had taken during the interview. However that might be, the story had enough in it to be copied everywhere, and I suppose that there was hardly a journal in the United States that did not carry a few sticks about the life and exploits of The Duster. And everyone wondered, somewhere in their articles, if The Duster really was in Christmas in an attempt to go straight.

That question he only answered to the editor, but to others he maintained a cheerful silence that enabled them to use their imaginations. Undoubtedly the newspaper talk raised The Duster in the minds of the people of Christmas a good deal, because they knew that the whole land was talking about him, and that made everyone feel a shade more important. I felt the same way, for that matter.

The morning after Duster appeared, just as the paper was distributed in the town, he went for a walk with me, avoiding the center of the village because he didn't want to be recognized and pointed out too much.

"Suppose I don't succeed in this job? Suppose I don't manage to stay straight, well, it won't help me a tremendous lot in the old life to have everyone know exactly what my face is like."

"Go straight!" I said. "Any snake in the world can lay a straighter trail than yours."

He only laughed.

We went on that morning around the southern edge of the town and away from the river, where it gets pretty hot in the summer, without much air stirring. That's why land and shacks are cheap in that part of the town, and we soon saw a lot of the old sourdoughs lounging around in their shacks, or sitting in the doorways. For Christmas was always a sort of a dumping ground for the worn-out prospectors, cowpunchers who had lost their nerve, broken-down lumbermen who'd had a touch of the heat in the desert, and all sorts of people who were busted up in life and still had to work some, but who wanted a pleasant place to settle down in. Everyone felt that Christmas was about as pleasant a place as you could find on the range, and therefore the town was filled with people like that.

The Duster recognized some of these fellows. He had a photographic memory that never failed to register everything that came in range of him. He stopped and talked to the ones he knew, and always asked what they were doing and appeared so interested that they told him the facts. One fellow with a squint in one eye and a limp in one leg pulled him aside and told him some wonderful story about a lost mine in the Christmas hills. The Duster gave that old-timer fifty dollars to finish fitting out a pack, but he wouldn't look on that as a grubstake.

"You pay me back after you've got the mine working," he said.

He handed out a couple more slices of money, here and there, because most of these fellows were so broke that they would pretty near have absorbed the gold out of the rocks.

Then, as he walked on with me, he told me to

keep my eyes open and, when I spotted a good fellow in trouble, to let him know.

"What are you going to win by this?" I asked The Duster.

He shook his head at me. "What could I gain except a little pleasure in helping out the poor fellows?" he said. "Baldy, are you always going to doubt me for everything that I do?"

He could be pretty pathetic when he chose, but that didn't bother me.

One thing at least he gained out of his charity to the broken sourdoughs and run-down cowpunchers. There were always a few of them cruising around the Ridley house, after that. No coming over to ask for charity right out, you understand, but just putting themselves to the windward of a chance for a good talk with The Duster.

That habit cost him money, of course. He seemed able to spread out his coin, however. To some people he gave thirty or forty dollars, and those people never came back to ask for more, but they blessed him with their eyes whenever they saw him pass. And to others, he would dole out just a few dollars at a time, sort of stringing them along. In this way, it was no time before "broke town," as the rest of Christmas called the section of shacks, was willing to vote for The Duster on almost any sort of a proposition.

But I think that what he gained, most of all, and what he had planned on most of all, was that same constant cruising of people around the Ridley house. Because those fellows were friendly, and they would have liked nothing so well as to blow to bits any crook or police officer, for that matter, who tried to get into trouble with The Duster. They were such a good guard that after a while I stopped worrying about The Duster's enemies—he had put up such a good strong shield of friends in almost no time.

That was a clever thing in him, any way you look at it. But the way that he handled the upstage townsmen was just as smart. He had known a good many of these people before he had come to the town, but he never would speak to any of them in the street unless they made it clear that they wanted him to. I heard several of those men stop and ask The Duster if he had forgotten them, and he would say something like this, looking at them very gravely: "A fellow doesn't forget a man like you, Smith. But I wasn't sure that you would care to remember me, after the minister publicly disgraced me ... to say nothing of the rest of my reputation."

He didn't whine, mind you, as he said these things, but he spoke so quietly and heartily that nearly every time the other fellow would shake hands with him again, in order to assure him that he was a friend of his and didn't care about the past record of The Duster, and for that matter, maybe The Duster had as good a record as most; as for the minister, he couldn't disgrace such a big man as The Duster—ten ministers like Lamont couldn't disgrace him. For his part, Smith was glad to see The Duster in town, and things would undoubtedly go better with him hereafter, and he trusted that Duster would come to dinner that same night.

But The Duster used to answer that he was mighty honored. Then he would edge the other fellow away a bit and say to him privately and deeply: "I don't want to spend too much time in the houses of honest men, Smith. I don't want to do that until I've stayed here longer, and have tested myself out.

Crime is a poisonous temptation, Smith, and I've got to prove that I'm worthy of conversation with decent men and women before I go about much."

That was just the line for him to take in order to have everybody feel puffed.

"There's something about me that The Duster likes and respects," was what their faces said as they walked away, and I know everyone began to comment on The Duster and say how really modest he was, and confound a man like Lamont who wouldn't let a dog try to swim to shore, and how really strong The Duster was.

Oh, he was strong, all right. He was strong enough to handle them as a cat handles birds. I knew it even when I couldn't see his deceit or the point to be gained by it. I knew it profoundly, and used sometimes to point a finger at him, and see him smile, admitting that I was right.

"However," he used to say, "maybe I can fool you yet."

Maybe he could. I set myself to be as sharp as a needle in probing his ideas and his ways, but, just the same, I couldn't fathom a great deal of The Duster. He was too much for me, as I've said before.

I must not go too far before I tell the results of that interview I had with Lamont on Monday. It had a good deal of bearing on the things that happened afterward. But in speaking of Duster's attitude in general, I ought not to finish before pointing out that whenever anybody mentioned the name of Manness, The Duster didn't complain about the cruelty of Lamont, but he would change his voice, lower his eyes, and start talking about something else, as though he were too much moved by the mere name of his dead friend to endure it.

X

After making the tour of the town that Monday morning, I went straight over to the minister's house and found him working in the vegetable patch with his sleeves rolled over his hairy forearms to the elbow and perspiration streaming down his face. He certainly looked a man just then.

I had ridden Dolly over, and, when he saw me climbing down out of the saddle, he came to me at once and held out his hand. It was a regular paw. I was glad to shake it, but he nearly broke my fingers for me.

"I was an old fool, yesterday," said Lamont. "I want to tell you that I'm sorry, Baldy, and ask you to pardon me for forgetting myself that way."

I slapped him on the shoulder.

"The old friends are the only good friends," I told him. "You don't have to apologize to me. I said a lot more than you did."

"I ordered you away from my house," said Lamont with a grin. "I never meant that, Baldy, and you know it."

"I know it now," I said. "You don't have to think about it any more."

"That hypocritical scoundrel, Thurlow, as he calls himself, got me so angry that I would have raged at my own girl, I suppose."

That wasn't as good as the first part of my reception, but I put it off as well as I could.

"She's a fine, upstanding girl."

"Her? She wouldn't stand up to a mouse," said the minister. "But whatever she is, she's true, may heaven bless her! I'm glad you came over here this morning, Baldy. We can have a talk about the old times and forget these scoundrels like the robber and murderer, Duster."

"I want to talk to you about a worse man than The Duster ever was," I said, seeing that I would have to take the bull by the horns.

He glowered at me for a minute, and then he said: "Are you going to make trouble for me, Baldy?"

"I hope not," I said. "But for old times' sake, I hope that you'll listen to me."

"I'll listen to you from now to the end of the world," he said. "Come into the shade."

We went in under the eaves of the house, and there we stood in the shade, but with no wind touching us, and my shirt beginning to stick to my shoulders, it was so hot. I remember that a cow was bawling somewhere on the edge of the hills and making the whole valley mournful with her tune.

"Who is on your mind?" asked Lamont.

"Manness," I said, and waited for the explosion.

It did not come. Lamont merely nodded and spoke almost as much to himself as to me when he answered: "You see how it is with me, Baldy? I don't even know for sure that the ashes are the ashes of Manness. There's no doctor's certificate. I stand inside of my rights in keeping the man from being buried there. It may seem to you a hard thing to do, but I hate crime and criminals, Baldy. All my life I've been fighting against creatures like Manness and that supervillain, The Duster. Now am I to begin opening the cemetery to them? We have the clean and decent men and women of the town there. Besides, there's no reason why he shouldn't go to any other church, where they're not so particular. You'll have to admit that, Baldy."

"It's because Manness died begging to be buried in that place."

"Did he? I doubt that. I'm not calling you a liar, Baldy, but still I doubt that about Manness dying and begging to be buried in my churchyard or in any other churchyard."

"I've heard The Duster say so, and in a way that I had to believe," I told him.

"I know you believe it, or you wouldn't be saying it to me now. But you're an honest man, Baldy, and you don't know the ways of the wicked people as I do. I've had to study them and fight them all the days of my life."

"The way I look at it," I said, "I don't see what's to be gained by that Duster, even if he does get the bones of his friend buried there on the side of the hill."

"I don't know what he gains exactly, either," said Lamont, "and that's part of the point. If I knew the scoundrel's game, I wouldn't be so afraid of it . . . but one thing I know, and that is that he doesn't mean well, and that he won't fail to get some advantage out of this deal he is making. What advantage, I don't know, but I refuse to make my church a stamping ground for hypocrites and their games."

I was even more convinced by his manner of saying this than by the words themselves, because he put a very great deal of quiet earnestness into his voice, and I knew that he would never be moved except by some great power.

"I wanted to say one thing to you," I said. "Whatever The Duster starts for, he tries for with his whole might, and you have to keep in mind that it's no big loss, except to your pride, if you let him bury Manness in the churchyard."

That seemed to move him a great deal, for he sighed and struck a fist against his wrinkled forehead.

"Aye, pride, pride is the sin that troubles me most, Baldy. Heaven forgive me for it. I was on the verge of going to ask the forgiveness of The Duster openly before the public, and I would do that . . . not for my decision against him, but for the excess of my words against him, do you see?"

I could see. He was ashamed of himself, and he wanted to make some amends to The Duster, although he wouldn't change his decision.

"But now," Lamont said, "you can take him the message for me . . . and . . . and"—he went on with an effort—"you can repeat it in just as public a place as you want."

"I wouldn't have the shaming of you, man," I said, "for the sake of one like The Duster. Certainly not. But I'll tell him privately what you have to say."

"Your way will be the best way," said Lamont. "Is it true that you're working for him?"

"Aye, it's true."

He was about to make a sharp answer, but then he controlled himself, and simply said: "Whatever you do will be all right for yourself and others, Baldy. You're a man I trust."

I knew that was a good deal from him, considering what had gone before, and I thanked him from my heart. Still, I was badly troubled, because I could see that there were stormy times ahead, what with the strange determination of The Duster to get those ashes buried in the accepted ground of the church cemetery, and what with Lamont's resolution against it. They were both strong. Indeed, Lamont was a regular bull. But a tiger will kill a bull.

I was about to go back to the Ridley house, when Lamont called out: "Hey, Margie, Margie!"

Marguerite came hurrying to the back door and looked out at us, and smiled at me.

"Give Baldy one of those loganberry pies," he said. She went to get it, and Lamont said: "You can tell The Duster that it won't poison him, anyway."

That was the sacrifice that Lamont made to atone for his rudeness to The Duster, and somehow it made me sad, for I could guess that, if The Duster ever had him at an advantage, there would be no mercy in those cold, bright eyes of his.

She brought the pie out in the tin, wrapped with brown paper and a string to hold it by. It would be better warmed up, but cold with milk it would be good, too, she told me.

"The Duster is mighty fond of pies," I said, and looked straight at her.

Well, it made me feel pretty sick to see her wince a little and flush. I glanced aside at her father, but, although he was staring full at her, I could see that there was so much love in his eyes that he would notice nothing.

So I went off back to the Ridley house, and, as I came close to it, I heard a sound of firing behind the place.

The Duster is wild at last! I told myself. And I got out my old .44 and went ramping out behind the house to hunt up the mischief among the trees, although what side I was to be on I did not quite know. You can see what a mixed state of mind I was in.

But there I saw on the far side of the oaks young Tom Lamont standing off with a revolver in his hand, and The Duster beside him, telling him how to handle the gun. No better teacher in the world, I suppose.

They had a broad blaze on a tree for a target, and just now Tommy let fly and must have hit the target, for The Duster said: "That's enough. You've dropped him this time."

And Tommy grinned as though he had heard a voice from heaven.

I heard The Duster go on: "A sure shot is worth two of your fast ones. The fast gunfighter plows up the floor and breaks the windows and the ceiling, but he's not likely to bring down his man. The fellow who starts by being sure can get the speed by degrees. It's no good being lightning-fast if you can't hit your target. Now you, Tommy, are going to be the sure kind, before I'm through with you."

"Am I?" Tommy said, worshipping the great Duster with his eyes.

"Of course you are. You've got a natural talent, and I'm going to bring it out. In a week it'll be a terrible fool who tries to bully you, Tom."

Tom took a breath that made his chest stick out like a pouter pigeon's. "You're mighty kind to me, sir," said Tommy.

The Duster dropped a hand on the boy's shoulder. "I've had enough experience in the world to tell a man when I see one," he said. "You're a man already, Tommy, and, when you get your size, you'll be a man and a half. That's sure."

They came back slowly toward the house, and, as they came, The Duster began to sing softly:

I'll sing you a song of Billy the Kid;
I'll sing of the desperate things he did;

'Way out in New Mexico, long, long ago,
When a man's only law was his own forty-fo'.

When Billy the Kid was a very young lad,
In old Silver City he went to the bad,
Right out on the street with a gun in his hand,
At the age of twelve years,
when he killed his first man.

So they went on toward the house, with the hand of Duster still on Tom's shoulder, and the song of The Duster trailing back to me among the trees.

I knew that the mischief was up, but what could I do?

XI

The boy went right on home, and, when he had left the Ridley house, I went on into it and saw The Duster sitting in a far corner of the room with his chin on one fist, while he looked at the distance. He started when he saw me and asked me what had been the result of my interview with old Lamont. I told him briefly what had happened and that Lamont had made friends with me but had persisted in a bitter hatred of him and all his ways and kind.

"Very tough old fellow," said The Duster in answer to me. "We're going to have a war that will be worth watching. Who will win, Baldy?"

"You'll never down him without murdering him," I told The Duster, "even if you turn his own children against him."

He drummed the tips of his fingers rapidly together and looked at me thoughtfully above them. "Tut, tut, Baldy," he said. "You ought not to make me a creature with cloven hoofs, and all. Leave something human to me."

I couldn't answer that. I merely snorted and pointed to the pie that Lamont had sent by way of amends to the gunman. You never could tell what would strike The Duster most hard. He got up and went to the pie. He leaned over it and breathed the fragrance of the berries and the baking.

"Beautiful Marguerite made it," I said pretty dryly.

"She picked the berries, most likely," he said. "She picked the berries while the sun poured over her, scalding her shoulders . . . in the dust and the thorns she picked the berries while the wasps rose into her frightened face, Baldy, eh?"

"Oh, rot," I said. I was interested, nevertheless, because it was a new mood to see him in.

"Then she carried the bucket of berries back to the house and hulled away the green stems that still clung here and there. She hulled them away and washed the dust from her berries, and tossed them a bit in the air, not hard enough to bruise the big, tender, wine-filled grains, but enough to let the air pass through and dry them. She couldn't succeed altogether, however. Some stain remained around the cuticle of the nails.

"With those stained hands, Baldy, now you see her mix the dough for the pie crust. Nothing is more difficult to do well. The shortening must be put in it in sufficient quantities . . . but not enough, say, to leave a horrible sense of lard in your mouth after you've eaten a bite. But the shortening is worked in, and the crust is rolled out. Now she greases the bottom of the pie tin, now she spreads the thin bottom layer. Now she packs in the berries closely, not stewing them first, but in great thick layers she spreads them, and mixes with them a few herbs known only to her . . . or perhaps gathered by her from some ancient family tradition . . . what would you say to that, Baldy?"

"I say I never heard such rot," I said. "What are you leading to?"

He went on without heeding me: "She puts in the layers of berries and the layers of spiced sugar, alternately. She builds up the body of the pie to a huge pile that threatens to overflow the edges of the tin . . . and then she adds the top layer of the crust, a differently tempered and flavored crust is this. See where she dimpled it down to the edges of the tin with her own small and careful fingers, and here she cut the air holes, so that the seething mass of berries will be able to breathe.

"The oven, in the meantime, is made furiously hot. The reek of heat passes through the kitchen, and, opening the door of the oven, with the great pie poised, she feels a blast-like flame, invisible, burning against her knees and pouring up the sleeves of her dress. However, into that furnace she thrusts the pie that she has made with such tender care.

"She stands back, thoughtfully, aware of what is happening. She knows that the layers of sugar are being drenched by the juice of the berries, and the rich liquid then is melting and boiling. She knows that the burned spices rise in vapor, part of them escape by the vents to perfume the oven, the stove, the room, the house, and even the road beside it, but some of the fragrance will remain in the pie itself.

"At last she opens the door at exactly the appointed hour. There sits the pie. It is turned to gold, and it is marked with crimson, for the juice of the berries has boiled and risen in steam and raged and burst upward through the vents, and here it has issued in a forceful little stream that has leaked down the side of the pie plate . . . do you see it? . . . and become burned to a crisp."

"Oh, dang it," I said, half bored and half curious.

"But at last," went on The Duster, picking up the pie and beginning to walk back and forth with it, "but at last the work is completed, and the priestess bears across the room the cooked pie, with clouds of steam and the aroma of cooked loganberries and spices steaming behind her . . . like a pagan princess, Baldy, offering up some mysterious sacrifice. . . ."

"Duster, I'm getting scared," I told him. "Are you clean daffy?"

"Inspired, and so a little crazy," said The Duster. "But see what this girl has done, this tender, innocent, charming, obedient, lovely, graceful, young, timid Marguerite has done? She has taken life . . . she has gathered it in her hands . . . she has made of it a sacrifice to please the other gods, the stern, brutal, cruel, avaricious gods, the men, in other words. And to one of them she has finally sent the sacrifice and now he holds it in his hands. . . ."

"Duster," I said, "she sent you one of six pies that she just made out of canned berries, and she sent it because her dad wanted her to!"

"Is that so?" replied The Duster. "However, who can tell what was in her mind when she sent it, and gave it into the hands of the honest, true, valiant, and faithful Baldy Wye?"

"Well, let's have a piece," I said.

"You can eat it," answered The Duster, "because

I'm not able to. Loganberries always give me indigestion."

It wasn't until later in the day that I was able to see that he had broken out into the tirade all because he wanted to cover up the effect of what I had said about his turning the children against their father. Right then I should have left The Duster. But how could I? The ten dollars a day, I would like to say, were not in my mind. As a matter of fact, they were, because this was the easiest and the best-paid job that I ever had had. However, more than the money I was interested in the show and in wondering what that fellow would do next.

Nothing happened for two or three days, except visits from Tommy Lamont, now and then.

It was only two days after the first lesson that Tommy came crashing into the house and yelled out to me—because The Duster wasn't there—that day he and his brother, the natural shot, had been shooting at a mark, and that he had beaten Bill all hollow.

It was a great day for Tommy. He was so full of it that he had to talk, and he told me that it was as though The Duster had been there beside him, quieting him, helping to steady the barrel of the gun. Every time he thought of The Duster, he knew that he would win, and he did. He shot the very heart out of the target, and out of Bill, also, it seemed. For the latter was so furiously jealous that he could not believe his eyes. Bill, up to that point, had been one half a degree bigger, tougher, stronger, more capable than Tommy, but The Duster had turned the scale in favor of the rider. To settle the matter, Bill had started a fight, of which they'd had at least a thousand in the preceding years, with Bill always the victor, except for that time when Tommy dropped a pumpkin on him from the second-story window.

But on this day, when Billy led with a smashing right, Tom ducked just as The Duster showed him how to do, and half blindly smote up and over. He was aware of the flash of his own fist darting like a swallow home over the shoulder of his brother, and then the punch whanged on Bill's jaw and sat him down with a thump. He got up again, bewildered and furious. But again he went down before the same uncanny hook. That had ended the battle.

"The Duster did it! The Duster did it! He could do anything!" said Tommy.

"How about Bill?" I asked. "Will he get over being upset like that?"

"I don't care. Aw, sure he will," said the boy. "Why shouldn't he? He licked me a thousand times. Why shouldn't I lick him once?"

Well, that was easily answered, but there was no good in answering it to that youngster. He was too sure of what was right and wrong—and all that was right was The Duster.

I put in a good deal about this scene, so that you can see how close the boy felt himself to Thurlow, and then you can understand better the meaning of what happened a couple of nights later when it had turned so chilly with a wind off the snows that we closed the door.

A tap came at that door and, when I opened it, in stepped Tommy Lamont. He had a bundle over his shoulder and a rifle in his hand.

"Hullo, Tommy," I said, "been hunting?"

"No," he said, "I'm just starting."

"For what?" I said.

"A job," said Tommy. He looked across at The Duster as steadily as could be. "You'll hear from others, so I came to tell you the straight of it, sir. My father heard that I'd been coming over here, and he forbade me ever to come near you again. I told him he didn't have a right to keep me away from . . . from . . . you!" He was on fire as he said this. "So I came to say good bye, Mister Thurlow."

The Duster looked down to the floor and I couldn't tell whether he was in thought or simply covering a smile. If it was the second thing, he ought to burn in fire for ten million years. At last he said: "Tommy, I'm sorry that you have had this trouble with your father, but I'm going to ask you to do something for me. Go out and rough it and do some hunting or whatever you please for two days, and then come back to me, will you?"

"Yes, sir," said the boy. "I'll do whatever you say."

"Good night, then," said The Duster, "before your father catches up with you."

The youngster flashed a smile at him, waved a hand at me, and ducked out through the door.

Fourteen, and in the hands of The Duster! It made my head spin.

XII

The next day at about noon we got the news of the hold-up of the Emmet stage. We saw the news, you might better say, because we were both down in the plaza, as the Christmasites called the little central square of the town, when the stage came rumbling in. It had picked up half a dozen riders along the road and they swept along in a vanguard, knocking up a lot of dust, and doing no good, and making a lot of noise, but all feeling pretty important, because they had got in on the main picture and could share in the excitement.

Tom Logan was one of those riders, and, when he pulled up pretty close to me, I asked him what it was all about.

He pretended to be perfectly cool and pretty much bored with everything, which is the way that your true Westerner likes to seem when there is action in the air. But Tom couldn't fool me. I could see the cigarette paper twitch in his fingers as he made a clumsy smoke.

"Nothing wrong," said Tom. "Only the stage has just been stuck up, Lefty Gainor is killed, and fifteen thousand dollars stole. Outside that, everything's just as per usual."

The people were piling out of the coach now. The driver was down off his seat, and giving orders and directions and advice in a very important way, and the job that he superintended was the carrying of Gainor out of the coach.

Lefty was a guard on that run, and for six or seven years he had sat on the driver's box with a riot gun at his hand. He had fired that riot gun, too. Three times, and no less, people had tried to stop the stage, and three times the riot gun of Lefty Gainor reached them and knocked the ambition right out of their hides. Brick Harper was one of those would-be robbers, and Brick had been left dead on the road's edge with a shocking lot of lead in his face and his brain. After that, there was no more trouble along that run, because the crooks felt that Lefty was bad business to interfere with. He was, too.

I was sorry to hear that he was killed, and, as a matter of fact, he was not. He had a bullet through the body, though, and the people that carried him didn't say a word. They didn't tell him to buck up, or that this would turn out all right, and they didn't say any other of the fool things that we usually do say in such times. All they did was to step slowly and softly, and give each other directions with looks and nods.

By that I knew that Lefty wasn't dead, but badly done for, and half an hour later the doctor sent out word that Gainor might die in ten minutes, or might live out a natural life. It was a gamble. The doctor didn't know on which side to bet, but he inclined toward a quick death. That was enough for us. When a doctor in a small town gives up as much hope as that, the thing looks finished.

We had the details of the crime by this time. It seems that the stage had just crossed from the Emmet onto the south fork road. It was over the first bridge on the Christmas run, and just as Chris Porter, the driver, slammed the brakes off with a jangle and sent his whiplash singing over the backs of his horses, a small man stepped out from the bushes on the right-hand side of the road and leveled a rifle at Chris and Gainor. He called out in a sort of muffled, deep bass voice for them to stop the coach and throw up their hands.

They did neither. Gainor jerked up the barrel of his riot gun for a snap shot, and Porter urged the horses ahead. But as he shouted to the team, he heard the shotgun roar and the rifle clang, and poor Gainor slid out of his place and onto the footboard of the driver's seat. That discouraged Porter a good deal. As he explained afterward, it would have been all right if his hands hadn't been filled with whip and reins. As it was, he simply had to jam on the brakes and stop the coach with a jar.

There were four men and two women inside of that coach, and men with women to watch them perform usually make a pretty good fighting lot. However, for some seconds the men inside had been listening to the groaning of Gainor and seeing red drip down. So when the robber ordered the lot of them to step out of the coach, they certainly stepped in order.

They had a good look at the bandit. He was small, and he had over his head a piece of red cloth with big eyeholes cut in it. It was the right kind of a mask to keep a man from being identified, because it covered his whole head, hair and all, right down to the chest. There was only one thing, in addition to his height, that would help to spot him. He was about five feet, three inches tall, and looked pretty slight. Also, his voice, which was very deep, was husky and thick, as if he had a cold. His hands were small, too, and very brown. But that didn't mean much, because most hands are brown in the West.

He was business-like and cool as you please. He told the two women to look after Gainor's wound, and, if they hadn't known something about first aid, Gainor would have bled to death in ten minutes. After that, he went down the line of passengers and fanned them for watches and wallets, and finally he had the pay box of the Christmas Lumbering & Development Company tumbled out and told the stage to drive on at once.

It was a pretty good haul. There were $12,000 in the box, and the wallets, watches, and the rest of the loot totaled up about $3,000 more. Porter drove the stage ahead, and they made good time into Christmas, you can bet, with poor Gainor groaning at every bump.

No matter how good an impression The Duster had made since he came to the town, and no matter how his description differed from that of the bandit, I must say that a lot of eyes looked pretty glumly at him after this robbery. But he had an alibi as big as a mountain, for plenty of people had seen him right in the main street of Christmas at the moment when the robbery was taking place.

He went on home, while I waited downstairs to hear what had happened to Lefty. A crowd of 100 people watched the little bulletins that were put out in front of the Gregory General Merchandise Store, where Lefty had been bedded down in a back room, and where they didn't dare to move him for a while.

Half an hour after the examination, it was announced that Lefty was sure to die, and, then ten minutes later, somebody came out and said he still had a chance, and would everyone keep quiet.

It was like watching a horse race. I never was at a more exciting thing than that.

A little after that, a sheet of paper was tacked up on the door of the store. It said that Lefty was now doing pretty well, sleeping under the influence of a narcotic, and people were requested to use back streets and alleys the rest of that day so that Lefty might have some peace. It was a sight to see the boots and shoes tiptoeing by that bulletin and every man reading the words for himself—if he knew how to read. Then the crowd stood about in little groups talking about the good character of Lefty—a thing they never had discovered before—and how a big posse ought to be organized to comb the country for the crook.

Then Jim Gregory, a white man if ever there was one, came out and announced in a low voice that the store would be closed that day and each day thereafter until Lefty was pronounced out of danger. Everyone nodded and smiled at Jim and swore that the store wouldn't lose any trade by this self-sacrifice. But I never noticed that good deeds pulled in trade as much as the price marks that show in a store window.

In the meantime, the posse was organized, and I was asked to join. But I could not see things that way. I had served on three posses before. I was with the gang that cornered the Finch brothers and Digger Smith, down in the Pecos, and I've had a scar and a lame hip ever since. It was Digger who potted me while I was trying to be a brave hero and make a name for myself.

Now that poor Lefty seemed in better shape, I went home to bring the news to The Duster, and I was surprised by the interest that he showed. He wanted to know every detail of the reports, and he nodded and walked up and down the room a good deal while he listened. In two minutes, I knew that The Duster did have something to do with that robbery, and that his share in it didn't please him a lot. However, I wasn't prepared for what was to come just after this.

I remember that I had raked together a lunch, and we were sitting down late to pone, and cold baked ham, and canned tomatoes, and plenty of coffee, when I heard the clicking of a trotting horse in the street, and looked out the door in tine to see Marguerite Lamont dismount.

She came up to the door almost at a run, and,

when I called to her to come in and mentioned her name, The Duster jerked his head a little and took on the look of a wolf that has been bitten to the bone.

He got up slowly and took about half a minute turning around to her, although it was he she had come to see, and not me at all, as you might surmise.

She busted out: "They're gone out . . . thirty armed men, and they're hunting for him, Mister Thurlow!"

"For whom? The robber?" said The Duster pretty blandly. "Is he a friend of yours?"

"Why, he's poor little Tommy, of course," she said.

Whang! What a jolt that was to me. The Duster acted pretty surprised, too, but somehow I could tell that he wasn't. He had guessed already, and that was why he had been so worried about the robbery and the condition of Lefty Gainor.

"Tommy? Tommy? Little Tommy, your brother?" said The Duster.

"When they talked about his size, and then about his big, husky voice, then I knew. Oh, Mister Thurlow, he's always wanted to be a man, and he's played at grown man so often, with just that voice. I knew at once, and Billy guessed, too. And my father is sure, and is half mad!"

"Did he send you?" asked The Duster, with an odd little ring in his voice.

"He knew that I was coming here," said the girl. She went up close to The Duster, with her hands clasped to her breast. "We'll work all our lives to pay back the money. And Mister Gainor will live, if praying can save him . . . but save Tommy, poor Tommy, dear little Tommy! No one but you can find him and bring him home."

XIII

The Duster took the girl back to her horse and helped her into the saddle, and then I saw him take one of her hands in both of his and look straight up into her face with those gleaming eyes of his. He said: "I'll never rest, day or night, until I've found Tommy and brought him back to you, Marguerite."

Actor? Why, he was one of the best. The way that he said her name would have parted thunderclouds and brought the sun right slam through. She smiled back at him and tried to thank him, but she was choked and crying, and The Duster stepped back and let her ride away with the mottlings of shadow and sunlight sweeping over her.

For my part, when I thought of how he had trained the boy to shoot and had talked up the wild life to him a lot more than I had heard, no doubt, of course it made me despise him pretty much, and I was on the very verge of leaving him and the job altogether. Then there was a good deal of sham in his talk to the girl, and sentimentality in the air. Still, I felt sure that he did mean part of what he said. He meant it at least enough to be certain that he would do as he promised: stay with the work until he had brought in Tom Lamont. That was a good deal—that was the important point.

When he came back into the house, he took a piece of paper and began to sketch on it, asking me about distances from point to point, and for two whole hours he went ahead making and correcting a map of all the district around Christmas.

I knew that this had something to do with his hunt for the boy, although I wondered why he would waste so much time. However, even when he had finished his map, he kept on figuring over it, back and forth, until I said: "Are you going to wait until tomorrow night for him to come back to you?"

"He hasn't a chance of keeping away from them till tomorrow night," said The Duster. "I've got to go out and find him. Will you come along?"

I was surprised that he wanted me—a man as smart as The Duster on the trail.

"I'll go along," I said, "but I'm not wearing a gun."

The Duster merely smiled. "We're not going to cut our way through, or shoot our way out," he said.

Under those terms we started, just after the full heat of the afternoon was ended. I rode Dolly, of course, and he took the other bay, and he headed straight-away toward the upper valley of the Christmas River, where the marshes stretched more than a mile across.

"He'd have to ride by full daylight up the valley to get there," I pointed out to The Duster.

"Kids always take the longest chance, if they are left to their own wits," he said.

He seemed so sure that I didn't argue, and we jogged the slopes and cantered the levels until we were on the outer border of the marsh.

There The Duster began to cut for sign. I found a set of hoof prints myself, but, a quarter of a mile inside the woods, I found the horse itself; it was a wild two-year-old with a shaggy coat and no saddle marks. I came back and saw The Duster sitting his horse in the shadow of a group of poplars and making a cigarette.

He was blowing out smoke and watching the rising wind snatch at it when I came up to him.

"I underestimated him," said The Duster frankly. "I knew there was mischief in him when he said good bye to me the other night, and I almost called him back and gave him a lecture, but then I remembered that he was only fourteen and I thought that camping out alone would be enough excitement for him."

"You used to sing a song to him," I pointed out, "about Billy the Kid killing a man when he was twelve."

He looked keenly aside at me, but did not answer this remark, and I had a pleasant and rather scared feeling that I had cut even The Duster pretty deeply.

"We'll never find anything by this light," I said— for it was sundown, and the west all golden fire.

"I've found the trail already," he said.

"The dickens you have!" I gasped at him. "How do you know?"

"Because it goes straight into the woods and dives through deep water, like a man who wanted to get into the shadows as quickly as he could."

"Then why are you waiting?"

"Until he's sure that we can't follow him very easily. If we come up on him by surprise, all right. If not, he's apt to drill us. He knows how to shoot."

He said that last with a grim touch of satisfaction that I admired. And there he sat and finished his cigarette while the sun dropped lower and the sky turned from gold to red. A blue jay flew out of the woods and flashed over our heads.

"That means mischief," said The Duster thoughtfully.

I stared at his serious, raised face. I wouldn't have

thought that The Duster, of all the men in the world, had the least touch of superstition in him, but then you never can tell about the fighters. Men who have taken their lives in their hands many times begin to get some funny ideas.

Then he led the way into the woods. I could see the trail clearly, as it cut into the soft soil, and we worked along gradually. The Duster went first. I was willing to try that place of danger myself, but I must say that he was generous and forced me to keep behind him.

The instant that we were well into the willows, the air was ten shades darker than it had been outside, but still we could see fairly well by the reflected, rosy light from the sky. The only trouble was that it already was pretty hard to tell solid scum from solid soil, but we kept on at a steady pace.

Finally the trail turned to the right and seemed to be following a ridge of good honest ground. The Duster stopped there and tethered his horse. I did the same without being told, and we went on again, with The Duster still leading. I knew he thought that he was close to the quarry by the way in which he paused, now and then. And the light was so very dim that he was continually on his hands and knees, examining, and even using his fingers to touch the sign.

We went through a stretch of naked stumps and into bigger trees again, when The Duster stopped me by raising his hand. It was almost as though he wanted me to listen to the chorus of the frogs, or enjoy the perfume of the steaming marsh water, which seemed to grow thicker and mistier in the first cool of the night. Then a horse snorted in the thicket, and the last half of that snort was stifled, as though a hand had grabbed the pony by the nostrils.

It was a jumpy moment. If The Duster was right,

that horse belonged to young Tom Lamont, and no matter how young he might be, he had proved that he knew how to shoot to kill. However, The Duster did not hesitate. He went straight into that thicket like a snake into long grass. I admired him a good deal for it. The most I could do was to get up my nerve to follow in his steps, right behind him. I don't think that he made so much as a whisper on his way through the brush, but I'm equally sure that I did.

However, presently I saw the gloom of the thick foliage thin out, and then I heard The Duster's voice saying suddenly: "Here are friends for you, Tommy."

Right with the last word, a gun exploded, and a voice cried out.

"Tommy!" I shouted, too sick to be afraid any more. "What have you done?" And I rushed straight out into a little clearing.

I could see Tommy standing at the side and the long glance of the rifle he had used. "I don't know! I don't know!" he said. "Did I hit you, Mister Wye?"

"You've killed The Duster," I said.

"The Duster! The Duster," said Tommy, dropping the rifle, and in a voice I don't want to hear again.

But at that, The Duster himself stepped out of the brush into the clearing, saying in a cool, daylight tone: "That was a good snap shot, Tommy, but never drop your gun till you've seen the white of the bear's dead eyes."

"You're not touched?" said Tommy, running toward him. "I didn't hit you, sir?"

"Not a bit. Still, it was a good quick shot."

"I thought I'd killed you!" said Tommy. "I thought . . . I thought . . ." His voice stopped. There was a queer sound—rather a pulse than a sound—and I knew that poor little Tommy was sobbing and shutting his teeth and his lips over that sign of feminine weakness.

The Duster was really wonderful, then. He kept right on talking, quite loudly and cheerfully, and remarked that we'd better be getting out of there, because night air in marshes made sure fever. He picked up the fallen rifle, too.

Then Tommy got his breath and gasped: "What about Lefty?"

"He's sleeping, and going to get well."

"Oh, thank God!" said the boy. "I didn't dream . . . I mean, you know what you said about a steady hand and a steady gun, and a deep voice paralyzing people like the look of a snake paralyzes birds . . . and somehow I never dreamed . . . and it was only a joke . . . and then he fired. I saw his gun move, and somehow the rifle suddenly went off . . . then I put the rest of it through because I thought . . . I've killed a man, and I might as well do all the rest. I went through it like a dream. And . . . oh, Mister Thurlow, are they gonna put me in prison for the rest of my life?"

He had got to The Duster, then, and was hanging onto him, and I heard The Duster say in a voice so gentle and low that I could hardly make it out: "Look here, Tommy, why do you think that I'm here?"

"To help me, sir, I hope."

"I'm here to help you, Tommy. And I'm going to put all of this right. You're going to be gotten out clean. You have the loot?"

"Yes."

"We'll return it all. Give it to me."

That was like a tap on the shoulder to me. I said to myself: *He's done all this for the sake of stealing the stolen money.*

XIV

We did not waste much time in the marsh, for the good reason that the longer we remained there, the more apt were the searchers to come on our traces. We got back to our horses and took the boy with us straight along the back trail on the same line that he had used in getting into the marsh. This was easier than hunting for another way, because the tracks of three horses marked this course even in the dull twilight, to which the day had come, but it would have been very hard even for a Duster to find another way out of the problem.

On the way we learned why the youngster had gone into the marsh. Once he had finished the robbery, he knew that the safest thing for him to do was to run for it as fast as he could leg it into the higher hills, and there live quietly for a couple of months, then gradually, with a different horse, drift away north or south and try to get across the border. But he remembered his promise to come back to The Duster at the end of the second day, and so he determined to hide somewhere near to Christmas. All of this, it appeared, had been worked out by The Duster, which was the reason that he had headed straight for the marsh after examining his own map of the lay of the land.

It was nearly dark when we came to the edge of the marsh again, but the outer trees loomed up a little blacker and starker against a faint rim of light on the western horizon, and it was by that light that we saw the danger ahead of us. Just as we reached the verge of the marsh, we saw a light flickering in an uncertain way over the ground ahead of us, and, a moment later, we could make out half a dozen riders following a man who went on foot, unhooding a dark lantern to read the sign.

I heard The Duster laugh softly. "A bullet through that lantern would be like stealing the one eye of the three witches," he said. "But they're already close enough to the marsh to guess what's in here."

If they went into the marsh itself, we could easily give them the slip, so we drew off a little distance to the right, and stopped there when they were so close that we were afraid they might hear the noise of the horses splashing in the water of the marsh.

Of course our hope was that they would follow the sign straight into the trees, and then we could slide back down the valley toward Christmas. But when they came close to the woods, they stopped. They were near enough for us to hear their voices in the moments when the wind allowed. It was blowing a gale, but only in puffs, and in one of the intermissions, I heard one of the posse say that, if they ventured in, they probably could get the skunk.

The voice of Sheriff Renney himself answered: "I wouldn't care to come at him in the dark like that. We'll wait for the daylight."

"You ain't afraid, Renney?" said the other.

He must have been a fool, asking that question of Renney, but the sheriff answered up very well. He said: "I'm always afraid when I come within gunshot of a crook. Besides, I shouldn't be surprised if The Duster himself is in there."

"Good gosh!" exclaimed the other, all his courage snatched away from him at once. "The Duster?"

"Exactly," Renney said. "I don't know, but I feel in my bones that The Duster had a hand in it."

"It couldn't have been The Duster himself. He was seen in Christmas at that time."

"It might have been a companion or a pupil," said the sheriff. "He's lost his old partner, and he ain't a man to do all the dirty work without help. Maybe he's trainin' up somebody to take the place of Manness."

I heard a gulped breath, and saw the head of the boy turn toward The Duster. He himself was not stirred by the words of the sheriff, but merely stuck out his chin a little more, as it seemed to me. The talking had not ended, and you can imagine that we were pretty near sick with excitement.

"Maybe he is," agreed another man in the posse. "But what makes you so sure that The Duster had a hand in this job?"

"Because it's the kind of thing that The Duster always does. Most great crooks do old crimes in new ways. But he uses the old ways and makes them new by salting 'em down with nerve. He's got the coolest nerve that ever held a gun, and this gent that stuck up the Emmet stage certainly used The Duster idea. There was six armed men in that stage, and only one robber takes on the job, steps out into the road, drops hard-boiled Lefty Gainor, and strings the rest of 'em out of the stage."

"It does sound like The Duster," said someone. "And think that I shook hands with him myself this morning."

"You won't die of leprosy on account of that," said the sheriff very dryly. "But this job either was done by a fellow coached by The Duster and tryin' out his nerve, or else it was done by some dang' young fool that never realized an instant the chances he was takin'."

You can lay your money that I was beginning to respect that Renney more than I ever had before.

"Shall we go on in?" asks another.

"We'll stay out here," said Renney firmly.

"Man, by morning they'll be a hundred miles away!"

"I don't think they will. I telegraphed to Emmet before I started for the marsh. They'll send down enough men to ring the other side of the marsh, and I'll have twenty more men in a few minutes to guard this section. Get a fire together, some of you boys, will you? And make it a big one. I want to send a signal back to Christmas."

Straightway they began to gather brush for a fire and soon had a huge heap of it together.

"Suppose that the crook or crooks see the flame?" someone asked Renney.

"He's apt to crawl out toward the edge of the marsh and see the cause of the fire," said the sheriff, "and, when he does that, he's pretty sure to turn around and try to break off on the far side of the willows. That will run him into the arms of the Emmet men."

"So that they'll get the credit?"

"We're not here riding for glory," said Renney. "We're trying to keep the law strong and clean."

I never had heard the law spoken of like that before, and it gave me a new idea. But when I heard Renney speak, it suddenly was pretty clear to me that there was another angle on the law, and that Renney must be right. You can tell truth when you hear it, almost like a light. In the meantime, I was getting more and more scared. A good man to have on the side of the law, that fellow Renney, but mighty bad when he was chasing you. That was the way that I felt, at least.

While the men were gathering the rest of the brushwood for the fire, The Duster spoke to us quietly: "That man Renney has grown a new set of brains. He's worked so long on Manness and me that he's grown intelligent."

He said it coldly, without any emotion, but in spite of the fact that Renney had numbers and position against us, I all at once felt sorry for him and would not have bet on his life for any odds you could offer. I think that Tommy felt rather a chill, listening to The Duster, also. For all the time he never turned his head away from his teacher whose lesson had produced all this excitement.

"What are we going to do?" I asked The Duster. "Go back into the marsh and try the other side?"

"And run into those Emmet men the sheriff has just been talking about?" answered The Duster. "I think not."

"Then what?" I insisted, because I was beginning to feel weak.

"Maybe we can see a way out by the firelight," was all he would answer.

He got off his horse then and kneeled in the mud, and seemed to be staring at the skyline that ran rippling over the hills toward Christmas and down into the flat of the valley.

"There are two lumps of horsemen rolling in already," said The Duster. "One up in the valley, and another straight down from Christmas."

He got back just as the match was set to the pile of brush. It set up a smoldering, softly crackling flame for a time, until it had generated enough heat to make the small green twigs explode in fire. Then waves of flame washed up into the air with a great crackling and snapping and hissing of sap.

"We'll ride out now," said The Duster.

"We'll do what?" I cried at him, for the noise of the fire covered our voices.

"We'll try to lose ourselves in an excess of light," he said. "They'll spend half a minute admiring the greatness of their work."

Then I looked closely at them and saw, as a matter of fact, that every man of the six was turned toward the fire, shading his eyes against it, and looking up to see the height to which the heads of the flame were tossing.

The Duster, without stopping to argue with us, rode straight out from the marsh and into the open, where the light of that fire swept us—like bullets, I could almost say.

The boy followed his leader blindly, and I could not stay behind to be picked up the sheriff's net, so I sent Dolly out into the open with about as good a will as I would have had in throwing myself over a precipice.

Even now, I can't believe that The Duster had the nerve to try this scheme. It was madness. Then suddenly I remembered what Renney had said about The Duster using old ways with a new courage. He did not even trot his horse, but walked it straight out into that sea of light. And I could not help remembering with a selfish satisfaction that all the loot was lodged in the saddlebags of The Duster.

Every step that we took I could feel the bullets searching my flesh. The light went through me. It seemed to me that I never had seen horses walk so slowly. They lifted up their hoofs as if they were walking in mud and appeared to be resting between steps. But we got on. The light grew dimmer. I could look back, after a time—I mean, I gathered enough courage for that rearward glance, and the posse had scattered back from the fire, here and there. I felt sure that one or two of them were looking straight toward us, and waited for the alarm cry and the shot. But I suppose that they were blinded, as The Duster had said, by excess of light. For presently we were trotting smoothly away, and not a soul followed.

XV

We got back to the Ridley house.

Approaching it from the barn, after we had put up our horses, was one of the hardest things that I ever did—for after what the sheriff had said on the verge of the marsh, I would not have been surprised if the dark of that house had blossomed with gunfire. However, we got safely inside the door.

I grabbed the arm of The Duster. "Duster," I said, "for heaven's sake put that money and stuff away! Bury it!"

He merely laughed a little. "This belongs to Tommy, not to me," he said.

"I don't want it!" Tommy said, rasping with emotion. "I won't have it, Duster. I want you to take it and do whatever you wish with it."

"Tut, tut," said The Duster, and lit a lamp.

On the wall of the room he hung up the saddlebags that had the loot in them. They looked to me like dynamite that might explode any minute and send us all to kingdom come. The Duster began to talk to the boy.

"What's before you, Tommy?" he said.

"I don't know," answered Tommy, who still looked white and sick and had to keep moistening his lips before he spoke.

"And what do you think?"

"If you don't mind, sir, I wish that you would think for me, just now."

The Duster stopped and clasped his hands before him and looked up at the ceiling with a frown. "That's a duty one friend has to another," he said.

I could have snarled out loud as I listened to the hypocrite and watched his pose.

But it went down with the boy. I could see him swallow the bunk like good food. He blessed The Duster with his eyes.

"Will you do exactly what I tell you?" asked The Duster.

"Yes, sir . . . even if it's to jump off a cliff."

"It's not that, but I want your solemn promise."

"You have it, sir."

"Then go home to your father."

Tommy rose out of his chair as if a big, hard hand had him by the nape of the neck. "Yes, sir," was all he said.

But still I did not hope. I wouldn't trust The Duster around the corner—not for a single second.

"You'll go straight home," went on The Duster, "and you'll go in and wake your father up."

"Yes, sir," said the boy, his voice very small and weak.

"And you'll beg him to take you back."

"I'd rather die," said Tommy. "And it would be denying you, sir."

"I have your promise?" The Duster said, cold as iron.

Tommy choked, and then nodded.

"Start brushing that dry sand and slime off your clothes and your boots."

Tommy obeyed. His lip was trembling, and he was green with anticipated humiliation.

"When you wake up your father, wake up your sister, too, and your brother."

Tommy leaned back against the wall, his eyes half closed. "Bill, too?" he said in a dying voice.

"Line them up," said The Duster, "and tell them word for word what you did and why you did it."

"To throw blame on you? I never would do that!"

"You'll do what I tell you. Tell everything that you had in your mind . . . about guns, and shooting, and perhaps there was a little remembering about Billy the Kid?"

Tom's face grew very hot and red, but the touch of shame seemed to give him more strength to stand up to the hard things before him.

"When you've told your story from the beginning to the end, I want you to beg your father to forgive you and take you back home, because you've decided that you want to be a good boy, and hope that he will start running your life again."

The thought of this made the boy bite his lip.

"Then," said The Duster, "I want you to turn to your sister and ask her to forgive you and promise . . ."

"Dear old Margie," said Tommy, with tears in his eyes, "it won't need any asking of her."

At this, The Duster made a strange pause, and looked straight at the boy as though he were seeing a ghost. Finally he recovered himself with a small sigh. "After that," he continued, "you'll turn to your brother Bill and you'll tell him that you realize that you've brought shame on the family and a smudge upon his name, and you hope that he'll forgive you, too."

"I'll punch his nose if he doesn't," said the boy.

"Remember," said The Duster, and lifted a lean forefinger.

Tommy sighed and nodded. "I'll do everything you say," he said.

"After you've finished," The Duster went on, "you'll say good bye to them all, and beg them to remember you, and start for the door, telling them that you're going to give yourself up to the law and confess everything that you've done, as the son of a minister ought to do."

"Jail!" gasped Tommy. "Jail for life, sir."

"Not a bit. Gainor's alive. They wouldn't give you more than five or six years in a reform school. And I'd manage to see you all the time, Tommy. Remember. You've had your fling. You've nearly taken a man's life. And now you have to pay for it."

The eyes of Tommy rolled upward, as a doubt, I suppose, appeared for the first time in his mind. But finally he took a big breath—big enough for a man—and nodded, and gasped out: "I'll do that. I'll . . . I'll go and wake Father up and tell him everything."

"Good," said The Duster. "That's the way I like to hear you talk."

"They'll want the money, sir?" the youngster said faintly.

"They'll find it here with me. Suppose you carried that money to them, and you were robbed on the way? They'd think you had hidden it."

Tommy shuddered at the mere thought.

"I'll do everything that you say, sir," he said. His

eyes brightened. "You're right. I need to be punished. I won't be a baby about it, either."

He went to The Duster and took one hand in both of his and looked up to him with worship, as nobody, man or child or woman, ever looked at me, or ever looked at you, either, most likely. Then, not finding any right words to say, he got out of the house and we heard him running down the path.

When we were alone, I gave The Duster the first blast by saying: "So you're turning him over to the law, Duster? You're gonna ruin the rest of his life for him, are you?"

The Duster merely laughed at me. "Baldy," he told me, "you make me feel like an old, old man. I want to say 'my child' and pat you on the head when I speak to you. It's plain that you don't understand anything that I've done in this little affair."

"I don't understand, except that you've turned that fine kid into a jailbird."

"Nonsense," said The Duster, laughing again. "Rub your eyes and wake up, will you?"

I blinked at him. Then suddenly I realized that I was a fool to try to follow the turns and the twists of such a brain as his. Already he had done things that night that I never would have dreamed of. And recently I'd seen him doing a pretty fair man-size miracle in the way that he had changed the opinion of the town of Christmas. When he came there, he had the name of a regular wolf, a killer. But now he was about the best-liked man in the town, by a lot of the people, and he was winning respect on all sides. He had excited everyone by this great game of his about going straight.

So I said no more, and The Duster began to walk

with a quick, light stride up and down the room, sometimes pausing and laughing a little to himself, and sometimes clapping me on the shoulder as he went by, as though inviting me to enjoy the joke that I didn't understand. I never saw him so happy or so excited.

"Let me tell you the finest thing in the world," he said, "and that's to bring a horse to the water and to make him drink."

"What do you mean?" I asked.

"You'll see in a few minutes," said The Duster. "Recantation, recantation is what I'm after." He laughed again, with that part in his laughter that I had heard there before and that usually gave me a nightmare the night after. I looked at him as at a strange sort of a monster. I never saw such mind power, if you follow my drift, in any man. It frightened me a good deal, but, also, I could not take my eyes or my ears from him. He was always a few jumps ahead of me, and that made it all the more interesting. Besides, I'd grown to like him.

No matter how he was to others, he was always fair and friendly with me, and gave me a good chance, and never sneered at me, no matter how often he might laugh. I knew that he would make the hardest enemy in the world, and I also guessed that he might make one of the best friends.

In the midst of his pacing he stopped short, listened a moment, and then scooped up a paper and sat down. I saw that he was only pretending to read and really fighting back a smile all the time, but I didn't guess why until I heard footsteps coming down the path—with his cat's ears he must have spotted them long before me—and then into the doorway came glimmering two figures, and dissolved in the lamplight into—who do you think?

Why, you've guessed it before me, I suppose.

It was the minister and Tommy, his son.

XVI

Old Lamont looked tired and worn; Tommy looked as grim and hard as iron. The Duster went to them as smooth and affable as you please. He could have a slick, kind manner when he liked. He said he was glad to see them; he wanted them to sit down.

"I won't sit down, Thurlow," said the minister, overlooking the hand which The Duster held out to him. "But I've come to ask you for help."

"Help?" said The Duster, and I could see that he was pretending a lot of surprise that he didn't feel. "Help, Mister Lamont? I don't believe that you would come to me for help."

Rage, weakness, and defeat came up in the face of the good minister. I was mighty sorry for him. There never was a better, simpler, truer, more honest man in the world than Lamont, in spite of his hot temper. But he was helpless with such a man as The Duster to handle him.

"I've come on account of Tommy," said Lamont slowly, and then looked at me.

"I'll leave," I said.

"No," said Lamont slowly. "You know everything already. And it helps me to have you here, Baldy. You're an honest man." He said that bitterly, and then went on: "I've had the whole story from Tommy. How you took him in and were . . . a friend to him. And then how this . . . robbery . . . and shooting . . . took place. And how you got him out of the marsh." He paused, and involuntarily admiration showed in his eyes. Then he continued: "Finally he has come to us and spoken exactly as you told him to speak. In the end, about punishment for his crime."

The teeth of old Lamont clicked. I almost thought he would throw himself at The Duster. But, of course, he didn't. People always manage to control their tempers when they're with tigers that are outside of a cage.

"In that," went on Lamont, "I see a great deal of justice. He should be punished. But when I consider that he will be marred and smudged with guilt all the rest of his days, I wonder if the punishment is not too hard for a child of fourteen? A child, Thurlow." He had to stop a little to control himself, which he did very well, going on: "A boy who never has given me one real moment of worry . . . until, shortly after . . . you came to Christmas."

"Are you blaming him?" cried out Tommy in a loud voice.

His father looked down at him and sighed. "I'm not blaming him," he said. "Not altogether. But now, Thurlow, my boy tells me that he insists on giving himself up to the law . . . which is throwing his life away. He must do it, because you told him to."

"No, no," Tommy said bravely, "but because he showed me it was the right thing to do."

"Thurlow," said Lamont, "you have more power over my own son than I have. I've brought him here to beg you to try to change his mind."

The Duster made a long pause, and in that pause

he looked straight into the face of Lamont, and Lamont met that glance for a moment, but finally dropped his eyes and his head, also. It was rather like a nod of assent.

Then The Duster spoke at last, saying: "Tom won't need any convincing. He's simply forgotten that, of course, a boy's first duty is to obey his father."

We all looked at Tommy, but he looked only at The Duster with the wildest pair of eyes you ever saw as he swallowed that idea and saw an escape from that horrible ordeal of the prison.

"As for punishment," went on The Duster, "if Tom went back to you and confessed and put his pride in his pocket, I suppose that he did about as well as any man could ask. That might be called punishment enough for a lad of Tom's pride. Do you agree, Lamont?"

"I do," Lamont said.

"Do you mean it, sir?" Tommy said.

"Of course, I do," The Duster said.

Tommy fairly groaned with relief. "Then I'll do just what you say, Father," he said.

"Go home," said Lamont. "I'll see you in the morning when you get up."

Tommy stopped long enough to give The Duster one brilliant smile of love and thanks, and then scooted.

It left the minister and The Duster together, and it hurt me to see the suffering in the face of the good man and the cruel triumph in the face of the crook.

"Thanks for staying," said The Duster. "I wanted to go back to the first talk we had together by the church. About the grave, you know, for Manness. At that time, it seemed that you didn't have a price, Lamont. You were one of those fellows a lot too proud to let their hands be soiled. Perhaps you've changed a little, since?"

Lamont closed his eyes and endured.

The Duster went to the wall and took down the two saddlebags. For the first time I saw what he intended doing, and it took my breath. "The fifteen thousand is in these bags," he said. "And an extra thousand besides, so that poor Lefty Gainor will get something big enough to make him wish to be shot twice a year. Enough, in fact, to keep him drunk for a month, once he gets well." He laughed a little as he said this, and went on: "Now, concerning the price of that grave plot for poor Manness . . . here is what I bid. This sixteen thousand, Lamont. And then the return of your boy to you. And the keeping of him out of jail. And his submission all around to you on every point . . . except perhaps one." His eyes were crueler than ever as he said this. It was plain on what point Lamont would never be able to control Tommy until death put an end to the career of The Duster.

"I'm offering this big price, Lamont, and in exchange you can give me the grave that you refused to Manness. And you can take your pride like a sheep and sacrifice it on the altar of a good deed, eh? That's a good, ministerial thing to do, I'd say."

I watched Lamont turn toward the door. Then he took two quick steps and I almost thought that he would go straight out. He turned, however.

"If I don't take that money to return to the rightful owners . . . then you keep it for yourself, Thurlow?"

"Exactly . . . with great enjoyment, old fellow."

The minister went straight up and picked up the treasure, but he looked as though he were lifting rattlesnakes by the rattling tails. He turned fair toward The Duster. "You've beaten me, Duster," he said.

"You've beaten me fairly and squarely, and on a point where I didn't dream that even angels could make me give way. But you have done it, and I congratulate you. Next Sunday I shall retract in church everything that I said against you. The day following you shall have the grave plot." He passed a hand across his forehead. "You struck me through my children, Duster," he said. "But I have been proud and I deserved the blow. I had been proud," said Lamont slowly again. "May heaven be merciful to me, a sinner."

With that, he turned and walked out the door, and with a good, steady step.

But as I watched his square shoulders and his fine gray head, I wondered if the fight were over, or barely beginning.

The end of The Duster's coming to Christmas was achieved, however, and the ashes of Hector Manness were to sleep in the hillside, watching Christmas River forever.

Twisted Bars

I

On the day of the burial every person in Christmas, I suppose, was out there to see the burial of Hector Manness, with the exception of the minister—you couldn't very well expect him to appear at such an affair, seeing the way that the burial plot had been dragged out of him by The Duster—and there were two or three people in Christmas who had suffered at the hands of Manness directly and in person. Well, naturally they wouldn't do him the satisfaction of appearing to make a bigger crowd at his burial. But everybody else went, knowing that Manness had been one of the worst and biggest crooks in the world, but mighty anxious to see the show that The Duster would stage for his dead friend.

He had a lot of great plans, too, but he found difficulty in carrying them out. In the first place, he had wanted to arrange for eight pallbearers to carry the casket of ashes and bones on a sort of fancy stretcher all the way from the house where he and I were living up to the churchyard. But he couldn't get eight men together. In fact, he couldn't get one—of a decent sort of man, I mean to say. He asked me to be one, but although I had a sort of sympathy for the way The Duster was taking care of the funeral of his old partner in crime, and although I really wanted to please him, I said: "Look here, Duster, being a pallbearer is a sort of a way of showing that you admired the dead man. Well, I don't admire Manness, and I never did. That's all."

He got a little angry at that, although I must say that he rarely lost his temper with me. He answered, with a pinching of his mouth that generally meant trouble. "You mean because Manness was a crook? Well, Baldy, I've been a crook myself, and the whole world knows it. I've been tried five times, for everything from shooting to highway robbery and safecracking. The jury disagreed . . . bless 'em . . . every time. But every time the whole world knew I was guilty. Still, you're not ashamed to work for me and live with me."

That was putting it up to me pretty straight, but I said: "You've been a crook, old-timer, and maybe you're a crook now. I don't know. But I do know that you've never been a sneaking, yellow crook, like Manness. You've done your shooting from in front and given your man a chance to fill his hand. Manness would rather get his man from behind. Indian style was his style. You've been a crooked gambler, too, like Manness. But he prefers to take on the tenderfeet and the greenhorns and the poor drunk cattlemen, and you've always used your tricks against the other professionals like yourself. Manness has cracked safes, and so have you, but if you busted the safe of the Kendrick First National, the way they say you did, it's also true that you gave back thousands of dollars through the mail to the poor folks with small accounts. They say that was how you were traced after that job, and they also say that was why the jury hung. Now, Manness never could have done a thing like that. He would rather've given up his blood than his stolen money, and you know it. Duster," I said, "for my part, I'd rather carry the dust and bones of a coyote to the grave than the ashes and the bones of a Hector Manness."

Well, everybody else refused The Duster in the same way, and he couldn't get the eight men together to carry that casket. He was a good deal upset by this, but he managed another way. He made a two-man show of it. One man was Hector Manness—the ashes of him, I mean, in the casket—and the other man was himself. This is what he did.

He let people know that the funeral would start from the Ridley house where we were living, and you can bet that a crowd gathered. They saw The Duster come out all dressed in black, just the way he was when he first came into Christmas town, with highly polished shop-made boots, and no spurs on them, and a white cloth wrapped around his neck like a stock. But he didn't have on a hat, in spite of the high, hot sun, and the pale face of The Duster flashed in the bright light. So did his eyes flash, too, but in a different way.

Out in front of the house there was a black horse standing that The Duster had hired for the day. He was a regular circus horse, and the blackest that I ever saw. He didn't have a white splash on his forehead, or a white hair on any stocking, but he was simply shining coal-black all over, and The Duster had rubbed him down with hard twists of hay until he glistened like glass.

He had a cinch around him and a small sort of pack saddle on, but this was so covered with flowers that you couldn't hardly tell what it was. Those flowers, The Duster and I had spent a lot of time picking and a lot more time making into wreaths. We had plaited flowers into the mane and into the long tail of the black horse, and we had wreathed the neck of the horse with them and worked them in to his bridle and along the check reins that kept his head down and his neck arched high. It was a sight to see that horse, and, when the wind touched him, he fluttered and rippled all over with color and beauty like a meadow in April. I'll tell you what The Duster had done. He even had burnished the hoofs of that horse with some kind of yellow gilding, so that it looked like he was walking on golden feet.

Well, out toward this horse went The Duster, bareheaded, as I was saying, as though out of respect to his dead friend, and carrying between his hands the casket, all covered with flowers, too. He put this casket on top of the horse, and fastened it to the saddle, and then we started off for the cemetery, with the whole town following us. Besides the town, there were people who had come in from the range all around, and from some of the other crossroads villages, and more than you ever would believe had come clear over from Emmet, fifty miles away. Such a crowd had hardly been seen in Christmas since the time of the Dorgan trials, the old people told me.

This crowd streamed along behind The Duster while he walked slowly along at the head of the horse, and the horse followed him. That beat me, to see that fool of a horse following The Duster, because, three days before, that horse would sooner have eaten you than followed you, but The Duster had taught him the lesson in that short time so well that the black gelding went along just a pace behind him all the way up Christmas Hill until we came to the gate of the cemetery.

Lamont was not there. The way he had resisted the burial of such a scoundrel and ruffian as Manness in his cemetery, you couldn't expect him to be present now at the burial services to do honor to a man he despised, and had a right to despise. The Christmas newspaper, which had doubled its circulation keeping track of the doings of The Duster since he had come to the town, said that the minister had gracefully given way to the force of public opinion, but I knew better—I and The Duster, and the minister's whole family.

At any rate, the minister was not there at the gate of the cemetery, and there was only the key left in the gate. It gave me a queer feeling, as if it said: "Open this gate if you dare, and walk in on holy ground."

For my part, I would hardly have dared, but you would not expect anything to stop The Duster. He only paused a moment to act his part a little better. He put his hand on the key and looked over toward the little spire of the church and shook his head, and sighed, so that everybody could see and hear him. You never would catch the Duster throwing away a chance like that to make an impression on everyone.

I heard people murmuring around me that the poor fellow really wanted the minister to be there, and that it was a shame, and that, after all, a dead man is a dead man, and that it was a noble thing to see an example of friendship like that of The Duster. There was a lot more rot like this being whispered and talked out loud, and a good many black glances cast over at the church, where poor Lamont was probably right at that minute doing some sort of good for other people and forgetting himself.

But the other people did not know The Duster as I did, because they weren't living with him, and they couldn't see that all this grief of his was just a sham and a pretense, and that he really didn't care a rap about Hector Manness's funeral and burial in holy ground. That being the case, the thing that ate me up with curiosity was why he had insisted on it and put up such a terrible fight for it. I would almost have given an arm to know.

Well, at last The Duster turned the key and opened the gate, and he walked in with the black horse right behind him and went very slowly on down the hill toward the far corner where he had bought the burial plot and put up the monument. On the way down, he comes to the place where there was the big rock that marked the grave of Silas Wrack, the great fighter of Indians and red-eye. When he got to that place, what do you think the old Duster did then?

Well, when he left the house in the first place, he had been carrying a couple of big, fine wreaths, and now, as he got opposite Wrack's grave, he stopped and faced the grave and the big, ragged rock where a smooth place had been chipped off and the name of Wrack hewed into the stone. The Duster faced that monument and somehow—maybe by touching the reins when I wasn't looking—he made the horse turn in, too, and face the same way. After that, The Duster went and laid one of his two wreaths at the foot of the rock and stood there a minute with his head bowed.

It sounds pretty cheap, to tell it this way, and, knowing The Duster the way I did, I understood that he had a good deal of respect for Wrack, or for any other brave man, but still I knew that he never would show his respect like this, except to impress the crowd. But in spite of what I knew, I couldn't help having a little chill settle in the small of my back, the same way it does before a fight or a base-ball game.

Everybody was as hushed and still as could be while The Duster stood there.

I heard someone say: "Beautiful tribute."

And another said: "Noble fellow."

Meaning The Duster, do you see? And not Silas Wrack who was noble, in spite of all his whiskey.

But suddenly I was wishing with all my might that something would happen to show up The Duster exactly as he was, and let the light into that queer nature of his. For once he had to stop acting and stop fooling other people, I wondered if The Duster would even know himself.

II

Now he went on down the hill until he came to the place he had found for Manness's ashes. It was a mighty good little monument. He had had only a few days to prepare for it, but he had got Tom Wilson and the Crocker boys to work day and night, smoothing off and polishing, as well as they could, several slabs of white limestone that were put together like the walls of a house, and into the front of this was let an iron gate, and on each side of the gate stood a couple of columns made to look pretty much like Greek columns. Nobody had seen this before, and it made quite an effect, shining in the sun this way.

Just now there was a sensation and a murmuring, and no wonder. For when I looked around, I saw young Tom Lamont standing there in the crowd. It was a good deal of a shock to see that, if the minister had not come, his son had. But that did not really surprise me so much. Because I knew that Tom worshiped The Duster for having taught him how to shoot. The thing that staggered me was the girl at Tom's side, for there stood pretty Marguerite Lamont as sure as I live. Well, that flabbergasted me. I wondered what Cain the minister would raise when he found out that his girl had been there? Or had he actually sent the two of them?

She looked pale and rather grave, although she managed to keep a little smile on her lips, as if to show that she was not noticing that everybody was staring at her. From her, I glanced back to The Duster, just as his eyes fell on her. I saw him start, and then flush strongly. Which it was a good deal more wonderful to me to see The Duster blush, than to have seen a mountain lean out of its place and fall down flat. For the tenth time I wondered what the girl meant to him? It wasn't half so hard to tell what he meant to the girl, worse luck.

This confusion of The Duster—the first I ever saw in his face, but not the last, thank heaven—didn't last a moment. He then stepped forward to the door of the little tomb he had built and unlocked the iron grating and put the casket inside while everyone forgot the Lamonts and glued their eyes on The Duster. They expected something, and so did I, although none of us could exactly have said why, just that it did not seem possible that The Duster would possibly stage such a show as this without having something worthwhile as the climax.

But now that he had put the casket inside the tomb, he stood by the door for a moment, with the second wreath in his hands. And just then I heard a voice I knew speaking aside to another man. I looked back quickly and saw it was Renney, the famous sheriff; his voice was not meant for anyone but his companion, but some freak of the air currents brought the words softly to my ear.

"Look now, and look sharp, because you're seeing face to face the greatest criminal in the West. The greatest in the world, from my point of view. There stands John P. Thurlow, who we all call The Duster. And, I tell you, I'd give ten years of life to know why he has made all this fuss about the burial of Hector Manness who was a low cur. There's a pile more here than meets the eye . . . or the ear . . . because that man Thurlow is as deep as the sea."

It was pretty thrilling to hear that what I thought myself was also thought by a smart fellow like Renney. But I wondered at myself, to find that my sympathy was with The Duster, and not on the side of the law at all.

The Duster knew just how long to make a pause last, and now he started in and said: "My friends, it may seem a strange thing that a man like me should stand here and speak at a burial. But the minister who might have gone through the proper ceremony was . . . unable to attend." He looked across at the little wooden steeple of the church as he said this, and the crowd buzzed softly, like flies on a windy day. Then The Duster went on: "I have placed the remains of Hector Manness in their last resting place, but before I lock the door on them, it is right that I should say something about this man. You all know that I am his friend. I put it in the present, because people we have known well are never dead to us. As well say that the man who has gone into the next room is dead, because he is no longer seen. But he is still in our minds, and we know his look, his voice, his personality. I know all these things still about Hector Manness and will continue to know them as long as I myself live . . . with the permission of Sheriff Renney."

This little sharp touch made everyone look at Renney, but he was used to the weight of eyes and it did not bother him. Besides, the turn that The Duster gave to his funeral oration by this stroke prepared the way for the things he was going to say immediately, and he went on.

"Lies do no one any good, because it's better to build a monument with grass and straw than to build one with untruths. I want to keep inside the truth when I talk about Manness. But I can begin by saying that of all the men I ever have known he was the one who led the most perfect life." He paused to let the shock of this pile up and accumulate, and then he went on. "What is the perfect life? Why, I suppose I may say that it is the one that fits most closely to the ideals and the wishes of he who lives it. And certainly Manness did what he pleased. He was a man who hated hard labor, and yet he was a man who has ridden, as I happen to know, a hundred and twenty miles in a single day for the sake of a stroke of business."

He smiled a little as he said this, and the crowd chuckled.

"His business was sport, and sport was his business. He succeeded in it so well that he never had to go hungry or thirsty . . . unless his day's hunting took him far afield. For he was a great hunter, and yet he chased nobler game than buffalo, which the

Indians used to love to ride after. In fact, in a great many ways my dead friend was like an Indian chief. In all his tribe there was no one more expert in skinning, for instance. . . ."

Here there was a subdued wave of laughter.

"He loved to take a scalp, and did it so swiftly and easily and painlessly that I have seen his victim still chatting and laughing with Manness, not at all aware that his hair was gone. Like an Indian, too, no white man could compete with him in the tricks of the trail. And a good many who thought they were chasing Manness found out that they were hunted, instead.

"He was never troubled by sickness and never kept awake at night by worry. His days flowed pleasantly, one into the other, and, when death at last came to him, it came in the middle of battle and he lived only long enough to name the place where he wished to be buried.

"Who would wish for a better life than this? To have what you wish, your hands filled with the business that you have chosen, and your nights with the enjoyment of the money you have made? To live richly on a small investment, too, is something that every man wishes. And who that is wise does not have more enemies than friends? Certainly that was true of Hector Manness.

"In a sense, he was an artist, for he took from the world what he needed in the way of hard cash and food. He returned to the world a great deal of amusement. What does the artist do more? And people have stayed awake all night to read the accounts of the adventures of Hector Manness. So, in the end, he comes to rest in the place that he himself chose to sleep the long sleep in.

"Down there he has the river to watch forever,

and the hills that walk through the water, and the cattle that walk on the hills, and the sky overhead. My wish for him is a long rest. I think he would be more interested in a long sleep and in pleasant dreams than in any awakening.

"And so, my friends, I thank you in his name because you have come here in such numbers to grace the last moment of Hector Manness before the door of his grave is locked after him. I would have been glad to make this a religious ceremony, but I am not a religious man. I would be glad to close with a prayer, but the only prayer that I can think of is the prayer that I many times have heard on the lips of Hector Manness himself...'A straight-shooting gun, a heavy bullet, and a light heart.' I wish all those things to all of you in a measure just as great as Manness possessed them. Amen."

The fact that he should wind up this whimsical speech with an Amen made a good many people chuckle. But their chuckling stopped almost at once when they saw that The Duster was closing and locking the door of the tomb. Then they trooped slowly out of the cemetery, for they seemed to guess at once that he wanted to stay behind them, alone, and spend a little time of sober reflection beside the remains of his old companion. I think that everyone appreciated the fact that, in making his speech, he had showed them the character of Manness and had proved that his own eyes had not been blind to the real soul of that man. Hard and bright and keen had been his words, and that was Manness. Harsh, too, and soulless, and mean. But that part could be left out.

I looked at The Duster until I caught his eye.

He had just straightened after placing the big wreath in front of the tomb. The other people had gone out from the cemetery, and, when he made sure that we were alone, he winked broadly at me.

"Baldy?" he said.

"Aye?" I said.

"What did you think of this show?"

I was surprised that he could be so frank, even to me. "I don't know," I said. "I can only see that you're pretty smart in fooling folks. I never thought it was a sad day."

"Haven't you? Well," he said, "it may be sadder than you think."

I began to grope for the meaning of this, but with a gesture he invited me to leave, and I went out, leaving him behind me to meditate.

III

The funeral of Hector Manness, as most people in Christmas town were willing to agree, was about the strangest thing that had happened there, next to the day when The Duster first appeared and was berated by the minister in his church. That had been the beginning of the long fight in which The Duster finally got his way, buried his friend in the church cemetery, and so discredited poor Lamont that a great many people were of the opinion that Christmas would do very much better without the good minister, and that some younger man ought to be given the headship of the church. I say that many people thought this, but, of course, the older heads and the men with any ability to understand character always realized that Lamont had a heart of gold.

When I got home to the Ridley house, I had spent a good deal of time along the way, and the reason for this was that people had stopped me in the street and in the alleys of the town to talk to me about Duster. Naturally they were more cautious than ever about him, and nearly everyone had a first question to put: "Is it true that The Duster is really going straight?"

I asked, in return, what they thought themselves, and most of them said that they had been reasonably sure of it until they listened to him that day in the cemetery, where he had delivered what might be called a justification of the lawless life. But I answered to him that The Duster simply was not such a fool that he would try to praise Manness out and out. He knew that the man was a crook, and it showed his intelligence and lack of sentimentality that he praised Manness ironically, so that the listeners could have a chance to smile.

When I said this, most men agreed with me and said that they thought more of The Duster than ever, and that they were reasonably sure that he was simply being perfectly honest in his speech at the grave of Hector Manness. In that way, I dodged having to tell them what I thought myself. But, to be frank, from the first time that I saw The Duster in Christmas, and through all the days I had been working for him, I never for a moment had doubted that he was still as much of a crook as ever, and that he had come to Christmas for a crooked purpose. How that purpose was forwarded by securing the burial of Manness in the cemetery I was not able to say, but my lack of information did not change my mind on the subject.

This is what I want to say before I bring in the account of the great night that followed the burial service. First, I want to state exactly what I saw and heard with my own eyes. Then I am going to relate what was seen and heard by others in Emmet, fifty miles away, and, if the reader is not half asleep, he can put two and two together pretty easily. To begin with the time when I arrived at the house.

I barely had finished throwing down a feed to my Dolly mare and The Duster's own bay, when something crossed me like a shadow over my heart. I turned around and saw The Duster standing there in the doorway, rolling a cigarette and leaning one shoulder against the jamb of the door. That's about as innocent and commonplace a thing as a man could be doing, but it didn't seem innocent and commonplace to me in The Duster.

When he looked up to me in lighting the smoke, it seemed to me that the veil that The Duster had been wearing ever since he had come to Christmas had been snatched away, and that I was looking at the real man. Just what the difference was, I can't say, but I might remark that there was less of a smile about him and that he seemed harder, more resolved, more alert. There was never a time when one could look at The Duster without a little shock of some sort. The Duster asleep looked more formidable than most men awake. But with this day, he was altered. The gun, you might say, had been drawn out of the case and was blinking in the open light of the day.

He looked at the two horses and said nothing except that they looked fit. I pointed out that they were all right, but that where his gelding had picked up the little wire cut a few days before, the flesh was now swollen and his leg seemed hot.

He looked at me with hard, straight eyes, almost as though I had cut the bay myself. Then he went and looked at the small cut and felt the swelling and the heat. When he stepped back, he said some careless thing, to the effect that it was all in the day's work, or that every horse was a fool about wire, but, as he went out of the shed, I got the idea that he was not nearly as careless about it as he wanted me to think, and that this condition of the gelding was a distinct upset for him.

Now, I don't want to pose as a prophet, but from that time onward during the day and the evening I was ready to expect something extraordinary, and was reasonably sure that The Duster intended to leave the place, or at least had intended to do so, until he discovered that his horse was hurt.

He said no more about the condition of the horse until during supper when he was at his second cup of coffee, if I remember right. Then he asked me if I thought the cut was serious, and if the gelding could stand a good twenty-mile run. I told him I thought that the horse might, but that when his leg got cold afterward, he might be lamed and crippled forever. He listened to me with a nod and a slight frown—he rarely frowned at all, but his expressions were mere ripples over ordinarily calm features. He said that it was true, and that after a brisk run, if he were tried again, the gelding might be found wanting.

I agreed. This sounds unimportant, but is useful to know in the light of what was to happen.

After supper, The Duster sat around with me for a while and talked. He told me stories about his boyhood. It was a hard boyhood, too, and, if ever anybody had a reason for going wrong, it was The Duster, I should say. It was like something out of a fairy tale. I mean, there was a bad step-mother, and a hard-hearted father, and poverty, and hard work, and all that sort of thing. He told only the funny side, but the cruelty leaked through like poison through a sieve.

He kept me amused for a long time, and I appreciated the stories a lot, but all the time I had a feeling that The Duster was being a little nicer and more amusing then he had any call to be. That he was bringing me over to his side, as you might say. It seemed to me that, while he was talking, he was always watching the effect of the words on me. After a long time—it was close to eleven—he suddenly said that he had had a long day and was sleepy, and that he was going to bed.

His exact words as he said good night were something like this: "Good night, Baldy. I'm tired out. You stay in and keep a watch for me, will you? If you manage to keep awake for a while, it won't hurt my feelings any. The fact is there are people in the world who would be glad to have me out of the way, even if they had to use bullets to do it."

That was not telling me any news. I wasn't even surprised when he said it, but when he went into his room and I heard the rusty lock screech as it was turned by the key, I was surprised. It was the first time that he had locked his room since he had started living with me in the old Ridley house.

Then I sat down and thought over my position, which was that I was commanded to sit up and guard the house—for the least request of The Duster had to be as much as a direct command to me—and that he would try to sleep himself out.

Very good and simple. But something about the very back of The Duster as he went through that door told me that he did not intend to sleep. You may think it is strange to talk this way, but backs say nearly as much as faces. Sleepy backs droop and the shoulders sag, but The Duster was a compact bundle of energy.

I put out the light at once and lay down on the floor, not to wait for enemies, and not that the hard floor would keep me awake, but so that I could listen with more desperate concentration to any move that The Duster made. I distinctly heard the bed creak as he threw himself on it. After that, I heard a few deep, muffled snores, like those that a very tired man often makes when he first falls asleep. After that, I heard not a thing, but I kept on listening with all my might, not for a short time, but for two whole hours while the silence ticked with my pulse as if with a watch.

By the end of that time, I was as nervous as could be, and finally decided that I had misunderstood what The Duster had said about the necessity of remaining in the house on guard. I got up, took a revolver bare in my hand, and slipped out of the open door. Then I went straight to the barn and by the slant moonshine saw that one horse was gone! Yes, sir. Somehow The Duster must have managed to get out of his bed and cross the creaking board of the floor to the window. He had—more wonderful still—got the sticking, screechy window open, and had climbed through without making a sound.

This may not sound very great to you, but it did to me. That old shack was as noisy as a drum if you so much as rubbed it.

One horse was gone, and now the one that was left lifted and turned its head. It was the gelding with the wounded leg. Yes, it was my Dolly mare that he had gone off on. I had been scared before, but I was angry now, so that I swore out loud, and the gelding nickered softly for company. That was the reason the cut on the bay's leg had troubled The Duster so much. He had planned on a night's excursion long before, but he had intended to take his own mount.

I went back to the shack.

The pale moonlight was bright on the ground beneath the window of The Duster's room, and I looked there into the dust, but I could see no mark. If he made one, getting out, he had turned back to smooth out the sign. Or else he had leaped like a cat from the side of the house clear out to the pine needles without leaving a trace on the soft earth.

I determined to light a match and look in at the window of The Duster's room, although, if I were wrong about his leaving, I would undoubtedly get a bullet through the head as an answering favor. I took that chance, lighted the match, and looked in.

The bedclothes were confused and rumpled. A quirt lay like a snake on the floor, and I saw a hat on a hook, and a bright-colored scarf thrown over it. I saw those things particularly as I looked in, but there was no trace of The Duster. He was gone.

IV

Starting with that moment when I looked through the window and made sure that The Duster was gone—and was scared to death for fear he might someday discover what I had done in spying upon him—it gets harder and harder to tell the facts.

The best way is to follow The Duster—not that I

know exactly what he did and said, but that I learned a good deal from him and others and can fill in some spots out of logical deduction, and such.

The Duster got silently out of the house by a sort of miracle, as I've said before, and, once outside, he set sail and burned up the ground on Dolly, my mare. It's hard to charge that against him, because he had not expected that his own bay would be laid up. He headed on Dolly straight for the town of Emmet, fifty miles away. You have to keep that distance in mind, because it's the point. It was something like fifty-five miles, to be exact, by the road, and, if a person avoided the road and kept to a straight line, he would have some rough going, but save about ten miles in actual distance.

That was what The Duster did. He rode an air line, almost, straight toward Emmet. Not all the way on Dolly, however. For after he had galloped her about five miles at a burning-hot pace, he broke through the trees into an open space where a man stood with a pair of horses. One of those horses was probably a long-legged speedster like my Dolly, and The Duster hopped to the ground, bounded into the saddle on the other runner, and was off again with a twitch of the bridle and probably not a word to the holder of the horse. Beyond this point, the way got pretty rough for fifteen miles, with the hills pitching up and down like waves, and The Duster must have kept in the hollows except at Snyder Mountain, where he would have had to climb the half-mile grade.

At any rate, he had ten horses to ride in covering the forty-five miles between the Ridley house in Christmas and the Muncie and Lang bank in Emmet. Nine men stood in the course, holding remounts for him, and so he shot like a train across the country. I have ridden a somewhat similar course afterward, and I could hardly believe that even The Duster made such time on horseback through that range, but the undoubted fact is that The Duster could not have left Christmas much before twelve o'clock that night, and it is equally unquestionable that he rode into Emmet at exactly half past two the next morning. He had been two hours and a half on the way. We know the time for several reasons, but particularly on the witness of Chester Porson, the grocer, who happened to be up in the night on account of insomnia, and, looking out his window, he saw a horseman riding at terrific speed through the soft dust of the street. He only had a glimpse of the rider, who kept in his saddle a little aslant. That was The Duster's style exactly.

When he came to the vacant lot opposite the Muncie and Lang bank, he rode his horse into the pines, left it standing there, and hurried out toward the bank. It was not like most banks. It did not have big plate windows in front or columns like it was a temple. It looked more like a store, and a junk store at that. Nevertheless, Muncie and Lang were about the richest bankers in that neck of the wood. Lang had retired several years before, but Muncie still kept his name in the firm. They both were worth millions, and they knew how to keep the money rolling. They never bothered with small accounts and they hated to make small loans. What they wanted was the big financing, and they were hot at that. Suppose you wanted to open up a track of timber and build ten miles of railroad to turn the trick. Well, Muncie liked to do that kind of work. Generally the timber paid big, but by the time you had finished paying for the railroad, you found out that you owned about ten percent and Muncie owned about ninety percent of the timber. You might say that he had winning ways about him. He would finance ranchers, too, and always liked to see people expanding their business, the point being that he knew how to gather the expansion into his own hands. So scores of important people really were working all their lives in the interest of that same Muncie and Lang bank.

One of the peculiarities of the bank was that it always kept a great quantity of cash on hand, because just as Muncie was an expert in sudden foreclosures of mortgages, so he was an expert in buying up people whose backs were unexpectedly jammed against the wall. He was an old-fashioned businessman, was Muncie, and he could have made money easily anywhere. In the West, he was simply in clover, where men can't believe that the other fellow may be a wolf.

Up to the front door of this bank The Duster went. The watchman came hurrying up, but, at a sign from The Duster, he turned his back and went off in the opposite direction. He did not go far, however. At the first corner he turned and made a signal down the alley, and instantly men came gliding out of a wood-and-coal shed that stood there. There were a dozen of them. Half of them went with their rifles to the rear of the bank building, and the other half sneaked across the road and got in among the pine trees.

It was as easy and neat a trap as you ever saw.

In the meantime, The Duster had walked into the deep shadow of the entrance and there he saw a man standing with his back against the wall, waiting. The instant The Duster came up, the other merely nodded, turned a key in the lock, and the two of them went inside. They went straight back to the safe room, The Duster's companion opening all the doors on the way.

"Where's the cashier?" asked The Duster.

"Turned yellow and stayed at home," answered the other.

"I don't like that."

"Neither do I . . . if the combination he gave me won't work."

But it did work, and just like a charm. The heavy steel door came softly open—with a little sigh, I suppose, as though it regretted having such a pair of crooks look at what was inside.

The wonderful thing was that Muncie should have laid such good plans all the way around for the capture of the crooks, but that, in spite of the fact that his cashier had warned him beforehand, he had failed to change the combination. That shows that even a regular Napoléon will make mistakes now and then.

The two were twenty minutes working over the contents of that safe. Each of them had a canvas sack—part of the furnishings of the safe itself—and they took out negotiable securities to the amount of $485,000, and hard cash that totaled $118,000. The sum of both items, you see, was just over $600,000, instead of the $1,000,000, or $1,500,000, that some of the newspapers reported.

They got the stuff and split it on the spot, working fast and never speaking, only their hands jumping, and each watching the other like a hawk, because it would have been easy to slide $100,000 into a coat pocket if the other fellow had not been on the look-out.

All this time, there were three men watching and listening inside the bank. They were the ones who could testify that not a word passed between the two as they worked over the spoils and divided them. But try as they would, they could not make out the face of The Duster. His companion they already knew. The cashier had betrayed him, double-crossing the crooks. But although they studied the flash of the lights, they could not catch a really satisfactory glimpse of The Duster at all. He wore a big hat, but the shadow on his face was not all from the brim, because he had on a skin-tight black mask as well.

The three men were, first of all, Jud Lake, the gunman. He was the sourest man I ever knew. He had done fourteen years and used to boast that was only a year for every man he had killed. He surely was a no-good murderer, to tell the naked truth about Jud Lake. The second man there in the dark, watching the robbers at work, was Larry Cross, of Butte. He was about as hard as they make them, but I can't say that he was quite up to the level of Jud Lake. The third man in that room was old Florence Muncie himself. Funny name for a man—Florence. But there was nothing flossy about that bright-eyed old reptile. He had rubbed his skinny old hands together when he heard the plans of the robbery revealed, but he was not content to stay at home and let the trap be sprung. In the first place, he had arranged the outside trap, which was sure to collect anybody who tried to get out of the building, front or back. In the second place, he had prepared a smaller inside trap, where Lake and Cross were to lie with a pair of double-barreled riot guns and simply blow the two poor crooks to pieces.

Well, Muncie must have nearly turned inside out when he saw the safe door open. He had not planned on that, and he remembered now that the cashier had warned him to change the combination. But then he seems to have been glad that they did get the door of the safe open, so that they could be shot to pieces with the stolen treasure in their hands. At any rate, that was the thing he whispered to the two gunmen who crouched beside him in the corner of the room.

The Duster and his helper pushed open the door of the cage and stepped out toward the front door. As they started along, The Duster gave one more ray from his lantern to light their way, and a flick of that thin pencil of light fell across the three in the corner.

A fine picture for The Duster to see there. I can imagine how the bulging, brutal face of Jud Lake must have looked, and Larry Cross, half simpleton and half devil, and, worst of all, I suppose, the lean, long face of the old man, white and pinched with lack of blood, in spite of the fact that he had lived on the blood of others all his life. A pretty thing he must have looked there in the dark, licking his pale lips and hungering for the killing to begin.

The Duster must have seen all of these faces, but, more than that, he saw the ready shotguns, and knew that he had been tricked. But even under those terrible, leveled guns, he thought of his companion more than of himself. The other fellow had not seen; The Duster kicked his legs from under him and yanked him suddenly to the floor.

V

The two of them were already toppling when old man Muncie pulled a cord that connected with the electric switch, and the whole inside of the bank was spilled full of light that flashed back from the windows and flamed and towered on the tall steel railings and spires that surrounded the different rooms and offices. The whole interior of the bank must have seemed on fire and a real trap to that pair of crooks. That was what old Muncie had intended—that he should occupy the star seat at a quick show, and enjoy the blowing to pieces of the robbers.

The same instant that the electric light was turned on, and while the two thieves were still toppling, Larry Cross laughed like a hyena and pulled off both barrels of his riot gun. Enough lead there to have battered in the side of a freight car. Not lead, only, for the old fiend, Muncie, had loaded those guns himself with extra heavy charges of powder, and with buckshot, of course, but also with little fragments of iron that would ruin the insides of the guns, but that would lacerate and tear the flesh horribly when the charge struck home.

Well, that charge did not strike home. I don't very well know how a crack shot like Larry Cross, an old hand and a cool fellow, could have missed in a deal like that. But the fact is that he was laughing himself, he was dead overconfident, and he was shooting at a toppling mark. The overconfidence must have been the thing that did the trick. Because he had a sawed-off shotgun in his hands, he simply did not take aim at all, I suppose, whereas, with a rifle or a revolver, Larry could not have missed at such a distance and by such a light.

The charge from his gun went with a *whang* and a ringing among the metalwork. It crushed the face of a big clock as though an elephant had stepped on it. It struck out a window, too, and rattled like terrific hail on the open safe. But not a single grain of the flying danger struck the two men on the floor.

Another thing happened when that gun exploded. The overcharge of powder was so great that it knocked Cross backward and bumped his head against the wall hard enough to make him dizzy for half a second. By the time that half second was over, the scene was a good deal different. A Colt was in The Duster's hands as he pitched for the floor and the charge from the riot gun rang and roared above him. He did not shoot at Cross, because he saw Cross toppling back from the kick of the discharge. Instead, he fired at the horrible, big face of Lake.

Imagine the nerve of that man! Pressed the way he was for time—using a hundredth part of a second—yet he would not risk shooting Lake through his huge body, because such a shot might leave a spark of life in him, enough to let him loose off the barrels of his shotgun. Instead of trying for the body, he made a snap shot at the head of Lake, and nailed him fair and true between the eyes.

Lake threw aside the gun without pulling the trigger, and made a couple of rushing steps forward before he crashed in the middle of the floor. That with a bullet through the brain, and the thing is proved by the fact that the body was found there afterward, and further by the statement of Muncie that was as accurate as you could imagine.

Muncie saw his pretty picture all spoiled by that last second's worth of action. It must nearly have broken his heart. Instead of parcels of dead robbers scattered on the floor, one of his own men was dead, and the other was out of action, and The Duster was picking himself off the floor like a wildcat, and leaping in.

You have to give even old Muncie praise where praise was due. He didn't flinch then, but dragged a revolver out of the nerveless hand of Larry Cross and tried a shot at The Duster as the latter charged home. But although Muncie's heart was as young and strong as any young fellow's just then, his nerves were a different matter. And his hand shook so that the bullet he fired missed The Duster by five feet and plowed right through the top of the cashier's desk inside the next steel cage.

Then The Duster was on them, with his masked assistant right at his heels. The Duster took Larry Cross, who had recovered enough wits to snatch out a second revolver just as The Duster crashed the hard barrel of his own gun against the forehead of the gunman. So down went Larry Cross.

It makes you stagger to think of it. Two such men as Cross and Jud Lake put out of action with a single shot and a blow by The Duster. I like to turn it over in my mind. It shows me what a man of action can be like.

The Duster's friend had old Muncie by the throat by this time, and shoved the muzzle of a revolver up against his ear to blow his brains out.

But The Duster jerked the gun away and said: "Here's the key to the outside door. Don't waste time!" At the same instant, he jerked out the lights, because although all this shooting had lasted not more than two or three seconds, from the snapping on of the lights to the grabbing of Muncie, still the outside guards had heard and were on the job, ready to help in the clean-up if any help was necessary. Help was necessary, you can bet.

The Duster leaned and whispered three words in the ear of old Muncie, and that withered old scoundrel began to mutter and groan and say he was too young and strong to die, and life was just beginning to have a full flavor for his palate, and such stuff. And he offered to double the amount of money that the crooks had taken, if they would let him live.

The Duster allowed that he might let the banker live, but it would only be on consideration that he would get them through the lines by his personal company.

That was what the old rascal had to do. He had to open the front door of the bank and step out through it with The Duster right behind him and the other fellow on his left side. The Duster kept the cold muzzle of a revolver pressed against the nape of old Muncie's neck, in case he should forget where he was.

At the same time Muncie put up a whoop that almost reached the skies. He yelled out that he, Muncie, had been taken, and that, if his guards and his hired men did not get out of the way, he would be horribly murdered right there in the street before their eyes. He told them to scatter and keep back and let them pass across the street into the trees.

All this had been too fast for a crowd to gather.

Doors were beginning to slam and windows to crash up, of course, but before the townsmen really had an idea of what was happening and where, old man Muncie and his two captors were marching across the street while the hired gunmen held their hands and ground their teeth, such a nice, open, easy mark that made.

Then Larry Cross came to his senses—such as he possessed—inside the bank. He stumbled to his feet, with a revolver still lost in the grip of his great hand, and plunged out through the doorway. The Duster should have taken it for granted that the inside of that fellow's head was not brains, but chiefly bone. The crack he had taken across the skull would have killed most men, but it merely addled the wits of Larry for a minute, and then left him all himself. He came with a roar, like a breaking sea, and the trio were just disappearing under the lip of the shadow of the pine trees when Larry spotted them and fired.

It had always been taken as a tribute of his wonderful skill with a gun that at that distance he should have been able to pick out in the shadow friend from foe and put a bullet through The Duster. But I've always felt that the savage fellow simply fired at the whole group and did not care who he dropped.

At any rate, old Muncie saw The Duster twitch over to one side as the bullet struck him, and expected to feel a bullet shatter his own spine the next instant. But The Duster held his hand. Then The Duster's companion, wheeling around, sent a .45-caliber revolver shot through the right shoulder of Larry Cross.

All the fine, interlocking bearings of that joint were smashed to pieces by the bullet, and it was a good deal worse than death to Larry, I suppose. With his gun hand out of action forever, and his strength withered out of his arm, he never was worth his salt again. The shock of the impact turned him halfway around, and he grabbed his poor shattered shoulder with his other hand. He would never fire a bullet again—and a good job that he couldn't.

Now, when these two bullets were fired, the party of three sank out of sight among the trees of the vacant lot, and all Muncie knew was that he could hear his men running toward them at full speed while he shouted and yelled to them to keep back. He saw the two robbers—mind you, he had no idea all this time that The Duster was one of them—come to the place where The Duster had left his horse and where his companion had left another. The two let go of him and jumped into the saddle, and there the smaller man poised his revolver and said he was going to kill the old man-eater, but the taller one—The Duster—would not allow this. He knocked aside his friend's gun for the second time, and the pair of them rode away into the dark of the trees, with the thick pine needles muffling the beat of hoofs.

They came out on the next street, where two men with rifles in their hands saw the pair go by. The two were brothers who had heard the shooting and run out into their front yard with guns ready. They saw the pair go by and called to them to know who they were and what was happening.

They got a shouted answer back, but could not understand it, and then as the two turned the next corner, the brothers saw the shadows of the masks across their faces. Moonlight or not, by that time it was too late to open fire, and that was the last that was seen of the two robbers.

In ten minutes, naturally, there were fifty mounted men on the search for the trail, but they never picked it up. The two had got outside the village unseen again, and the night swallowed them and their $600,000 in loot.

VI

Easy money, you may say, no matter what had been in the night's work, but I don't agree. If you can shoot as straight as a die and move as fast as a cat's paw, and don't care a rap about the little matter of life and death, then an adventure like that night's work in Emmet is all very well, but, as a matter of fact, ordinary people with ordinary ideas and ways of thinking never could do such things as The Duster and his companion had got through. Besides, I can tell you more of what The Duster paid for that business, and for that purpose I'm glad to get off the region of other evidence picked up here and there and tell you again exactly what I heard and saw of the game.

It was exactly at two-thirty that The Duster rode into Emmet. It was precisely three when he rode out of it again, a third of a million richer than when he entered. And at five-thirty in the morning, he arrived back at the Ridley house in Christmas. I know the exact hour, because, as I heard his step on the front porch, I looked up at the face of the clock and saw the hand pointing at the halfway mark between five and six.

As a matter of fact, he had ridden back from Emmet—wounded as he was—in two hours and a half, which must have been just about the time that he consumed in riding over. He had ridden forty-five miles of pretty rough going at that terrific rate, burning up horses as he went along, and all this with a gaping wound in his side!

I'll never forget how he came in by the dull dawn
light of the day. I had lain down at last on my bunk,
not expecting to sleep, but hoping to rest a little, and
as I sat up, on hearing the step, in came The Duster,
wavering like a drunkard. It was so unlike his usual
easy step and straight bearing that I did not recognize him for half a second. He was helping himself
slowly in, his left arm gripped against his side, and
his right hand fumbling from the door to the back of
a chair, and then on to the central table.

I was up and with him in a moment. He was
white. His face looked long and his eyes sunken and
black-shadowed, and he looked straight past me as
though he were seeing his own pain a good deal
clearer than my face or anything else. But, even
then, with all his strength gone out of him and only
his nerve left, he was able to make his voice as
steady and sure and controlled as ever. What a man,
that Duster.

He said to me: "Baldy, go out to the stable and
you'll find Dolly there, pretty hot. Start working on
her. Get her dry. Keep on working until the sweat no
longer stands on her."

I said: "Duster, you look as though you need more
working over than Dolly ever can. You . . ." Here I
stopped with a sort of groan, because I saw his left
side, the clothes all plastered with red. But in spite
of what I saw, that man had such a wonderful command that, when he waved his right hand toward
the door again, I did not have the nerve to stand
against him but went out and took charge of Dolly.

She was everything that he said. But although her
head was down and the sweat running in rivers and
her eyes dull as death, and although I loved her like
a human being, still, when I looked at her, my won-

der was only that The Duster had been able to ride her as furiously as all this when he himself was hardly strong enough to stand. That's the only way I can describe his ride across the hills, by the finish of it, and by that you can judge for yourself the agonies that he must have gone through on that terrible ride.

I started to work on Dolly, just as he said, and I had hardly begun, when I heard the boy that brings the milk sing out loudly at the door of the house: "Hullo, Mister Thurlow?"

"Very well, thanks," said The Duster, his voice almost more cheerful than I'd ever heard it.

"Sleepin' late this mornin'?" asked the boy at the door.

"Just a wink or two extra before breakfast," The Duster replied.

The boy had been able to see him stretched in bed from the doorway, and The Duster not only talked to him, but went on: "Have you tried that snare for the rabbits, Charlie?"

"Have I tried it? I sure have!" cried Charlie, in a ringing voice. "I tried it, and it caught me three the very first day. Well, I never seen anything like it. Why, a man, he wouldn't need anything but that snare to live anywheres."

"And it'll work with birds, too, if you make it smaller and lighter, Charlie."

"I'll try that, and thanks for showin' me how, Dust . . . I mean, Mister Thurlow."

"You call me Duster if you want to," he said, "because most people do, Charlie, to my face or behind my back." And then he laughed.

Gosh! When I think what that laugh must have cost him.

Of course, Charlie was about the happiest boy in

the town of Christmas as he walked off from the door, and I'll bet that his one thought was for the time when he'd have a chance to get the great man in a crowd, and call him Duster right in front of the whole bunch. That would make him almost as distinguished among the boys of Christmas as The Duster was among the men.

I stopped my grooming of Dolly to listen to this talk, and to wonder why The Duster showed himself in bed, and, if he did, why he opened up that talk with little Charlie, and why he continued it, and brought in about the snares, and what name he could be called, and all that. I knew that he liked Charlie, but I also knew that every breath he drew was costing him the most terrible pain, and that his exhaustion must be making his mind reel, but the point of it was that he wanted Charlie to have him firmly in mind that morning. I was to find out why, later on.

I worked close to forty minutes over Dolly, rubbing her down, walking her in the cool breeze, sluicing water over her, and finally I was able to rub her down and dry her off and leave her as dry as you please, just as The Duster had directed. All that time I was so interested in getting back to The Duster and finding out how he was with his wound that I hardly noticed the small cuts on her legs and the whip across her shoulders, where she had been sent flying through the tall brush at full speed. I would have about killed, I think, any other man who had taken her out and treated her so, but The Duster was different—on this morning, at least.

As I worked over her, I wondered and wondered where she had been, although I'd washed some red clay off the inside of her knee, and there was no color like that in the earth up the valley, so she must have gone down it.

When she was dry and comfortable and enough herself to begin munching at the hay in her manger again, I turned around and rushed back to the house and found The Duster—half out of bed, trailing toward the floor, naked to the waist, with his arms flung out from his body, and across his left side the red furrow of a bullet wound, caked with dark red above and below, and with the red still welling up slowly and dripping onto the floor.

I'm not a boy. I've seen my share of wounds, but suddenly I said to myself that The Duster was a dying man, and, by the dizziness that whirled my brain, I knew then for the first time how fond I'd grown of him.

Luckily there was water heating on the stove, because the fire had smoldered all night long, and the kettle over it. I fixed a basin of warm water and went to The Duster, who I'd first straightened out on the bed. He must have used up the last of his strength in talking to Charlie, and, as the boy went off whistling and singing, the happiest kid in Christmas, The Duster had flopped in a dead faint. I began to swab off the caked blood, and, at the warm, soft touch of the water soaking into the wound and soothing its torn edges of flesh, The Duster groaned with relief.

He opened dim eyes and looked up at me, seeming to recognize me through a mist. "Bless you, Baldy," he said. He had gathered his willpower so hard that his teeth were still locked like a bulldog's, and he groaned out these words through his set jaws. Somehow that sounded like a real blessing, and not just merely words.

I kept on working and said nothing, but as I cleaned the wound and got some adhesive tape and soft cloth to make a bandage, he began to talk, a phrase at a time, something like this:

"I have to be able to stand, Baldy, in an hour."

"Man, you're crazy," I said. "You'll be in bed for a week or two with this little affair. What'd you do? Scratch yourself on barbed wire?"

"No," The Duster said with a grin, "the barbed wire scratched itself on me."

"You'll have a rest, after this," I warned, "or else you'll be endangering your life."

"Already endangered," he said.

"Is it?" I asked him.

"You'll learn later," he said.

"I'm not asking questions," I said.

"Trust you?" he muttered.

"I won't turn you down, Duster," I had to tell him, "no matter what you've done."

"Gotta walk, stand, talk, in an hour," he repeated.

"Can't be done," I promised him.

"Has to be."

"How?"

"Pull the adhesive tight as a drum."

I did as he told me to do, laying on the cloth first. But it certainly hurt me and made me shrink to draw the tape tight on that side of his—because it was swollen and inflamed and feverish from his shoulder to his thigh. But I did as he said and saw his face turn wet and shining with the agony that he went through. But when he looked up at me and saw some of his own pain reflected in my face, he was able to smile.

"Good old Baldy," he said.

VII

A dog that runs to every hand and voice is not a dog that interests most people. They prefer the sulky fighter—you win a wag of the tail from him after six months. That smile from The Duster meant more to me than a dozen compliments from ordinary men, because it showed me that he trusted me.

Still, no matter what I thought of him and how much I wanted to help, I was pretty much at sea until he said to me, as I worked: "Along with another man, I robbed the Muncie and Lang bank in Emmet last night. My alibi is the time I was back here. Charlie is my alibi. As soon as I get fixed up a bit, you go downtown and find out what's being said of the robbery. It must have been on the wires from Emmet a long time ago."

Mind you, he didn't ask me to promise that I would keep the secret. He asked nothing, in fact, but he didn't have to ask. I knew my own mind, and so it seemed did The Duster.

There were plenty of things to do now. The Duster thought of everything. There had to be signs of a breakfast eaten, for one thing, and so I built up the fire, using the bloodstained clothes that The Duster had used on the ride, after soaking them pretty well with kerosene. I soaked them too well, as a matter of fact. They went—a belch of smoke and a roar of flame—up the chimney and turned the stovepipe red-hot in no time. I was afraid that the roof might catch on fire and ran outside, and stayed there for a minute to look around the countryside and notice if anyone were near to spot the arm of flame that was wagging above our chimney, but I could not see anyone, and took it for granted that things must be all right.

When I came back into the room, The Duster saw me, and he was braced up in one end of his bunk, looking as far gone as a man can look, but setting his teeth against exhaustion and pain.

What do you think he was doing? Why, he had out some rouge and stuff and he was coloring his face, so that the pallor would disappear out of it, and his lips, too, would lose that pale-purple look. Making up like a girl! I lay ten to one no other man would have thought of doing that, or had the skill to do it if he had. But The Duster was ten men in one.

When he spotted me, he simply said: "Don't look as if your whole family had just died, Baldy. It's not as bad as that. And what difference does it really make to you if they do catch me?"

Not that that made me wish any less that he'd escape, but it let me down a little. I really had begun to feel that I was in the middle of the storm, but he simply pointed out that whatever happened no hand would fall on me. Somehow that eased me a good deal, which may show that I'm as selfish as the next man.

I got back into the kitchen in time to find that the coffee had boiled over, and the bacon was burned in the pan, but, at any rate, the white-hot chimney was now turning red, the clothes had burned down to a packed heap of glowing rags and ashes, and there was enough smell of cookery in the air to do for an army of sheriffs to smell.

I gave the rags in the firebox a poke to raise a flame out of them again, and, while they were going up in a rush of flame and oily smoke, I rescued the last of the bacon from the edges of the pan and took it together with some coffee and pone to The Duster.

When he saw the bacon, he nearly turned green through his artificial coloring, which he had spread over his face by this time. He made a gesture to push it away, but I caught his hand.

"You can't live on coffee, Duster," I said. "Not straight through the day to the night. You gotta eat this bread and bacon, and then you can have all the coffee you want."

He gave me a desperate sort of a look but nodded almost at once. "You're right, Baldy," he said. "You understand."

I felt a good deal of pride in having made him do my way, for once, and I couldn't help sorrowing a little over The Duster as I saw him tackle the food with shaking hands. He was forcing every mouthful, and yet he didn't complain once he had started.

Finally I said what had been cropping up in my mind for a long time: "Duster, if you're well enough to go through all of this, you're well enough to get out of Christmas and ride for your life. If it's your life that's in danger."

"It is," said The Duster, "because one man was killed last night. That was Lake. Did you know him?"

"Of course I knew him. But that didn't make any difference, because they'll hang you for bumping off an ex-murderer as quick as they'll hang you for killing the President. Duster, you'd better get out of here and get quick. I'll go with you, if you want, and try to take care of you. But with that scratch on the side of you, they've got the evidence that they want for putting a rope around your neck. Heaven knows it would please them to kill you if they could, Duster. And what's to keep you here in Christmas?"

"Unfinished business," said The Duster, and looked me in the eye in such a way that I had to turn away.

What was his unfinished business? Then, in spite of myself, I saw the pretty face of Marguerite Lamont in the cemetery, looking with all her soul toward The Duster.

I was called back by The Duster and had the spot pointed out to me where the blood had spilled from his side onto the wood. That I scraped off, and, when I had finished this, I had to bring in dust and rub it onto the white place until it was the same color as the rest of the floor.

"It still looks a little shiny," said The Duster, "you'd better roughen up the surface a little. . . ." But then he jerked up his head and listened, and his eyes were as bright as coals. "It's too late," he said. "You'd better get out in the kitchen and start cleaning up . . . no, start for the shed to saddle the horses. And I'll be in here . . . reading . . . and smoking." He stood up from the bunk as he spoke. But the effort made a ghastly change in his face, and his head fell straight back. It must have been like the thrust of a sword through his side. Yet he didn't say a word, but just got into the homemade chair by the table and grabbed a magazine and started rolling a smoke.

I could hear them coming, by this time, the boom of voices down the wind and the creaking of saddle leather. So I grabbed my hat off a peg and went out the door and managed to raise a pretty good imitation of a cheerful whistle. There I saw them coming along under the trees.

Renney was in the front, and alongside of him was old Muncie, humped over in the saddle, and with his long face fallen between his shoulders. Of course, the minute I saw them my heart sank. I didn't care so much about the rest—there were seven or eight riders—but I knew that Muncie was about as wise a man as stepped in the West, and I had heard The Duster himself say that Renney was off by himself as an officer of the law. And they were to walk in on poor Duster when his strength was gone and when his wits must be pretty nearly addled with exhaustion and with pain.

When I saw them, I waved a hand at them and gave them good morning. They didn't answer until they got up close, and then Renney said in a rather subdued voice: "Good morning, Baldy. Has The Duster come back?"

That was a neat question. I don't know where I got the sense to answer it, but I said: "Come back from where?"

The sheriff bit his lip. "Ain't he been out?" he asked.

I shook my head. "Not that I know of," I said, and didn't even regret the lie, but only wished that I could make my voice sound as though it was the truth.

"Why d'you talk to this fellow?" said Muncie. "He's with The Duster and bought up by him. Is The Duster here?" he snapped at me.

"Why talk to me?" I said, pretty hot under the collar.

"We don't need to," replied Muncie. "Let's get at the house, Renney."

Renney was short enough when he answered: "I'm running this party, Mister Muncie."

"But I've already paid for it," replied the old banker.

Which in a way he had, not that Renney had got anything out of it as yet. But we learned later that Muncie had offered ten percent of every penny recovered from the crooks, and that he had a flat offer of $10,000 apiece for the robbers. That was a lot of money, in those days, although you didn't need to hang up any golden reward to make a fellow like Renney do his duty.

The rest of the riders had come up. I knew most of them, but they only gave me nods or a grunt, like men who had their minds filled up with old acquaintances. They were a hand-picked lot, and just the sort that you would expect Renney to have out to ride with him. Old hands, they were, tough as crickets and still just as lively—men that knew trails and guns and the ways of animals and men on the hunt.

All those suspicions and those brains were about to concentrate on The Duster, and I gave him one chance in twenty. No, not as much of a chance as that, because one in twenty is worth some sort of a bet.

"You'd better come along with us," said Renney to me, "because I'll have to keep you under my eye."

"What's happened?" I said.

"Nothing much," said Renney. "Million or so stolen from the bank of Mister Muncie, here. That's all. And Lake killed, and Cross shot down. Not much else worth mentioning."

"And The Duster did it?" I said, opening my eyes at the sheriff.

"We're going to find out," said Renney.

So I went along with them, and watched them dismount.

I wasn't with the first to get into the house, but I heard the voice of The Duster sing out a greeting to them all, very cheerfully, and then Muncie, in a sort of scream, yelling: "There's the man who killed Lake!"

VIII

Of course I knew that The Duster was desperately hurt and done in, but, when that voice of Muncie shrieked out that way, I tensed myself to be ready for the roar of a gun in fast action, and I expected to see what was left of the first part of that posse come tumbling back through the doorway, while the rest scattered for cover.

Nothing like that happened.

I heard The Duster say: "Lake? You mean the gunman? They've got him at last, have they?"

Oh, he was calm as ice, but Muncie barked again: "I'll swear on a stack of Bibles that's the man! Arrest him, Renney, and take him off to jail. Emmet's jail. That'll hold even The Duster."

By this time the rest of the group had squeezed into the room, and I was along with them.

The Duster had not stood up—he hardly had the strength to, I suppose—but sat rather sprawling in his chair, holding his cigarette in one hand, and with the other hand lying on the table and drumming lightly there.

I wondered, at first, that he didn't show surprise, or anger, or curse them for bothering an innocent man, or something like that. But he did not assume any such airs at all, and I could see why, after a moment. They all knew that he had been through the wars, and if he pretended too much, they'd be suspicious. A man who has been tried for robbery or murder five times does not throw up his hands in horror when he's arrested again. And The Duster took this as calmly as you please. Renney had answered the last remark of Muncie by replying that he was running this party and that Muncie would have to wait until he was back in his bank before he started in giving orders.

Then he said to The Duster: "Where was you last night?"

The Duster kept on drumming on the table with his fingertips for a moment and looked over Renney and Muncie, and then the rest of the faces in the group. "If I had chairs enough, I'd ask you gentlemen to sit down," he declared, "but you don't look in a sitting humor. Is this a joke, Renney?"

"Come, come," answered Renney, but not with any heat. "You're too old a hand to try bluffing with me, Duster."

"I wouldn't dream of it, Renney. I respect your brains too much. But I hope that you respect mine a trifle, too."

"Of course I do," said Renney. "And I've begun by asking you where you were last night?"

"Here, of course," said The Duster.

"You lie!" shouted Muncie. The old man was so full of venom that he couldn't hold it in.

But Renney simply raised one hand to quiet him. "Parkins," he said, "go out and look at the horses in the shed and see if they look as though they've been used last night."

I could appreciate the forethought of The Duster when I heard this, but I hoped that Dolly had got back a bit of strength by this time, and that she hadn't broken out into another sweat—which as likely or not she had.

Then Renney went on, as Parkins left: "The rest of you scatter and search this house and the ground around it, and the shed as well."

"All of us?" said one man. "You want to be left here alone?"

Renney blushed like a girl. "I've gotta take my chances, even with The Duster," he said.

So they all left the room and went stamping through the kitchen, and The Duster's sleeping room, and then up the ladder into the little attic, where I hoped that the spider webs would choke them.

"Now, suppose you tell me where you were last night and just what you did?" Renney said to The Duster.

"Let me see," The Duster said. "I was pretty wakeful last night."

"Aye, you were!" snarled Muncie.

The Duster looked him slowly over, from head to foot. "Cats eat birds, Muncie," he said, "but you'll never get your teeth into me."

Renney grinned from ear to ear. No matter how keen he was to get Thurlow, it was plain that he had no use for Muncie. Who did, for that matter?

The old man champed like a horse on a bit, but he couldn't think of anything to reply to this last remark, and The Duster finally went on: "Yesterday was a pretty big day for me, Renney. I buried the last of Manness yesterday."

"I know that." Renney nodded.

"Then, when I came home, I spent an easy day, and last evening I sat up pretty late with Baldy Wye, here."

"Is that so?" said Renney, turning suddenly on me.

"Yes," I said very heartily, because at least this much was true. "It was after eleven when we turned in."

"Where did Thurlow sleep?"

"In that room."

"And you?"

"In this bunk, yonder."

"After The Duster went in there did you go to sleep right away?"

"Not for over an hour," I said.

"Did you hear anything from that room?"

"Not a sound, after the bed creaked when The Duster lay down."

"An hour. That would make it twelve?"

Renney thought for a minute. It was plain that he was subtracting twelve from half past two and wondering how The Duster could have got to Emmet in two hours and a half. He didn't know, and I didn't, either, about the relay of horses that had been used.

"Could he have got out of that room except through this door?"

"Not without waking the house up by getting through the window."

Renney went into the bedroom, and I heard the floor creak under his foot, and then the screech of the sash as he raised it. Finally he came back. "Impossible for most people, but we're dealing with The Duster," he said with a smile.

"What difference does Baldy Wye's chatter make?" broke in Muncie. "He's the bought man of The Duster."

"How early did The Duster come back this morning?" Renney said quietly to me.

He couldn't catch me, however, although he almost did.

"Do you mean, when did he come out of that room this morning? The next time I saw him, it was about five-thirty."

"You did?"

"Yes." This was true enough. I wasn't asked how I had seen him or where.

I saw Renney look up into the air, troubled. "Did anybody else see The Duster here at about that time?"

"Yes," I said, "there was Charlie . . . the kid that brings the milk. He came in a little later and saw The Duster through his door, still in bed. He was taking it lazy this morning."

Renney nodded, and I saw his eye taking a note of Charlie, but it was pretty plain that he accepted the fact that The Duster had actually got back to Christmas two hours and a half after the flight of the robbers with the loot from Emmet. That would have upset any man's calculations a good deal. Two hours and a half for forty-five miles of open country.

A couple of men came in then to say that they'd found no money or anything else suspicious, but that in the ash box of the stove they'd found some buttons, and they took out three of them and showed them—buttons that looked pretty charred and warped, but buttons they were.

"Do you feed clothes to your fire?" Renney said harshly to me.

"Clothes? Of course not. Hold on! There was a couple of old rags I shoved into the stove yesterday. May've been buttons on them. I don't remember."

As I said this, my glance trailed across the face of

The Duster, and somehow I could feel the gratitude shining out like a sun at me. And immediately afterward, Parkins came in from the shed. He said that the gelding seemed fresh enough, but the mare looked tired and done up. He had taken her out and offered her water, and she drank pretty deep, with her knees shaking a little. Her coat was clean and dry. Matter of fact, it was too clean. Her eye was dead. He would say that the mare might have been used and used hard, last night, and been groomed down later. There were little cuts on her legs and welts on her shoulders, but he wouldn't say they were marks of last night. They might have happened any time during the last few days.

I was glad to hear him say that, while the eyes of Renney kept flashing from the face of The Duster to mine. Finally Renney said: "Good work, Parkins. You have a pair of eyes and you've seen a horse before this. But . . . suppose that mare was off her feed?"

"Aye," said Parkins instantly, "she'd be exactly the way I've said. And particular if she was enough off not to lie down last night."

It almost scared me to have the sheriff put in a word on The Duster's side of the case, but here old Muncie broke out: "What's the use of all this nonsense? It was The Duster, I tell you, and he was hit in the side by a bullet last night as he dragged me across the street. Why don't you examine him?"

"Tut, tut!" said The Duster. "Hit in the side by a bullet, did you say?" He chuckled a little, very softly. A real laugh would probably have shaken his face into a twist of agony.

"You can tut, tut all you want to," said Muncie viciously, "but I'm gonna have you examined."

"Renney," said The Duster, "is the old coot to be favored in everything that he wants?"

"I'm sorry, Duster," said Renney. "But he's so sure of himself that I have to favor him in this one thing."

"Danged nuisance," The Duster stated, but still keeping his voice as calm as you please. "I'm to be stripped and searched because an old dotard like Muncie says so?"

Renney nodded. "I hate to do it," he admitted. "I came here sure that Muncie was right. I don't mind saying that I've changed my mind since, for several reasons. Mind you, Duster, I don't want to plague you, but I do want to be pretty thorough. I'll have to ask you to let us see you stripped to the waist."

IX

The sheriff was mighty apologetic, as though he knew that he was in the wrong and did not want to have it held against him, but he had to go to the ground with every clue.

As for the posse, it was clear that they did not like this business. Muncie apparently had promised them a clear case, and they had found nothing that they expected to find; all they had done was to show themselves to The Duster as enemies, and everybody on the range knew that The Duster never forgot a good turn, and certainly never rested until he had repaid a bad one.

So the whole party was giving up hope just at the verge of success, and the whole band was cursing

Muncie silently at the very instant when he was bringing them to the wishing gate, as you might say. It was a strange business.

Old Muncie said: "If there's such a thing as instinct, instinct is showing me the right road. I tell you all, I've seen gunmen work before, but there's only one real tiger on the range, and that's The Duster. I saw him working last night, and nobody but him . . . I couldn't be fooled. I saw him before, mind you, on the big day in Tucson. Well, I can't be fooled about him. Duster, stand up and let's see you."

I remember that just at this moment a band of cattle were being driven down the road, and their mooing and the swearing of the cowpuncher, who was riding point, and the clacking of the hoofs made a bad racket, just when one wanted silence for the crisis of this scene. It was so bad that I even turned my head a little and saw a big brand on a bald-faced Hereford. It was a parcel of cows off the Larsen and Douthit ranch.

I looked back at The Duster as he put a hand on the table and leaned forward.

"Is this going to be done, Renney?" he asked coldly.

"I've gotta ask you to do it," said Renney, really confused.

The Duster stood up. He had a hand on the table to help him, and he moved slowly, but I thought that I could guess under the clever make-up on his face the cost of that move. Like another bullet plowing through him, I should have said.

When he stood up, old Muncie made a sort of a rush toward him. The malice in that man was so great that it looked as though he were going to try to rip away The Duster's clothes, but he met Thurlow's eyes, and that was enough to stop him.

For my part, I had edged out to the side of the crowd nearest to the kitchen door.

Bullets were going to fly, if I knew my man, and I didn't want to be in range of them. I was willing to lie for The Duster, and take care of him in every way that I could, but to draw my gun on honest men for the sake of a fellow I knew to be guilty was more than I could go. I was ready to jump for the kitchen door when I heard The Duster say:

"Well, if it has to be, I'll stand for it . . . and remember you for it afterward, Renney. You . . . Muncie"—it was exactly as if he spoke to a dog—"where did the bullet strike me?"

"In the left side . . . the left side. I remember it as clear as day!" How old Muncie yipped it out, like the hungry old coyote that he was.

I saw the hand of The Duster reach down and seem to grapple with the lower part of his shirt. To pull a gun, I made sure. For I knew that when the worse came to the worst, he would certainly die before he would surrender. But I was wrong.

He was wearing no coat—just a shirt with a bow tie at the neck that looked mighty out of place there in that Western shack. Now he threw up the side of his shirt and held it high.

And I found myself staring like a man in a dream. I could see the white of the skin, and the lean ribs of a man in hard condition moving as he breathed, but there was no sign of the great strips of plaster that I had dragged so carefully over the wound.

"There you are, you cur!" said The Duster. "Does that satisfy you? Now get out of here, and you, Renney, along with the rest of your pack!"

They got, let me tell you, and crowded out past

me, where I stood still gaping—crowded out from the set face and the burning eyes of The Duster as though lightning were apt to crash on their heads as they went. I shall never forget old man Muncie muttering aghast as he stumbled through the doorway: "I was wrong. I was wrong."

He wasn't wrong at all, as I very well knew, and yet, by some miracle, The Duster had made him seem so.

As the last of them got hurriedly through the doorway, I, still gaping at The Duster, whose shirt-tail was hanging down on one side, suddenly understood. It was so simple that it ought not to have fooled a child. But it had fooled a lot of excited and half-frightened men, and all through the confidence and the scorn with which The Duster had acted. He had pulled up his shirt and showed them his body, well enough, but it had been the right side that he raised, and not the left.

When I saw that, I slammed the door behind the last of that crew, for I heard The Duster's lips whisper: "The door."

He was wavering where he stood and trying to lower himself into a chair again, but could not manage it.

How he had held out that long I can't really guess, but now, when he slumped, he went altogether in a heap, and I dived for him and barely caught him in time. It was an odd thing to lift The Duster in my arms. Him that had made such a name and could overawe so many hard-headed, hard-fisted gun-fighters and veterans of the trail, why, he was hardly more than a kid as I picked him up. I wouldn't put his weight above 150 pounds, at the most. He looked bigger. Standing on his own feet, he looked fit to go up against anything or any man, but here, as I held him in a dead faint, he was nothing at all!

I packed him over to the bed and laid a hand over his heart, but it wasn't beating. I mean, I couldn't catch the pulse of it, and I thought that this last grand bit of acting must have killed him, after all. For it wouldn't have been strange, considering the weakened condition he was in, and the great stretch and strain there had been on his nerves and his brain.

I ran into the kitchen and got some cold water and came back and sluiced it all over him, regardless. And then for the first time I saw his chest heave a little. Next I fetched a flask of old red-eye, strong enough to peel paint off a fence, and I wedged the muzzle of the bottle between his teeth and poured down a good stiff dram.

He felt that. A mule would have felt it. He groaned and stirred a little, and then stretched out on the bunk with a sigh.

The second time in one morning that he had fainted, mind you, and both times alone in my hands. That was more than anybody else could say about his relations with The Duster.

I raised the wet shirt and looked at his wound—I mean at the plasters that held it, and I saw at once what was increasing The Duster's troubles. The pull and the gripe of those straps had certainly corseted in his pain and enabled him to get through the scene he had had to face, but it had also set up a great irritation, for the red edge of the inflammation now extended beyond the edges of the straps.

I ripped those straps off, and some of the skin they were hitched to, so that The Duster muttered in his unconsciousness. But when the bandages were off, and he could breathe more easily, I saw at once in his face that it was a great comfort to him.

So I bathed the wound over again—it was still bleeding a little—and put around him a proper sort of bandage that girdled him and fitted easily, and would give a chance for the lungs to stir and for air to get at the edges of the wound. There's nothing like air to help along a cure, if you'll believe me—the clean, dry Western air, I mean to say.

I was just finishing this work, and still The Duster had not opened his eyes, when I heard a rap at the door. It fair stopped my heart.

I didn't answer, and the rap came again, and then the voice of Sheriff Renney.

I had to go answer the knock, and I unlocked the door and opened it a crack.

"Baldy," said Renney, who looked pretty troubled, "there are still some things to be cleared up about this, and I want to talk to The Duster for a minute."

"You can't," I said.

"Can't?" Renney said, and lifted his eyes at me.

"Renney," I said, "you're a brave man, and I know it."

"Thanks," he said shortly. "But what in the world has that got to do with the case."

"A whole lot," I went on softly. "You're a brave man, and I know that you take every chance that you have to take, but I'm sure gonna beg you not to run into trouble when you don't have to. You've given The Duster a pretty hard run this morning, ain't you?"

"Yes," he admitted. "He took it pretty hard. I gotta admit that it humiliated him a good deal."

"Maybe more than even you think," I said. "The fact is, Renney, that he's in the back room in a ragin' temper. And he's sworn that the next time he lays on you, he's gonna go for his gun and finish off his account with you, because you've been houndin' him and persecutin' him for years."

"If he feels like that," Renney announced, "he can have his chance with me now. Open the door, Wye, and stand back."

It staggered me a good deal, but I stuck to the knob of the door with a frozen grip.

"Renney," I said, "just think it over a minute. Tomorrow he'll be calmer. But right now, if he sees you, one of you two has gotta die."

It was true, and the one would be The Duster—by means of a hangman's rope.

"Baldy, you're right," said Renney, the anger clearing out of his eyes. "I'll do this later." He turned away from the door.

X

Although Renney did not come the next day, or the next, we lived in a besieged house, always in fear of every voice that passed down the road, expecting it would turn in and call at our place. In my anxiety, I lost pounds, until I discovered that The Duster, that fellow, actually was enjoying this affair. The suspense that nearly drove me crazy was a sauce that made life taste to his palate. When I learned that I did not worry so much—although I still had enough to think about.

For one thing, it was amusing, always, to follow the twists and the turns of The Duster's mind as he evolved one expedient after another. He had little to do, and he trusted me thoroughly, so that he used to talk out his ideas aloud to me, and, brilliant as I knew he was, it was astonishing to hear the childishness of some of his proposals designed to assure us a quiet time at the Ridley shack.

For instance, he suggested at one time that we should quietly dig out a small cellar and get him down into that while I gave out word that he had gone off into the higher Christmas Hills on a hunting trip on foot.

Again, he thought that we might hire a doctor to declare that he had a very dangerous contagious fever, like smallpox, for that would effectually keep the people away. I had to point out that the doctor, the instant he was aware of The Duster's wound, would know that, after all, he had been at the robbery of the Muncie bank.

He had half a dozen other ideas like that, but, in the meantime, he hit on one expedient that would prove really useful. He got me to make him a sort of canvas camping chair in which he could lie back almost prone. The idea was that if anyone should come to the house, he would simply be lying down in the chair, taking a nap. That idea was simple, but it was pretty sound, and, when we fixed him up with his clothes loose and everything comfortable, it was just about as though he were lying in bed, as far as rest was concerned.

It was wonderful to see what care The Duster took of himself. When he moved, it was only an inch at a time, for fear lest a strain on his side should part the healing tissues again. He always spoke softly and laughed with care, so that the jar of the heaving chest should do no harm. He watched his diet like a hawk, keeping himself a little hungry, and going in for a lot of green stuff to eat. He said that bacon and soggy pone and coffee were all right when a man had a chance to exert himself and work out the poison, but he wanted light food when in bed. He would not touch coffee, and used to make himself drink milk, although he could not keep back the wry faces.

His amusements were making his foolish plans, cleaning and re-cleaning his guns, and, above all, lying with his eyes turned up and watching the ceiling while his thoughts brightened and darkened in his face.

It was plain that he was good company for himself, and he used to show me, in spite of himself, little glimpses into the truth about his nature. A dangerous truth, I tell you, and about a dangerous nature; sometimes when I watched his secret, faint smile, I could almost see sharp cat's teeth behind it. It was mischief that he lived for and loved.

Sometimes, too, he would content himself with badgering me about any crazy thing that came into his head, and his steady, bright eyes always fooled me, so that I never knew when he was serious and when he was joking, until I lost my temper in self-defense, as you might say, and then always saw him quietly smiling at the end. He was a rare one. All velvet, you know, one way and cactus thorns the other.

He knew that he baffled me, of course, and that was one of the things he used to annoy me with. He said one day: "Look here, Baldy, if I took off this shoe would you see a foot or a cloven hoof under it? And if I shaved my head, would you see small horns sprouting?"

Well, that was nearly the way I felt about him. He was almost always entertaining to be with, but he always scared me a little.

We were staving off the people pretty well. I usually told them, when they came, that The Duster was out shooting, or that he was just taking a walk, or some such thing, and they used to go off again, seeing me in a grouchy humor, because a Westerner would rather sit on tacks than talk to you when you're out of sorts.

One afternoon The Duster said: "Baldy, I want to tell you a story."

"Go ahead," I said.

"Down the Christmas Valley," he went on, "there's a point where a little creek runs into the river, and a hundred yards above the junction there's a pair of big poplars growing, and at the foot of the southern poplar there's a big stone, and, if you lift that stone, you'd find under it a strong canvas sack, and, if you were to go get that sack and bring it up here to me, I'd be mightily obliged to you."

"Why not leave it there?" I said. "It's safer there than it would be here."

"For one very good reason," he said. "The fact is that it's a fairly damp place and the contents of the sack may mildew."

"That's a pretty good reason," I admitted.

"There's still a better one," he continued. "My partner in the little Emmet job is as sharp as a fox, and by this time he knows that I'm back in the Ridley house and that I undoubtedly have put away the loot somewhere along the trail. He's going to nose out that trail, and sooner or later he'll find that stone and lift it."

"Who is he?" I asked.

The Duster smiled and shook his head, for it was a thing that he never would tell, no matter how much he trusted me.

I said: "You ought to get men you can put your faith in when you tackle a job like that."

"Should I?" replied The Duster. "Let me tell you, old fellow, that it's pretty hard to find a man with three hundred thousand dollars' worth of trust in him."

I had to admit that that was right.

"What about honor among thieves?" I asked him.

"That's a thing that the thieves like to talk about."

"Isn't it there, then?"

"Most men have mighty few temptations. It takes courage to tempt oneself," he answered. "But your good upstanding robber is almost always in such a position that he will line his purse thicker by cutting a throat."

He always smiled, when he talked like this, but I knew that he half believed what he said.

"And now about your little trip," he said; "if you start at night . . ."

"I'm not starting, Duster," I told him.

"No?" he asked, and raised his eyebrows at me.

I shrugged my shoulders. "I do what I can for you," I said, "but I can't make myself into a thief for your sake."

"Thief?" he echoed.

"By handling stolen money," I replied.

He gave me a long, thoughtful look, but said not a word more about the subject.

I wish he had, for then we should have been able to dodge the tragedy that followed. He might have persuaded me, I think, with that clever tongue of his. About not letting $300,000 rot away, for instance.

Well, he gave up persuading me the instant I spoke like that, and I had no more trouble with him about it.

It was the next day that the real trouble began,

and not at all the sort of trouble that I had been expecting all the time.

That day he arranged a new kind of dressing for his side. The bandages came off, and, instead, he had me put on his wound a dressing of herbs that he had directed me to pick and steep in hot water, and, over those herbs, he had me put a dressing of—what do you think? Mud!

When I looked at the wound that morning, the edges still were not united, and the whole affair looked mighty angry and worried me, but I did as he told me to do. It was an Indian cure, he said, and perhaps it was, or else just one of the childish ideas that he got from time to time.

The middle of that morning, I saw young Tom Lamont come up the path, and I sang out to him that The Duster was not at home. He hesitated for a minute, and The Duster called: "Is that you, Tommy?"

The boy answered that it was.

I swore from the kitchen to find that my lie had to go for nothing. "You can warn people off yourself, after this," I said.

"Good old Baldy," said The Duster. "But you see, old-timer, that a fellow has to see a friend, now and then. Tommy isn't people. He's a partner of mine."

I might have guessed by this, I suppose, the course that he was going to follow with young Tom, but I didn't. In another minute Tom was through the door and grinning with a pretty, bright-red pleasure at The Duster.

You would have thought that he was meeting Santa Claus, and I really think that Tom would rather have spent his time with The Duster than with an angel from heaven. The Duster had a way with all kinds of youngsters—animals or men.

He said: "Tom, I'm having a lazy, sleepy morning. You don't mind if I don't get up?"

"Not a bit," answered Tom. "But somehow it seems to me that you look a little pale, sir."

"Do I?" said The Duster. "Well, perhaps I do. Stomach is upset a little. What have you been doing with yourself, Tommy?"

"Getting to be fifteen," said the boy.

"Hold on. Have you had a birthday?"

"Yesterday."

"And you didn't tell me."

"No, I didn't. It would have been like asking for a present, sir."

"I've asked you to call me Duster, Tommy."

"Yes, sir . . . Duster, I mean," said Tommy, pink with pleasure.

"Because we're friends," said The Duster, "and friends like to know about the good things that happen to one another, eh? Take that gun off the wall," he went on, pointing to a fine new shotgun, light as a feather and strong as iron. "That's to prove you're fifteen, Tommy."

I saw Tommy take the gun, like a boy in a trance, but all at once I told myself that Tommy would have to pay for that weapon, and pay for it through the nose.

XI

The biggest one day in my whole life was the time when I got a new knife. I was eleven years old, and I had had knives before, but most generally they had been ones cast off by somebody else, with one blade broken and the other ground down to a sharp bevel, or else they had been toy knives, and I've always admired the trouble that toy makers must go to get the stuff that they put in toy knives. It would be too cheap and easy to put in plain steel or even iron, so they work up a tinny stuff that turns its edge on your fingernail and the frame of that knife falls apart and the blade wobbles on its pinions. It doesn't even look like a knife to a real boy. But this new knife that I got when I was eleven years old was a corker. It had a strong horn handle that gripped your hand to the blistering point and a big blade, three and a half inches long, made of steel that would cut rhinoceros hide like nothing at all, and it had two smaller blades, to say nothing of a leather pouch. When I brought that knife to school, the whole crowd of boys envied me for a week.

Now if a knife like that meant so much to me, imagine what a brand-new double-barreled shotgun meant to Tommy Lamont, the minister's son, who never had more than half a pair of suspenders at a time. He was older than eleven, but still he was a boy, and everything that goes by that name has only one brain and heart and soul. In the country of a boy, the currency is canceled stamps, and the crown jewels and badges of honor are guns. Well, Tommy grabbed that gun, and his hands shook, and he could hardly see it, there were such tears of joy in his eyes.

He sat down beside The Duster and had the fine points shown to him, and he listened religiously to how it should be cleaned and cared for. You can't buy the love of a grown man, I know, but you can buy some of the love of a boy outright, if you know how to go about it.

I growled to myself as I worked away in the

kitchen that there was something wrong in this. The Duster was fond of Tommy, and he was generous enough to give away ten shotguns, for that matter, but I had seen his eye when he was making that presentation, and I was not satisfied.

Pretty soon I heard The Duster saying: "It isn't really that I'm tired and sleepy. I can't very well get up, Tommy."

You can bet your life that I stopped work and listened with both ears, after that.

"You can't?" said Tommy.

"I've had a bullet scrape along my left ribs," said The Duster.

I heard a gasp, then: "But I thought you showed them your side and they saw no wound?"

"I showed them my side. But it was the right side, Tom."

Another gasp. "That was an idea!" cried Tommy, full of admiration. "But you did it, Duster? You broke the Muncie safe open, Duster?" That was in a whisper.

"I'm telling you," said The Duster.

"Why, I'd rather die than let anybody else know," Tommy promised.

"I know you would," said The Duster in a grave, deep voice. "Once in a while a man finds a friend in this world, Tommy. And I've seen enough pikers and quitters to know the real people when they come my way."

"Thanks," said Tommy, nearly choking with pleasure.

He was fifteen, mind you, and how could he be anything but wax in the hands of The Duster?

I listened, and I guessed what was coming, and I swore to myself that for once I would interfere.

"I broke the safe open. And why not? Everybody knows that Muncie is a thief and a robber, except that he hides behind the law while he robs. He uses foreclosures, instead of guns and bullets, but I'd rather be hit with a Forty-Five-caliber slug of lead than with a foreclosure, for my part."

"So should I," said Tommy, willing to agree to anything.

What did he know about foreclosures? He only knew that his god on earth was speaking to him.

"It must have been terribly exciting," said Tommy. "I mean, there in the bank, when Muncie turned on the light."

"Things happened too fast to be very exiting," The Duster explained. "But it was warm for a while."

"Old Muncie, they say he's nearly dead with spite and rage and hate for everybody and everything, Duster." The boy chuckled as he talked, and then laughed, a crooning laugh. You could tell that he wished he had been there. Well, most boys are two-thirds Indian, and Tommy was a little more than most, I suppose. Just The Duster's talk about bad-men and guns and shooting had made Tommy, not so long before, actually rob the Emmet stage, and Lefty Gainor was still getting well from the bullet that Tommy had put through him. Yes, I must admit that Tommy had in him the possibility of going wrong, but only out of the bigness of his heart, if one can put it that way.

"He's lived and fed on hate the whole of his life," said The Duster. "All that I'd ever regret would be not that I robbed him, but that I couldn't get everything that he owns, I'd rob him as quickly as I'd rob a wolf."

"So would I," agreed the boy.

The Duster said quickly: "No more talk like that, Tommy."

"No, sir," Tommy answered humbly. "I haven't forgotten."

"And you haven't forgotten," went on The Duster, "that you ought to get on through your schoolwork, and find a business that you're interested in."

"I like railroading pretty well," said Tommy. "I might be an engineer someday."

"Maybe you will be, and a mighty good one," The Duster confirmed. "But the thing for you to remember now is that you're only a boy. And you won't yet know your mind as a man. Is that right?"

"Yes, sir, of course it is. I haven't forgotten what you said to me at the time of the stage business. Oh, Duster," he broke out, "what sort of a fellow would I be, if I didn't do exactly what you said about everything, seeing the way that you got me out of the trouble that time, and what a friend you've always been to me, in spite of everything?"

"Tut, tut," The Duster said, "I can't help loving my friends, Tommy, and I count you for one of the best. That's why I was willing to tell you about the Muncie business."

"Who was with you that night?" asked Tommy Lamont eagerly.

"Why, Tommy, I'm surprised," said The Duster. "Of course I don't mind telling you what I have done, but would it be fair if I were to tell what other people had done?" He added: "Of course, it isn't a matter of my trust, Tommy. It's for the other fellow. Suppose you had ever been with me in a job, would I talk to anyone in the world about you? I should say not."

"Of course you wouldn't," Tommy said. "And

now I understand. I'm sorry I was such a fool as to ask. But there's been a whale of a lot of talk about that other man."

"Has there?"

"Yes, and you wouldn't hear it, laid up the way you are, and Baldy is about half deaf, poor old gent."

I wanted to run in and give Tommy a piece of my mind, when I heard that. I'd prove to him that I could hear as well as any young snip in the world. But I held myself in. I remembered that he was a boy.

Tommy Lamont was going on: "I'll tell you what they say . . . that this partner of yours, who was surely the man who was working in the bank just before the robbery and disappeared afterward, is a new man that you've picked up to take the place of Manness. And they say that though he's a new partner for you, he must be an old hand, because he did everything so slick, and covered himself up so well. So that if it hadn't been that one of the men he bribed double-crossed you, then you would have had the money without any trouble and danger at all. They say that maybe it's a brother of Manness."

"Do they say that?" said The Duster with a slight rise in his voice.

"They do, because he's about the same general cut, but older, and gray, and all of that."

"People get queer ideas," said The Duster, yawning.

"I guess it isn't important, but I thought I'd tell you."

"I'll tell you something," said The Duster. "That other fellow who worked with me is such a fox that he'll soon be along my trail to pick up the loot I left behind, because, of course, he knows mighty well that I didn't bring the stuff home with me."

"Would he do that, when you're so true to him?" questioned the boy, full of indignation.

"He's that kind," said The Duster, almost sadly.

"But when you . . . when you were wounded? And after you'd done all the fighting for him?"

"What's that compared to the chance of getting three hundred thousand dollars for himself?"

"It's pretty hard to believe that you'd work with such a cur," Tommy stated fiercely.

"One doesn't find square shooters every day," said The Duster. "It simply doesn't happen. You'll find that out, Tommy."

"Aye, Duster, I suppose I will. But . . . d'you know what I could do?"

"What, Tom?"

"Well, if you'd trust me, I mean."

"I could trust you with my life," The Duster declared in a simple way.

"Then tell me where you hid the stuff, and I'll go get it for you."

There it was—the cat out of the bag! I had guessed from the instant that the gun was given what The Duster had in mind, but see how he had worked up to it and made the suggestion come from the boy himself. A clever fellow was The Duster.

"You get it for me?" repeated The Duster. "Why, Tom, I couldn't let you do that. Suppose they caught you with it?"

"They'd never catch me."

"I'd rather lose the three hundred thousand dollars than have you come to any trouble, old fellow."

"But I could go by night, Duster. They'd never catch me."

"Yes," agreed The Duster, as if letting himself be

persuaded against his will. "Of course, you could go by night, all right."

"And I will, if you'll tell me where to go."

"I could do that in a minute."

And, of course, he did.

Then I stepped into the kitchen doorway and I growled at them: "Duster, you're a low-down crook . . . and Tom is a simpleton. He ain't going to take a step to get that stolen coin!"

XII

If you want real hundred-proof trouble, scratch a Scotchman. The Irish can give you plenty of work, but they get over being mad quicker, and they have a sense of humor that helps them a lot. But a Scotchman is all steel down to the middle of his heart, where there's a small place that's kept tender for one or two old friends, and for Bonnie Prince Charlie.

I thought that the youngster would send a double charge of buckshot into me at first, and then that he'd go for me with his bare hands. He was dancing with rage.

"The Duster is a crook, is he?" said the boy. "You baldheaded, squirrel-brained, monkey face, you! I'll show you who's a crook!"

He would have gone for me, right then and there, but The Duster stopped him—thereby putting himself more than ever in the right, of course, from the boy's point of view. "Buck up, Tom," he said. "I can stand hard talk from a fellow like Baldy Wye. He means well, Tom, no matter how he talks."

"No matter how I talked before," I said, "I'm through with you now, Duster. You got this boy ripe for a stage hold-up before . . . and now you're going to load him down with stolen goods, so's he can take a ten-year trip to a reform school and be a ruined name the rest of his life."

"Shut up!" Tommy said to me, grinding his teeth. "The Duster didn't get me to rob the stage, and you know it. But he got me out of all the trouble when nobody else in the world could have done anything for me. And you know that, too. Go on and leave The Duster, then. You're just another quitter. But I'll take care of him."

He was fairly quivering with excitement, and loyalty, and devotion, and willingness to die for his friend. I didn't get angry at him. I sort of pitied him and loved him, there was so much man and baby mixed up in that lad.

"No," said The Duster. "Let Baldy Wye be. He's right, after all. He's completely right. Suppose they caught you . . . why, they'd have you in a reform school in no time. No, no, Tommy. It was my first idea, and the right idea, and I'm sorry that I ever mentioned the thing to you."

That soothed me down a good deal, and I began to have a better idea of The Duster than I had had a minute before.

"The contemptible coward!" Tommy hissed, his lip lifting as he sneered at me. "To jump on you when you're helpless, Duster."

"No, no," said The Duster very earnestly. "Baldy is the straightest fellow in the world and one of the best friends I've ever had, Tommy. He's stuck by me here, through thick and thin, and driven people away from the house, and nursed me, and cooked for me, and watched me day and night, and treated me like a son."

As he piled up these details, it began to take my breath a little, and, as for the boy, he was completely flabbergasted. He took me in with a long look, and it was plain that he was seeing new things about me. Then he set his teeth and marched up to me with a mighty resolute look. "I've been wrong," said this little gentleman. "I certainly beg your pardon, sir, for all the rough talk I've used on you. Will you forgive me, Mister Wye?"

I took his hand and squeezed it. "You're a young fool," I assured him, "but an amusin' young fool besides. And, of course, I forgive you, son. And I'm not Mister Wye, either. Only . . . no more talk about goin' after that money, that's worse than poison for you to touch, Tommy."

"No, Tom," The Duster said impressively. "I won't have you endanger yourself on my account. I forbid you to go there, Tommy."

Did he mean it? Oh, I don't know. But I'd put up my money that he didn't, and that he was just playing one of his smart parts, and making himself appear a thousand times better than he ever was, and melting my heart, and making Tom worship him more than ever, but all the time really knowing that the lad would never give up the purpose that The Duster had suggested to him. There was too much obvious bulldog in Tommy Lamont for that. Is a Highlander loyal to his chief and ready to die for him? Well, The Duster was in the place of chief to Tom, poor boy.

But to go back to that moment, we were all thick friends in an instant, with young Tommy still very apologetic for the way he had talked to me, and with me, of course, forgiving him. If another man's dog bites you, you ought to blame the man and not the dog.

Tom went on to explain that the reason he had come over was to tell The Duster that his brother Bill was mighty anxious to come to call, because he wanted The Duster to teach him boxing and shooting and a few wrestling tricks, the same as he had taught them to Tommy.

"Do you want me to teach them to him?" said The Duster.

It was a hard test for Tommy. His brother Bill had always been able to keep the upper hand until The Duster's tricks put Tom on top at everything— riding, shooting, fists, and even at running. We watched the youngster struggle with jealousy and pride on one side and with a sense of duty on the other, but I think we both knew how the fight would come out. The best nature always won with Tommy. He was that kind of a lad.

He said at last: "Bill naturally can do everything better than I can. He'd learn a lot more from you than I could, sir."

"You're pretty fond of Bill, Tommy?" said The Duster.

Tommy rubbed his nose. "He's licked me all my life," he said, "until you taught me that straight left and right cross. But there's nobody like Bill. There's no yellow in him, Duster."

He could see his own Waterloo ahead of him, but he faced the music with a smile, and I made up my mind on the spot that I'd never known a boy who was worth one-two-three compared with Tommy Lamont. How could he help being, since he was the son of such a man, and the brother of such a girl as Marguerite?

While this was going on, The Duster had made

up his own mind, and he said that, when he was well enough, which wouldn't be for a few days more, he would start in with Bill, as he had with Tom, but he wanted to know if the minister gave his consent to all this?

He did, it seemed. Old Lamont was a good Christian and knew how to forgive an enemy, even if he couldn't forget one. He had told the boys that they could see The Duster as much as they chose. He had gone one step further and wanted The Duster to come to dinner at his house. That was humility with a vengeance, considering the proud sort of a Scotchman that Lamont really was.

The Duster said that he would be delighted to come, but that would have to wait, also, so Tommy went off with his head high. He had been trusted with the confidence of the most important man he knew anything about, and that made him walk on air, to say nothing of the shotgun under his arm that would break the hearts of all the boys in town, when they saw it.

"That boy is going to be one of the best men you ever met," said The Duster.

"Now tell me what you mean by that?"

"I mean that he will if he ever gets bridle-wise and learns to stand a cinch and a saddle."

"Every man is not a beast of burden, Duster," I said.

"Every good man is," he answered. "And every man who's worth his salt to society is a chap who's willing to stand the spur, and carry a load uphill, and all that sort of thing. But if he bucks the saddle off, and breaks the bridle, and runs off and jumps the fence into the next pasture, then he turns into a man like me, and society gets its guns and ropes ready to hunt him and hang him. And mighty well right society is."

It was a wonder to hear him talk like this, condemning himself so openly. He knew what was wrong with himself. As a matter of fact, badmen are nearly always better than good men in one respect. They know their sins and they're not proud of them. But your all-around good man gets all mixed up and is apt to think that nothing he does can be wrong.

That night I changed the dressing on The Duster's wound, and I was surprised at the change in it. The inflammation had disappeared completely. The edges of the hurt looked clean. And you could fairly see the healing going on.

So I went out without grumbling, this time, and got the same herbs together and stewed up another dressing just like the first one.

He allowed himself a little bigger supper that night, and, when he went to bed, he said to me: "I'll be able to go to church tomorrow, Baldy."

I told him that he was crazy, but he insisted. "A few prayers won't do me any harm," he said. "Besides, it's time that I showed myself to the people, or they'll think that there's something wrong. The thing you don't understand is always the evil thing, Baldy, and the thing to be feared."

He was right there, too. He had about as much practical wisdom as any man I've ever known. So I prepared to go up with him to the church the next day and to face the crowd with him, and see the admiration and the host of eyes that would settle on The Duster like bees on a lump of honey. For the way he had put down Renney, the posse, and old Muncie had made a great impression on everyone. It was felt certain, by this time, that he intended to go straight, and Christmas was getting ready to be proud of its favorite son.

I had put the fresh dressing on The Duster and was smoking a pipe in the doorway when I heard the whistle of Charlie, the milk boy, coming down the road. You could always tell the whistle of Charlie. He was just learning the high notes and put a lot of breath into them.

I called out and asked him for the news, so Charlie came gasping and panting with haste up the path and stood in the faint light of the hooded lamp, which shone from inside the house, where The Duster was reading.

"News?" said Charlie. "Why, there ain't any news except about Tommy Lamont."

"Tommy?" I said, getting a chill right then. "What about Tommy?"

"You've heard all about it. Why, everybody in the town knows all about it!" Charlie cried.

"We're off here on the edge of the town," I said. "So we haven't heard. What is it? We're fond of Tommy, here in this house. Mighty fond of him."

"You won't be now," said Charlie. "He's turned out a robber. And he was one of the two that robbed the Muncie bank. And they've caught him with the goods on him."

XIII

When Charlie had gone, I went back inside the house to pack my roll and leave, because I realized then that The Duster had known that the boy would go straight ahead, no matter how he was forbidden, after the idea was suggested. Inside, I saw The Duster stretched on his bunk with his hands folded behind his head while he looked up toward the ceiling with that faint smile that I had come to know so well.

I knew that he had heard everything that was said at the door, so that it looked as though he were amused by what had happened to Tom Lamont. However, he couldn't be such a monster as that, so I put down that smile to hard thinking, and thinking that must have a cutting edge.

That instant I made up my mind to stay. There was some plan in The Duster's mind, and I must stay and help if I could.

When The Duster saw that I was there, he didn't refer to Tommy at all, but asked to have his bandage and dressing shifted again, which I did and, once more, was astonished by the change in the wound. He gave me directions then for preparing a dry dressing, and it was a queer mixture that I had to pound up—tarry fennel was one of the things, I well remember that. I laid on this dry dressing and asked him what else he wanted.

"Sleep," said The Duster, and closed his eyes.

That would have been a fake—or a prayer—in another man, but not with him. Just as you can lighten or darken a room by raising or lowering a blind, so The Duster could sleep instantly, or instantly come awake.

I knew by his deep, regular breathing that he was unconscious, and I sneaked off and lay down in my own bunk with all my clothes on. I was too upset to sleep for a long time, for somehow this quietness of The Duster was more exciting to me than the sound of guns, since I guessed that he was planning some desperate deed.

In the morning, when I got up, he ate a light

breakfast and then got me to help him dress. He moved with very particular care. I had taken off the dry dressing, found that the wound had still further progressed, and then, at his command, corseted him in stiff strips of adhesive tape. I had protested against doing that, but he stopped my talk with a move of his hand, like one who doesn't intend to waste any strength on unnecessary actions—even words.

I got him fed and shaved and bandaged and dressed, at last. He was very particular about everything, and finally, having viewed himself from head to foot, he shook his head at the image of his pale face in the mirror.

He sent me out to harness up the team to his rubber-tired buggy, the one that all Christmas had gaped at when he first appeared in our streets. When I came back with the team spruced up and the buggy behind them, well dusted, I found him putting the finishing touches to his make-up.

When he was through, he looked as if he'd just come in from several days of hard riding and hunting, say, under the open sun. He was able to paint a picture, that Duster.

"It's about time for the church service to begin," said The Duster. "The rest of Christmas is going to be there in order to see how the minister takes it, now that his boy is in jail. We'd better go there, too."

"Duster," I said to him, "as sure as there's blue in the sky, you're going to crack your side open again. And if you do, it'll be the death of you. D'you know that?"

"I do," The Duster replied. "Give me my hat."

Quietly he said that, in a matter-of-fact way, but I knew what it meant. When he lay awake the other evening, smiling at the ceiling, he had been considering all the dangers and strains he must subject himself to the next day. He had considered them and determined to go through with them.

That instant I stopped talking, because I saw that I was merely making a fool of myself. I helped The Duster out to the buggy, and got him up into the body of it. He kept himself quite limp, and let me do much of the work, so that I was boiling with heat before I finished. Yet, he would not let me drive.

He sat up straight as a string and smiled down at me while he held the reins in his gloved right hand. A mighty calm smile—but I'd been with him enough to see the pain behind it. There was a cold fear in him, too, for he mighty well knew that I was right, and that if he broke that wound open, he had one chance in a hundred.

I must say that he drove slowly toward the church, which was the one concession that he made to his condition, but the way he took was straight through the most crowded portions of Christmas, where everyone could see him driving up the hill toward the church.

He had only been partly right. Maybe half the town had already started wandering up the hill for the cruel reason that they wanted to see how Lamont would face them under this disgrace. But when The Duster was seen on the way, the rest of Christmas grabbed its hat and started after him.

That church was jammed, this morning, even tighter than it had been on the day of The Duster's first arrival. You could hardly squeeze in.

For my part, I wondered if old Lamont would hold the service this day and try to face Christmas with his son in jail. But before we were halfway up the hill, we could hear the bell wrangling and jangling against its clapper and pealing farther and wider than ever.

I remember that it was a beautiful morning. It was a morning for birds! To get off there beyond the treetops, I mean, and sag away into the blue of the sky, and take a handful of ice crystals out of one cloud and go sit and eat them on the soft top of another. It was a morning to be young in, or old, too, and I felt the blood jump in me like a grasshopper in a stubble field.

Well, we got up to the church, as I was saying, and waded in through the crowd that was as silent as could be, it seemed at first, with all eyes glued on the empty pulpit where Lamont would have to stand. But now and then, under the silence, I could hear the whispers begin softly.

He ought to burn with shame, they said, to preach morals and religion to others, and not be able to teach them to his own son. A fine sort of a man he was to have roared and berated The Duster. And he raising a son who would be a lot worse! For The Duster, at least, was able to change his way of life.

We heard rumors like this, as we squeezed into places. It was going to be a hard thing for the minister to face that congregation. They were angry clean through. I don't know why, really. But you get more than five men together and you have a mob. And mobs are children—or a lot worse.

Here were these people, mind you, who had seen that good man slave among them for years, giving away the food out of his mouth to the poor of the town, and every day and night turned over to the interests of his people, and yet they were ready to turn on him now because he happened to have a fine, high-strung, wild-spirited lad for a son, and that son had done a wrong thing. Not so wrong, either, when you come right down to it.

We heard other things about young Tommy Lamont while we were in the church. The sheriff, Renney, had been on hand at the jail to question Tommy and find out if he really had been one of the two at the Muncie robbery, or if he merely had been sent by one of the robbers to bring the money, but Tommy had refused to speak. He was still as a stone, when a word from him would practically have set him free. He would be loyal to The Duster to the finish. However, the crowd could not see what was in Tom's mind. They jumped to a conclusion, and they were as wrong as poison.

There was a murmur through the whole crowd just now, for Marguerite Lamont and her brother had just come into the church from a side door. They looked pale and drawn. You could see that their eyes were swollen—even Bill's, although he stuck out his chest and tried to look fierce as he stood up and looked around the church. But that was only a babble of courage. You could see that Bill's heart was broken, like his poor sister's.

You'd think that sight would make the congregation pity them. Not a bit! They were hard as nails, these people of Christmas on this morning. They growled to one another that there must be bad blood in that family.

Well, it made me clean tired to listen to them and to watch their scowling faces. But when they looked over toward The Duster, they changed, and brightened, and nodded, and smiled at him, and hands were waved in our direction—where I sat on The Duster's left side, trying to keep off all pressure on his hurt. The Duster stood ace high now, and the minister was down in the dirt,—he who had been able to put his foot on The Duster's neck in the beginning.

I suppose that crowd thought The Duster had come there to triumph over Lamont, and they did not blame him. No, they sympathized, and the sight of him made them all the fiercer against poor Lamont. Well, I'd rather deal with dogs than with people, take them as a whole.

There had been some sort of a choir singing, or something like that, a few nights before, and the church had been decorated for it, and there were still wreaths and strings of flowers and greenery, here and there, tied up to the poor, bare rafters of that shack of a church. It seemed to me as though it were all arranged like a funeral, where the minister was to be the dead man. This here looked like the end of his work and his real life. I tried to get that idea out of my mind, but I couldn't.

Then the old man who played the organ began to play something, but at about the second strain it wheezed, coughed, and then squeaked like a rat you had stepped on. The music ended, and the organist began to fumble around.

But I pitied Lamont worse than ever, for now it meant that he had to enter the church in silence, without any music to cover up his coming, for sound can be like a veil to a face.

Everybody grew quiet—fiercely quiet—and waited, and waited, like so many tigers about to spring.

A door creaked, after that. The minister was coming, walking slowly out of the side aisle and toward the pulpit. The silence was so terrible that you could hear the little squeak when a nail in the heel of his boot struck a nail head on the floor.

Then the people drew in their breath all at once, as if they had been drinking. And drinking they were—the misery of Lamont.

XIV

Surely they all saw—tigers or not—that their minister had become an old man overnight, and that, when he came to the pulpit, he was pulling himself up with his hands until at last he stood straight before them. But still they would not pity him, or the awful misery in his eyes, or the weariness in his face.

I had seen The Duster with a bullet wound in his flesh on the verge of collapsing. But Lamont was wounded deeper. You couldn't bandage or dress his hurt. Even opium wouldn't reach that deep.

Well, I prayed that he wouldn't break down, but that he would make a good game finish, like a hunted animal that turns around and tears a few of the dogs before the end. I hoped that he would pour himself out and scald a few of the sneaks and hypocrites who were sneering at him from the benches.

But when he opened his lips, his voice was wonderfully mild, wonderfully steady. He spoke like this: "My brothers and sisters, we are forced to begin our service today with a silence, because the organ has broken down after many long years of service. It used to wheeze sometimes, and groan sometimes, but somehow or other it managed to get through its work on Sundays, and on Friday nights. Perhaps there was a flaw in its making . . . and today the flaw showed through. However, for my part, I can't forget its long years of service."

He paused for an instant here. It wasn't much of a joke, but it was a pleasant beginning, and, of course, any blind man could see that he was comparing himself with that organ, which might break down after long service. I only hoped that he would have the strength to push the thing through.

I looked around the congregation. Well, sir, I'm ashamed of humanity when I have to say that not an eye understood him or would pity him. They were hard and bright and shone like the steel of gun barrels.

Poor Lamont cleared his throat and went on in the same quiet, deliberate voice: "We will begin today with the reading of the Twenty-Second Psalm, in unison." He added a few words, telling them on what page of the church Bibles it would be found.

I looked around me. There was no Bible in the rack in front of me, or I sure would've read—if I had had my reading glasses. But all the rest of that congregation didn't put out a hand—except a child or a woman here and there, instinctively. But there would be a growl from the men, and the hands went back and lay flat and empty on the knees once more.

You see what it meant? They were going to let old Lamont suffer alone. They had come there for that purpose, and not a voice would be lifted to help him out. Why, even now, I turn hot and then cold, just to think of it, and the infernal meanness of that gang. Not bad people, mind you. Only, the mischief was in them that morning. Take the best people of the world and form them into a crowd, and they'll give you a new stoning every day in the week.

Now Lamont began to read, his voice clear, steady, and slow, so that others could follow him in unison, but with a terrible lot of meaning in it. Two voices did follow him, and with a dying flutter, you might say—there was the boyish, heavy bass of Billy Lamont, and there was the sweet low sound of Marguerite.

It gripped my heart so, I can't tell you. I wanted to get up and shout to them that they might torture the minister if they wanted to, but why burn those two poor kids alive? But I couldn't cry out. I couldn't say a word. I was frozen.

For Lamont wasn't dodging the issue this day. He was going to meet his misery face to face, and, just as he had berated other people in that church, so now he had the courage to stand before them and show them his own misery.

It was a tremendous thing. It was greater than The Duster facing the posse with a painted face and no life in his body. I don't know one psalm from another, but the words of this one, they crashed on my mind like the roar of a waterfall and made me shake all over:

"Why hast Thou forsaken me? Why art Thou so far from helping me and from the words of my crying?"

Heaven knows that should have touched them, but it didn't. I looked sideways, and I saw the horrible sight of a man with his mouth a little opened by a grin and his eyes glittering and small with enjoyment. Eating the minister's agony, do you see?

The slow, big voice of the minister went on, with a ring of grief in it that struck in my heart like the sound of a dead bell.

When he got to—"They trusted in Thee, and were not confounded. . . ."—there was a sob of a woman's voice that was like that of a child, but more mournful, and more wanting to be comforted, so that your hand goes out before you even without your will.

It was Marguerite. I saw her head drop, and the hand of Billy go up to his face. Their voices stopped there, but not a sight or sound of sympathy did I hear in that whole church full of brutal people.

You might have thought that they were at a dog-fight.

That sob of the girl ruined her father. He had carried on that far, but here he wrecked suddenly. I saw his face twisting with effort, and his lips framing words that would not come out.

But, by Jiminy, still not one ounce of sympathy did he get from that crowd—not from the fathers of it—not even from the mothers, mind you.

The silence lasted two or three thumping heart-beats. You could count them. Then right beside me a clear voice picked up the words, saying: "But I am a worm, and no man . . . a reproach of men, and despised of the people!"

I could not believe my ears. I turned, and there was The Duster, without any book to read from, sitting straight, with his lean face raised toward the minister and all the sincerity in the world in that actor's voice of his.

Well, that cracked them! The crowd, I mean. They could listen to a good man like Lamont, a true and honest man like their own minister, and they could see him show his grief before them without stirring, but when they heard this "reformed" crook speak from the same text, they were done up.

You could hear the rustle of the turned heads; you

could hear the little shrill gasp of the women and the children; you could hear one deep, thick murmur from the men.

Yes, The Duster had rung the bell with his first shot.

After The Duster began, there had been a sudden sound of turned pages, like the still, soft rustle of rain through dead autumn leaves that come twisting and tumbling down to the ground, and now voices of men and women struck in, and the thin voices of children, saying like a great chorus:

"Be not far from me; for trouble is near; for there is none to help!"

Yes, from the whole crowd—except some like me that had left their reading glasses at home—up came that voice, and you could hear the tremor and catch of women's tears, pitying. Pitying what? Why, the "reformed" crook, of course, who was here professing penitence, as it seemed. And then taking up the great words and laying them on their own hearts—because who is without trouble and the need of help?—and pitying themselves next of all.

But finally they woke up and saw what had happened, like light breaking through darkness. I suppose that whole gang, even the roughest, suddenly saw that they had tied the minister to a stake and applied a match to the wood to burn him. For now all their eyes were on him.

Now, what the words were did not matter, for the minister was able to speak again, and the congregation sat in the palm of his hand and even forgot The Duster, who sat back with his head dropped a little, and pretty far spent, as I could guess.

We got out of that church among the first, for most of them stayed—the men with troubled faces, feeling that they had done wrong and not knowing what to do about it to make amends, and the women flocking around the minister at the end of his sermon, and crying over him, and, I suppose, more real religion was stirred up in that one session than in a year before.

By whom? Why, by The Duster!

XV

As we got out of the church, I knew that no matter what happened to Tommy, Lamont was stronger in his church and in his town than ever before, and yet it seemed a sort of miracle that The Duster had been able to do this by speaking a few words out of a book.

We headed straight for the rig and the team, when Marguerite Lamont, who had slipped out through the side door near the pulpit, came straight toward us, all blind with the tears that were still running down her face.

The Duster, when he saw her, gripped my arm, so that his fingertips grated against the bone. But then he made himself turn and face her, while she came up and took one of his hands in hers and pressed it against her heart.

"I know why Tommy loves you," said the girl.

When we got to the rig, The Duster didn't mind me driving, and he sat all the way home with the look of a man who is trying to see through a fog on a dangerous trail.

I didn't speak, neither did he, until I got him to the Ridley house and stretched on his bunk again.

"What will you have?" I said.

"Sleep," he said again. And he had it.

I put the horses up, watered, unharnessed, and fed them. Then I went back to the kitchen and cooked lunch, moving around softly to keep The Duster from being disturbed. When I had finished, I woke him up. He ate a little, and then went back to sleep, after I had looked at the corseting of adhesive again. It bound him hard, but there was no sign of inflammation. At least, it had not spread past the edges of the bandages.

Still, I was terribly worried, but I would no more question him about his purposes, and such, than ask an eagle in the air where he was bound. I couldn't see the game, but I knew that it was in sight for the mind of The Duster.

I had to turn away two or three people that afternoon, who wanted to talk to The Duster, but he was still sleeping sound, and it was not until the twilight began that he woke up and asked me suddenly for coffee and cigarettes. That was what he always wanted when he had some game on hand, and I knew that the time was close when he would make a decisive move.

It was all so complicated that I had thought myself into a stew through the course of the day. Suppose he wanted to get Tommy off scotfree, the best he could do would be to make a full confession that he himself had been the robber, and then Tommy would only be guilty of carrying stolen goods, a crime they wouldn't press too hard, probably, against the boy. But that was the only way out, so far as I could see, and somehow I knew that, no matter what else The Duster might do, he never would be able to make such a confession.

His whole life had been one long game with the law and the long arm of the law was what he had played tag with. It was not so much a matter of failing generosity, I suppose, as it was a principle of instinct. You can teach a dog to lie down with a cat, but you can hardly expect him to give her his bone.

The twilight dulled toward night, and there was only a faint rim of horizon light, at the last.

Then The Duster said to me: "Take a lantern. Cover it with a sack. Go to the edge of the woods and face across the valley. Cover and uncover the lantern three times."

I took the lantern without a word. There was some crooked purpose being forwarded, I knew, but I didn't much care. All that I wanted was the freedom of Tommy Lamont from that jail.

On the outer edge of the woods, therefore, I sent the three beams of light flying across the valley, wondering what eyes might be watching for them. Then I lingered a moment to watch the stars, stepping here and there on the still shallows of the Christmas River. After that, I went back to the Ridley house and found The Duster laying out some regular punching clothes. They were old, battered, shapeless things, sagging out at the elbow and knee, the way cloth does when you've ridden in it through the rain.

The Duster stepped into them at once. After that, he sat down with a pot of make-up and worked on his face. He made it a mahogany color that didn't quite come down to the lips. It was a pretty crude effect. You could even see the smears where the stain was streaked across his face, but The Duster seemed contented enough. I don't think he worked five minutes, giving his hands a final wash to make them the same shade as his face. Next, he got out from his bag a scrap of white beard. He put this on, and then he looked pretty much like nothing at all.

"Is that a disguise or just a joke, Duster?" I asked him.

He grinned at me without answering. Then he lifted a board of the floor—I hadn't even known that it was loose—and took out from beneath it a little canvas roll, darkened with oil stains. This he unfurled and took out some steel tools. I only had a flash at them, and, therefore, I could not name them, but I very well knew that they were to be used as keys or levers to get poor Tommy Lamont out of the jail.

Just then I heard a noise outside the door, and The Duster hooked a thumb in that direction, so I went to look. No man was in sight, but a fine big horse with the earmarks of a runner was standing there, half in lamplight and half in shadow.

"There's a horse there," I said to The Duster.

He nodded and, getting up from his chair, left the house and took the path, leading the horse behind him.

As soon as he stepped into the darkness, I could see the effect of his make-up at once. It made him look like an old weather-beaten man, and he reinforced that idea by walking with a shuffling step.

"So long, Baldy," he said.

"Good luck, old-timer," I replied.

"Good luck for what?" The Duster asked, and faded out among the trees.

I was on the point of running after him and asking him what I could do, but I didn't. Inside the law is the best place for me to stay, no matter what your Dusters may be doing. However, I can tell you exactly what he did that night, as though I had been with him every step of the way.

XVI

He went straight across town. Most people were inside having supper, but he was seen in three places—an old man leading a fine big horse, as though he were afraid to trust himself in the saddle. Then, near the jail, he put the horse in the young grove of poplars that had jumped up in the space where the post office will be built, someday. With the horse lodged, he made a circuit of the jail and found out exactly how things stood by getting a peek at the window, here and there. This was what he found.

In the front room, or office, where the safe stood, was an armed guard with as tough a face as you ever laid eyes on. He had on a pair of Colts, and in his hands there was a cavalry carbine, and on his mug there was the look of a man who's willing to use his tools. That was Sam Lucas.

In the cage or prison room, there was another man, called Bobby Saunders. Bobby was the regular jailer, and he was busy now collecting the tinware that the prisoners had just eaten from. He had three in his keep. A couple were tramps picked up for vagrancy, and the third man was young Tommy Lamont, now smoking a cigarette and pretending that nothing made any difference to him.

Clear outside the jail there was Renney himself, sitting on the steps of the building, not smoking, and heavy with guns. He had volunteered for this job of keeping the prisoner and the $300,000 worth of recaptured money safe until the people from Emmet arrived to take charge.

So there you see the job that lay before The Duster—a building to crack open in the middle of the town, with three professional and expert fighters to defend it.

The Duster did not hesitate, although what he did seemed the most obvious and clumsy thing in the world. If he wanted to get inside, he might have jimmied one of the windows. He didn't. He simply walked up to the steel-barred and re-barred cellar windows that opened on the side of the jail that faced the street, and fell to work with a long saw that had a jeweled edge. Right on the street, mind you, with his sleeves rolled up over his stained forearms.

That saw was a priceless thing. I've heard The Duster talk of it at other times. Now, with a drop of oil here and there, it melted away through rough steel bars as though they were mere wood. There was only a little creaking, now and then, to tell what was happening. He cut straight down through the left-hand side, and then was halfway across the bottom when Henry Pfeffer, the butcher, came by and saw him at work. He asked what he was doing, and a thick mumbling voice answered that the window was to be walled up by orders of Sheriff Renney and that he'd been given the job, and a danged tough job it was, working that way through the night. But Renney wasn't taking any chances with his new prisoner in that jail.

The butcher thought that sounded logical enough,

so he walked on and would have gone straight home if he had not happened to see Renney sitting on the steps in front of the jail. He stopped for a word with him and, after he had talked for a few moments, asked him about the walling up of the cellar window.

Of course, that was the first the sheriff had heard about it. He got up to investigate, and loosened a gun in its holster as he went along. But when he reached the window, he found that the steel frame of bars had been partly cut through and partly torn away. Renney did not call for help. He simply dipped his head into the syrupy blackness of the cellar, and then climbed through to investigate.

The Duster, the minute Pfeffer passed him, guessed that his time was short, and, leaving off the cutting, he grasped the bars and twisted them with a turn of his muscular arms. At the very first pressure, the rotten cement that held the bars in their sockets gave way.

The Duster leaned that frame of bars against the wall of the jail. And here I know that he actually stopped to replace his tools in their wrapper of oil-stained canvas, and tied the string around it, and slipped the thing into his coat pocket. Then he climbed down into the dark cellar. He had with him a little dark lantern, and, unhooding this a hair's breadth, he sliced the blackness with the ray, and found the slippery steps that climbed to the floor above. So he went on. I hold my breath even now, as I think of that man going forward after he had been accosted by Pfeffer, and when danger was gathering on his back trail so fast.

He went up the steps to the locked door at the head of them. The Duster had it open in the twinkling of an eye and looked through in time to see the jailer putting out one of the two lanterns that lighted the inside of the building. Then he turned down the second light, leaving the interior all awash with shadows, and sauntered down the center aisle, where he stopped a moment to talk to one of the tramps—a big redhead who had graduated out of the prize ring a couple of years before and taken to the road. The redhead promised to punch Bobby's head when he got out of the jail. Bobby laughed. He was the sort of a fellow who didn't know what fear was. He had the red eye of an angry bull, no matter when you met him, and he would have fought a cage full of wildcats for the fun of it.

He went on, chuckling, and, as he turned the corner of the aisle to go into the office, a shadow rose up off the floor beside him. He dropped the lantern and swung his heavy bunch of keys for the head of the shadow, but just then he was slammed along the jaw by something that was not hard, but that struck with terrible impact. If you've never been tapped with a sandbag, you can't describe the effect. And The Duster had sandbagged Bobby.

Bobby lay on his face, as a man does when he's really knocked out, and The Duster didn't waste time tying him. He had no time to lose, he guessed.

So he picked up the bunch of keys and ran down the aisle. He had to spend a whole minute there, trying key after key, until he got the one to open Tommy's door, and, as he worked, he gave Tommy instructions.

Tommy hung onto the bars and whispered with a gulp: "Duster, I'm sorry I was such a fool. I never should have let them take me. But the hammer stuck in my gun . . . I didn't have it properly clean, I guess."

"Thank heaven that it did stick," said The Duster. "After this, you'd better ride without any gun at all. You're going north, Tommy, and you're going to keep on riding until you're across the border. Take this money. . . ."

He had the door of the cell open by this time, but young Tommy stopped then and there to argue the propriety of his taking the money from The Duster. One deep, short curse silenced him, however. I suppose for the first time he realized that The Duster was taking his life in his hands by being there in that jail.

He did not stop at Tommy. He immediately unlocked the doors of the two tramps as well, and showed the whole three of them the way down the cellar stairs.

He did not follow. He had something else to do in the jail before he left. Thorough was The Duster's motto, from first to last.

Now this was just the time that the sheriff was fumbling across the cellar floor through the darkness, and, hearing the opening of the door at the head of the stairs, he looked up, and saw several forms file smoothly out and downward. He tossed up his gun to shoot.

"Who's there?" asked Renney.

The big redhead was the first of the procession, being the sort that leads. When he saw the dim gleam of the gun beneath him, he tried to check himself, slipped on the wet stone steps, and shot downward like a bullet—200 pounds of him.

Renney fired, of course. But almost of course, he also missed. And just as he was pulling the trigger the second time, the redhead, with a yell that cut through half the ears in Christmas, landed with one shoulder in the pit of Renney's stomach.

They went across the cellar floor like one man, but, on the far side, the sheriff was the cushion that broke the force of the tramp's landing. So Renney lay there sound asleep, while the tramp eventually got up and followed the other two through the window. Tommy was first now, and, finding the horse that had been left for him, he slid out of Christmas like snow down a mountain.

In the meantime, Lucas in the safe-room heard the distant commotion, the shots, and the yell of the tramp. He had been told not to leave that room under any circumstances, but this was too much temptation for a natural fighting man, and he jerked the door open just in time to let The Duster put the cold lips of a Colt .45 against the hollow of his throat. Lucas was a rough fellow and a fighting man, but he didn't need to be a professor of philosophy to know the best thing to do. He dropped his gun, let The Duster fan him for the rest of his weapons, and then rendered the key that opened the safe itself. He even held the light, by which The Duster saw his way to $300,000 in cash or convertible securities.

"Shall I gag you?" The Duster asked. "Or will you give me ten seconds to get away?"

"Gag me," said poor Lucas, "or I'll have to change my name and go to China."

Well, sir, the amazing thing was that The Duster actually did it—with all the town of Christmas spilling out into the streets and making for the jail with the first guns it found ready to hand. The Duster spent thirty priceless seconds tying and gagging Lucas to save the poor man's face and reputation. Then he made for the cellar, and out into the dark.

I didn't see the money. That had been cached on the way home. But I did see the tool kit replaced under the loose board of the floor.

"Suppose they look there?" I said to The Duster.

"They won't," he said, stretching himself in his chair. "They know I'm a lot too subtle to use an old woman's hiding place like that under the floor."

He was right. Renney came there, looking sick as a man might after having 200 pounds of shoulder hit him in the stomach, and, with his men, he fairly tore up that house. He had nothing against The Duster, really, but he knew, and so did everyone else, that no other man in the West had the nerve and the coolness to make that jail break except John Thurlow.

But when the search ended nowhere and the rest of the men had gone, Renney sat down and actually smoked a cigarette with us. He rubbed his stomach frankly, but he did not seem to hold any grudge.

"You've done a smart thing," he said to The Duster, "and most likely you've spoiled my digestion permanently. But there's another point . . . you've turned young Lamont into an outlaw by this little trick."

The Duster merely smiled. "Crooked young trees can always grow straight," he said.

The sheriff did not argue. He merely studied the upward twisting of his cigarette smoke.

"Aye," he said at last, "sometimes time is a doctor."

The Duster's Return

I

The face of Renney was never greatly welcome around the Ridley house while The Duster and I were staying there. But this afternoon I was less glad than ever to see the sheriff riding in from the road through the trees.

For one thing, it was hot, and when I say that I don't mean what they call in the East "that dreadful humidity." No, I mean the dry heat that they tell you in the West is so healthy. Maybe it is. So is an oven then. Everything felt it. The blue jay that went overhead like a jewel seemed looking for shade more than mischief, and the two squirrels that used to scold me every day at the top of their lungs now moved slowly through the branches of the trees and only swore at me now and then, softly, as though they were saving their breath. It was so hot that the sun fire heaped up higher and higher on the naked ground outside the grove, so that you could see it shimmering like water, and looking through it the mountains appeared out of joint, as though they were reflected in a cheap mirror. Now and again, the wind rose just strongly enough to topple that pile of flame and send it invisibly sliding and pouring in among the tree trunks. When it reached me, it burned the damp back of my hand dry in a minute and made the hairs stand up and the skin prickle; it burned my eyes and slid like scalding water down my neck.

On that day, there was no comfort except in smoking a pipe and in looking down the hill through the trees to where the Christmas River was running pale blue, like the sky, with a white cloud or two stuck in the quiet shallows at the bend. Talk was the last effort that I wanted to make. I had finished the lunch dishes and scrubbed out the kitchen and had everything shipshape, and I swore that the only hot thing The Duster should have for supper would be coffee, so that the afternoon lay ahead of me as restful as the run of the river itself. Even thinking was hard, and it was better to watch the brown trunks turn into green leaves and needles, and the foliage turn into the sky, and the sky turn into the great white sun flare that was traveling slowly west toward the horizon.

But there came the sheriff on the same runty mustang that he usually rode, biting at its bit, jerking out its head to make the reins slip through his hands, and always hunting for half a chance to get hysterical or just plain mean. He had an eye as red as a ferret's, and looked as though he lived on raw meat. But there was Renney in the saddle, looking tired, not of the horse, but of things in general.

He looked like a tramp. He hadn't shaved for a week, and his nose was whiskey-red from the weather, and he wore an old red flannel shirt that was sun-faded to a dirty pink over the shoulders, and caked with dirt and dust.

He came up, drew rein, and dismounted with a jingle of spurs and groan of stirrup leathers, while the mustang tried to take a piece out of his shoulder. It missed, and threw up its fool head, and stuck out a stiff upper lip, ready to receive what it deserved. Renney was too tired and hot to bother with that though, and he only made a threatening motion with his hand. I waved my pipe at him by way of greeting.

"Is The Duster here?" he asked.

"The Duster ain't," I said.

"Rode out?"

"Yes."

"When is he due?"

"Don't know."

"You're glad to see me, it looks like," said Renney. "Shall I sit down and rest my feet? Thanks, I will. You got a pretty cool place here," he added as another wash of the sun fire came drifting through and burned me to the bone. He wasn't joking, either. He'd been out where the air was all aflame and this shade felt good to him.

"How are things?" said Renney.

"Fair," I said, seeing that he was bent on talking and making sure that I wouldn't say a word. Because I guessed that he wanted me to talk about The Duster, and I knew too much about him to get going on the subject.

"You got a toothache, maybe," suggested Renney, arranging himself beside me on the doorstep, "and don't want to open your mouth and let in the cold air?"

"Renney," I said, "what are you after?"

"Ideas," he answered.

"About what?"

"About The Duster."

"I'm glad you let me know," I said. "I thought that maybe you'd ridden over this way for the sake of the scenery, or the exercise, or something."

Renney grinned, but the smile didn't last long. "Old son," he said, "how long are you going to stick with this?"

"I'm leaving in a coupla days," I told him.

"You said that last month."

I sighed. It was true. Every day I told myself that The Duster was a crook and that, if I didn't look out, he'd make me another. But every morning I put off leaving until the next day.

"He's got a hold on me," I admitted.

"He has on me, too," said Renney.

"Aye," I answered, "but not as big as you'd like to have on him. With handcuffs, if you could make them fit."

"Sure . . . at first," he said. "But I'm not as certain of that now." He stopped in the making of a cigarette, a sure sign that a man is dreaming. It began to seem to me that he was thinking out loud. "I don't make him out," said the sheriff. "We know that The Duster is the best all-around gunman and slick gambler in this part of the world. He'd admit it himself. But in the midst of his fame, as you might say, and while the world is still at his feet, what does he do but chuck everything, as far as we can see, and come here to settle down."

I thought of the Muncie bank robbery, but I didn't speak—naturally.

"Then," went on Renney, "he makes a grand play to get permission of the minister to bury the ashes of his old partner, Manness, up there in the cemetery, and, although the minister fights hard, somehow The Duster manages to get the thing done . . . I don't know how. Then he makes a play to get young Tommy Lamont over on his side, and, the first thing you know, we find Tommy carrying hundreds of thousands of dollars of stolen money . . . and Tommy's jailed . . . and The Duster gets him loose."

"Does he?" I said innocently.

"You know he did," said the sheriff with a good deal of decision. "In the first place, there's no other man in the world who would've been able to do that job. Well, The Duster did it, and the whole town is sure that he did, and the whole town loves him for doing it. Isn't that clear? He made a fool of me that night, but I don't carry a grudge on that account. Only . . . I'd like to talk things over with him."

"He'd like to, I'm sure," I said, lying pretty easily. Because I knew that no matter how often The Duster had fooled Renney, still he was pretty much afraid of the brains of that man. I couldn't see why, when he'd showed the upper hand so often.

Just as we were talking, along comes a couple of riders flickering down the road past the tree trunks, and they stop in front of the house. We can hear their voices, and the first is that of the minister's daughter, Marguerite Lamont, saying something to "Duster, dear!"—and The Duster answers. We hear them laugh like a song together, and I look at the sheriff and see him wearing a frown that is half painful and half mere thought.

Then The Duster comes toward us, and the girl gallops away. The Duster comes toward us, singing, and this was the song that he sang. It comes up into

my memory like a sound up a well shaft, hollow and
sweet:

> *Oh, my name was William Kid*
> *As I sailed, as I sailed;*
> *My name was William Kid*
> *As I sailed.*
> *And I murdered Mister Moore,*
> *For I hit him from before,*
> *And I left him in his gore*
> *As I sailed.*

It wasn't the sort of a song that sounds cheerful,
particularly when a fellow like The Duster is doing
the singing. How many did he leave in their gore?
Well, I never heard from him, and what others say
you never can believe. Gossip always talks in head-
lines and capital letters.

When he saw the sheriff, he reined his horse
straight over and dismounted and shook hands. He
was such a fine actor that you would have thought
that he was meeting one of his best friends. I mean,
he was cordial, and grave, and considerate. Renney
went to the mark like a bullet.

He said: "Duster, what's it all about? Come clean
with me and tell me what you aim at here in Christmas?"

"Why, Renney," said The Duster, opening his eyes
very innocently, "I want a quiet home after a hard
and troubled life. That's all that I want."

Sometimes I thought that he overdid his acting,
but perhaps that was because I'd lived so close to
him and began to know him so well.

Renney narrowed his eyes. "That's what I want to
be sure of," he said.

"Or?" The Duster said, raising his eyebrows a little. He was mocking Renney, demanding what he could do, as you might say, flaunting his safety under the nose of the sheriff, but Renney didn't lose his temper.

"Not to you, Duster, at present," he said. "But I'm wondering about others. Straight men make others straight. If you're really settling down here, then perhaps the boy was sent off to go straight, also. Tommy Lamont, I mean."

"I don't know anything about him," The Duster stated.

"You don't know where he is?"

"No, of course not. Poor Tommy. Since he broke jail, I have not heard from him."

Renney smiled a little. "I can tell you, then," he said. "He's up in Canada in a logging camp, in British Columbia."

II

That was a stroke. It hit The Duster between wind and water, and such a look as he gave the sheriff I hope I'll never receive. You could see the cold, hard consideration in his eyes as he asked himself whether it would not pay to draw a gun on Renney. He decided not in the next instant, but he was so hard hit that his color had changed, and his nostrils quivered.

I never had been quite sure of The Duster's attitude toward Tommy Lamont. At first, I thought he simply used the youngster as a leverage to work on the minister, and, after that, as a hold on the affection of Marguerite Lamont. But this day it showed in his face that he loved the boy.

Even that calm, steady voice of his, always under such good control, now went out of hand and shook as he said: "You're going to extradite him and bring him down here, Renney?"

The sheriff made a long pause. "It's my duty to do that," he said. "I owe that to the law."

"Baldy," said The Duster to me, "will you fix me up a cup of coffee?"

I was gathering my heels under me with a groan when Renney interrupted with: "You might as well let him stay with us, Duster. You can't buy me off with cash."

That was another stroke. I felt that for the first time in my life I was watching Duster play a losing game, and I got excited and curious. My respect for Renney went up 1,000 percent, at least. I remembered what The Duster himself once had said—that a crook always has a big advantage over an honest man, because the crook is always dealing from the bottom of the deck. Yet here was Renney taking tricks.

The Duster made a little gesture with both hands. "What can I do, Renney?" he asked.

"Be good," said the sheriff.

I thought it was a joke, and got ready to smile. Then I saw that I was wrong and that Renney meant what he said. Be good.

"What has that got to do with Tom Lamont?" snapped The Duster.

"This. I've had my eye at long distance on Tom ever since he reached that lumber camp, and it appears that he's trying to do what's right. Which makes me think that you gave him some right advice when you took him out of the jail and sent him away. But I'm not sure. I'm watching both ends of the line . . . Tommy up there, and you down here. A wrong step from you, and I get you, if I can . . . but most certainly I get Tommy."

The Duster took out a handkerchief and wiped his forehead. He was thinking as hard as he was able, I knew, and fighting something inside himself.

"You've made yourself a factor in this town," went on the sheriff. "The boys think you're the greatest man in the world. The tramps and dead-beat 'punchers, they love you because you've ladled out money to them and shown them through a good many tough spots in their going. And even the old-time respectable citizens are now willing to say that probably John P. Thurlow is no longer The Duster, but an honest man trying to go straight. It may have been the bright example of The Duster that sent Tommy Lamont wrong . . . but it's also fair to say that The Duster seems to have brought Tom back onto the right trail. Now, Duster, I've come to you and I'm asking you for surety."

"What?"

"Surety that you'll stay straight from now on."

"And then?"

"Then I forget the past. My duty is to arrest poor young Lamont. But I don't want to. I ride in the name of the law, but I want my work to count among good men. I'd rather keep one man straight than arrest a thousand crooks. I want to see Tommy Lamont go right. But a thousand times rather than that, I'd like to see The Duster really turn into John P. Thurlow, honest citizen of the town of Christmas."

Now, take it by and large, that was the most surprising speech that I ever heard from any man. It suddenly popped my eyes open. We can't help looking on the police as our enemies, but suddenly it occurred to me that really they're our best friends. But they harden up their hands and their words for crooks, and that's the side of them we see. It dawned on me that the sheriff not only was honest, and brave, and smart, but that he had a heart of gold. He was the enemy of no man except the thugs.

"You want surety," said The Duster. "Well, I'm here living peaceably in Christmas."

"You may drop over the hill any day and bust a bank to smithereens."

The Duster took thought. "What sort of security do you want?" he asked.

"The security that most men give, for they take root like a tree and bind themselves to society."

"That sounds rather educated and difficult to me," The Duster said with a trace of a sneer.

"You understand me perfectly," said the sheriff without any anger in the face of that mockery.

"You mean, Renney, that I should settle down and raise a family . . . give my bond to society in that way?"

"You hit the nail on the head."

"Lead up the girl, then," announced The Duster. "I'm to step out and ask the first comer if she'll take a chance with an ex-crook?"

"You know I don't mean that," replied Renney. "And the strongest reason that brought me here today was a girl. I mean Marguerite Lamont, Duster."

Well, it would have done you good, knowing what The Duster was, to see how the sheriff paralyzed him time after time in this way. If he had been upset by the mention of Tommy, he was simply staggered by this talk of Tom's sister. He looked fighting hot again, snapping out: "What of her, Renney?"

"I'm not insulting you," Renney said gently. "But the whole town except her father has seen what I've seen. Her eyes are always on you when you're around, and she gives away her hand every second . . . as every good woman does, I think, and thank heaven for it. Only, Duster . . . suppose she gives her hand away to the wrong man?"

The Duster glared at the sheriff, then at me, as if he would have struck us both. Then he started up and walked back and forth with long, quick strides, and his horse started to follow him, making a lot of clumsy evolutions to keep up with his master.

There was a good deal of meaning to that—the horse and the man—the pricked ears of the beast, and the dark, working face of The Duster. People and animals both had reason to fear him, and yet they loved him, too.

Renney said not a word. He reached over and made a little stack of pine needles, like a child building a house. He was building a house, for that matter, and I certainly admired his craft.

"I suppose you haven't talked about this in other places, Renney?" said The Duster at last, coming to a halt in front of the sheriff, and still looking as though he would love a fight with almost anything.

"Of course not," replied the sheriff. "It's your business, Duster, and not mine at all. I'm only asking you. In the first place, do you know a woman you like better?"

"Better than that child?" said The Duster, throwing up his head.

"Aye, better than Marguerite Lamont."

"Renney, do you hear me?" said The Duster.

"Suppose a marriage to her would seem to you a proper giving of hostages to society. But what of her? What hostages can I give her? What surety?"

"Your word, man, which you've never broken, so far as I know."

That was a good touch. It surprised me. But when I came to think of it, I couldn't remember that The Duster ever had been accused of making his way by lies.

He gripped his hands and stared desperately at Renney. "Man, man," he said, "you know what I've been. I've come when I chose, and left when I chose. I've had what I wanted and when I wanted it. I've picked out a road and never asked where it led. I've ridden by day, but I've ridden by night, also. I've worked when there was spice in the job. I've lazed when I felt like it. And the thing's in my blood. How can I give it up?"

"You've been hunted like a fox," answered Renney. "You've slept in snow . . . like that trip you made west from Alberta . . . and you've ridden rods in February . . . as when you jumped from Detroit straight through to Butte. You've starved for a month at a time, as you did in the Pecos country three years ago. You've gone in rags, or hardly clothed . . . the way you got out of Phoenix not so long back. You've had your money by the hundreds of thousands, but you've lost it, squandered it, fooled it away, used it to bribe or buy weak good men, lavished it on fine horses, dropped it at races, spilled it out like water for a few bright days in New Orleans, or New York, or Denver. You've learned to be startled by your own shadow . . . to jump up wide awake when the wind whispers at night . . . to never sit except with your back to the

wall . . . to keep away from windows and doors . . .
and always to have your right hand empty, and
ready to grab the butt of a gun. Do you call that a
happy life?"

The Duster reflected. "Aye," he said then, "better
than eight hours a day . . . carpet slippers and a
newspaper at night . . . a baby squalling at dawn . . .
and the first of the month like a gun at your head."

How would the sheriff answer that, I wondered?
He had the answer pat.

"She would make up the difference, and more,"
he said.

I saw The Duster fumble at his throat like a
schoolboy puzzled by a hard question. "I can take
the chance when I'm gambling only with myself,
but how could I gamble on her happiness? Suppose
I made some wrong step . . . or that she had a look
into the story I've lived . . . or that I stopped lying
and drawing the curtain over what I've been. It
would break her heart."

"You talk," said Renney, "like a child. There's
only one real wrong that you could do to such a
woman, and that would be to stop loving her."

He stood up as he said it, and The Duster went
and caught him by the shoulders. "Renney," he said,
"could I do it?"

Imagine The Duster, if you can, saying such a
thing?

"I can't answer you," Renney said with a twisted
grin. "You'll have to ask Marguerite."

The Duster did not speak again. But he got to the
back of his horse and into the saddle with one
prodigious leap, and was gone away through the
trees like a frightened wildcat.

I waited until the dust of his going had settled

down, and the last dead leaf had fluttered back to a place on earth. Still I stared after him, seeing in my mind the way that bay must be turning the curves under the spur, and the look of The Duster as he leaned over the pommel and jockeyed an extra bit of speed out of the gelding.

"Kind of dry, that timber," I said to Renney at last.

He was looking the same way with me, but none too happy, I should've said.

"Aye," he said, "and he'll burn without any smoke, I hope, and last a long time."

"He will," I declared, although I wasn't at all sure. "Tell me, Sheriff," I said, "how you come to know so much about women?"

"I don't," he said.

"You certainly seem to have Marguerite Lamont by heart," I argued. "I never heard any woman talked out better."

"Well," said Renney with a sigh, "there's some of them that carry their title on their forehead. Besides, she used to smile at me once in a while before The Duster came up like the sun and turned the other men black for her."

III

"To thine own self be true!" said someone.

A friend of mine says that is Shakespeare, although it sounds pretty Bible to me, but you never can tell the two apart. One sounds like a pulpit set up in the mountains, and the other sounds like the mountains brought into the pulpit. Which I mean to say that whatever The Duster was, he was true to himself in the pinches, and that's about all that a man can ask of another, I suppose. For my part, I'd only ask a man to be honest for about once a week, but when The Duster came charging up to the house of the minister like a tiger out of the jungle, we know what he did and said, because there was another man present.

Who? Why, the same man he had cheated, scoffed at, beaten, and then upheld in his church as if for the sake of sport. The girl's own father—the minister himself. Why did The Duster do that? For lack of shame? Or to show his own power over men and women? Well, I don't know, but my job is simply to set down the facts.

Beside the minister's shack, he pulled up the gelding on his two hind legs and hit the ground before two more were down. He went up to the front door and gave it a whang, and the voice of the minister bawled out and asked him in.

When he went in, there sat Lamont behind a deal table that served him as a desk. He was in shirt sleeves, his hair tousled up by his shoving his big hands into it as he thought, and a scowl on his face as he drafted out next Sunday's sermon with an indelible pencil on cheap, rough paper. Which was as much as to say that he hoped his ideas would be immortal, but had his doubts. He had wetted the lead of his pencil from time to time while he worked, and the result was a round purple patch in the center of his mouth.

"What d'you want?" said Lamont, and then saw that it was The Duster himself, which must have made him come as close to trembling as a Scotchman can.

"I want to talk to you," The Duster said.

"Do you need a crutch for that?" Lamont asked. "Or will that chair help you out enough?"

The Duster did not take the chair. Instead, he stood behind it, with his hand resting on the top rung, and his hat in his hand, acting humble. But he never could really be humble. There was too much proud fire coldly lying in his eyes all the time.

"I have come to tell you a story," The Duster began. He gave a bow toward the kitchen door, where Marguerite showed herself, slim and white against the dimness of the rear room of the house. She had her sleeves tucked up over her round arms, and an apron tied around her, and in her hand there was a dishtowel with which she was polishing up a glass. I imagine her standing there and glowing at The Duster like a star in the dusk of the day. "And I should like to have your daughter hear about it, also," The Duster added.

Lamont turned around in his chair so that it squawked like a puppy that has been stepped on. "What have you to do with this?" the minister asked, glowering at her.

"I don't know, Daddy," she answered, mild and meek as usual.

"Come on, then, and we'll soon find out," the minister said, and in she came, too fascinated and shocked and delighted with the presence of The Duster to even remember to put down the towel and the glass, but from time to time giving it a rub, looking down at its brightness, or hesitantly up at The Duster as though his face were a dazzling light.

"Now?" Lamont said, looking grimly back at The Duster.

He answered: "I wanted to tell you a story, sir."

"About what?" said Lamont.

"About a sheep, sir."

"If you have to put in the sheep, leave out the sir," said Lamont. "Now, what is it?"

"Once upon a time," said The Duster, "there was a sheep born with teeth like a wolf."

"Go on," said the minister. "I like the beginning of that story because it sounds like a confession."

"The truth always does," said The Duster, "because it comes as rarely as Sunday."

"Stuff," Lamont scoffed. "Go on with your yarn." He gave his daughter a hard look, but got no more out of her than if he had looked at the zenith of the sky.

"This sheep," said The Duster, "one day got through a hole in a hedge, meaning no harm, and began to eat the neighbor's grass . . . and, when the neighbor saw it, he sent out his dogs and they gave it a terrible run, but, when it could run no longer, it turned around and fought, not with its head and its feet, but with its teeth. It killed a couple of the dogs and hurt two more of them, so that they went howling home.

"After that, the sheep was so frightened by what it had done, and so delighted to be free, that it scampered on back to its home flock. But when it came through the hole in the hedge, the other sheep smelled blood. At once they set up the cry of . . . 'Wolf! Wolf!' . . . and the rams ranged themselves on the outside of the flock, and the wethers behind them, and the little lambs inside them, and the bell-goat in the center of all, and they kept on shouting . . . 'Wolf! Wolf!' . . . until the farmer came out with a gun and saw the red on the white thing by the hedge, and fired at it, and sent a slug through its body, and another slug through its face."

As he said this, The Duster paused in the making of a cigarette and absently touched his cheek where there was a little white scar. Then he went on: "The poor sheep that was born with teeth . . . which was not his fault at all . . . ran away as fast as he could, and would have been found and killed by the dogs of his own master, if it hadn't been for the coming of the evening. When he got off in the woods, he licked his wounds and wondered at the strangeness of the world, and stayed there, starving and wondering, until his wound was well.

"When he came out of the woods again, he found out that the simplest way to live was on the bodies of his fellows . . . that is to say, the other sheep that he found, here and there, most of whom didn't have teeth, but a great many of them with very long wool. He collected enough fleece to keep him warm and sold the rest for food, and lived very well, and would have been extremely happy if he could have forgotten the warmth of the old nights when he slept in the fold with all of the other sheep, breathing and blinking around him. You understand how it is?"

"I don't understand a thing you're saying," said the minister, who was such a clever man that he didn't mind being stupid now and then.

The Duster turned slightly toward Marguerite and made a little bow, which was one of his ways.

This sudden and grave appeal made her lift her hands—the glass and the dishtowel with them—up to her breast. "Yes," she said. "I mean to say, I think that I understand you perfectly, John."

"Is that his name?" roared the minister, suddenly frightened and, therefore, speaking very loudly.

She shrank back into her chair. "Duster, I mean," she said, whispering.

The minister made a face, but he kept the words from coming out and sat up in his chair, scowling first at The Duster, and then at his daughter. He changed color, too, and he had mighty good reason for that. "Go on about this eternal sheep," he commanded.

"Certainly, sir," said The Duster, appearing to like his humble rôle on this occasion. "The poor animal outcast sheep went . . ."

"The one with teeth, you mean?" asked the minister.

"Yes, sir."

"Drop the sirring and get on!"

"The poor outcast sheep, sir," said The Duster gently, "went up and down the face of this earth, not sadly, but kicking up his heels and even bleating a little now and then, but still, as I was saying, remembering from time to time the sheep fold, like a safe little village, and the farmer's dogs, like the strength of the law, and the farmer himself like a powerful judge. Do you follow me, sir?"

The minister growled, but said nothing. He was too busy watching Marguerite, who was sitting on the edge of her chair with the glass pressed against her breast like a diamond beyond price, and her eyes staring wildly at The Duster—and something more.

"This sheep," said The Duster, "that went wildly wandering up and down through the hills, taking what he wanted, going where he wished, laughing at the law, and at the little churches, and the men that pray there, and all such things . . . this same fellow, one day came back and looked over the rail of a fold, or a village, as you might say, wondering how many fleeces he could pick up there in his regular occupation."

"I suppose you mean that he was a robber?" the minister said harshly.

"That was his occupation," said The Duster very mildly, "and, as the poet says, there's no harm in a man following his occupation, sir."

"What poet says that?" bellowed Lamont, getting red in the face.

"Shakespeare, sir," The Duster answered.

Lamont was silenced. For even a minister will accept quotations out of Shakespeare, it appears, although I never could learn why.

"To go back to the poor lost sheep that looked into the village," went on The Duster, "he was used to seeing all sorts of people. There were men he had robbed in banks, and there were men he had robbed on trains, and there were men he had robbed at the card table, and men he had robbed on the highway. He was used to reading the minds of men through their faces. Except for ministers, who he always found extremely difficult, sir."

"Confound you, you rascal," Lamont declared, and then coughed and glared at his daughter to warn her that she was looking like a frightened and enchanted goose.

But Marguerite did not heed him. She would not have heeded fire from heaven if it has suddenly poured down between her and the face of The Duster.

"Get to the point," Lamont demanded abruptly.

"I shall, sir," said The Duster, "at once."

IV

"You were looking over a fence into a village wondering who you could rob in the last sentence, if you want to find your place," said Lamont.

"The sheep was," said The Duster.

"The sheep? Bah," muttered the minister.

"That was about what the sheep said," replied The Duster. "I don't want to conceal that he had grown rather hardened in spirit from walking the hills by day and night."

"Chiefly at night, I suspect," sneered the minister.

"Exactly, sir, so that he was familiar with the stars," The Duster said. "And when he looked down into the crowd of the people in Christmas, he saw a great many good men and women, and some not so good . . . but most of them were concealed or dimmed by a mist that rises up from human faults and sins and sorrows, except on Sunday mornings, when, of course, you brush them all away from your good sermons, sir."

You see that The Duster had brought the scene around to twelve o'clock, as you might say, and struck a gong with his last words that echoed into the minister's heart, and certainly into the heart of Marguerite.

"Your sheep . . . your stars . . . your mists . . . I wish you'd get down to the facts of your case," said the minister.

"I hoped," The Duster explained, more gently

than ever, "that you would have some sympathy for this poor sheep."

"We'll tell in the conclusion," said the minister.

"That sounds more legal than Christian," The Duster said. "However, I want you to know that the sheep had been out in the weather so long, and was so long unwashed by such things as good Sunday sermons, that he had weathered very dark. In fact, you might have called him a black sheep. But this black sheep, when he looked over the fence into the village at the people inside, and saw their faces, dim with sin and complacency, and wind, and good works, and talk, and scandal, and gossip, and back-biting, and treachery, and envy, and hatred, and petty cheating, and lies, and all the other things that go to make up the dust in a village street . . . among all these, so bright that it was like the stars he was so accustomed to see shining over the midnight hills, he saw one face always before him. . . ." He made a slight pause, and looked straight at Marguerite, and, as he did so, the glass trembled from her hand. She made a vague gesture to recapture it, but it crashed on the floor into a million pieces, and she sat there holding the dish-towel against her breast like a cross, say, or a child.

The minister leaned in his chair and looked at the girl with despair and fear, but she did not regard him a whit. Her lips had parted. He could see her breathe, and with every breath the light waxed and waned in her eyes.

The Duster was looking straight at her now, and for once in his life I suppose he was not acting as he went on in such a voice as no man and no woman ever had heard from him before. "She was so gentle, so good, so beautiful, that my heart stopped like the hands of a watch that will always point to a Sunday morning, and the church on Christmas Hill, and Marguerite."

The minister came to his feet with a lurch, like a steer that has worked free from the mud at the edge of a tank. "What do you mean, Duster?" he cried. "What are you saying here?"

"I am simply telling you a story of a black sheep who fell in love," said The Duster.

Her own name seemed to have frozen up speech in the girl, but, at this, she uttered a little cry, and the poor dish-towel fell from her, and she sat with her empty hands turned up, looking partly like a child and partly like a saint, which is exactly what she was.

"Do you love my girl?" the minister asked.

"I do, sir," said The Duster.

The minister turned toward Marguerite, but when he looked at her, there was no need whatsoever of asking a question.

All the labor, the disappointments, the pain, the loss of his good wife, the disgrace and disappearance of Tommy his son were probably less to him than the shock of seeing in the face of Marguerite that she did truly love this man. He was no fool, and, if he knew anything in the world, it was that his daughter would never love twice. She was the sort of a sword, you might say, that can cut through a mountain of steel, but it is only good for one stroke.

So Lamont stood there for a moment, swaying, gripping his big labor-roughened hands and breathing harshly, like a man who has been running uphill. All he could say for a moment was: "You've spoken in front of me. I want to remember that. You've spoken in front of me." Now he rubbed his knuckles across his forehead. "Marguerite?" he said at last.

Of course she heard the pain and the loss and the misery in his voice, and the fear that he felt for her sake, and the cherishing which he had given to her, like a father and like a mother, too. But, after all, there is one time in her life when the best of women is strong enough to be cruel, and this moment had come to her. All she felt for her father made her voice low, but it was audible as the breath of life or the beating of a heart.

"Ah, Daddy," she said, "may I have him?"

Those words I have turned in my mind a great many times, and I would not change them. It was like a child asking for a toy.

The minister, like a man fatally hurt but still marching in the ranks, went straight on to do the duty that lay in front of him. "I have no right to give you or to keep you, dear," he said. "You love The Duster. . . ." He had to pause there, and fight with himself for a minute. For I suppose the very name Duster brought up into his mind his own struggle against this man, his defeat, the disgrace of that burial of a heathen outlaw in the sacred ground of his cemetery, and all the killings and lesser crimes that were counted into the record of John Thurlow. However, he was able to go on again presently: "All that I can do is to try to see that your future will be fairly safe in the hands of your husband. I think that I should try to do that, Marguerite."

Even if she had been able to find breath for an answer, I suppose she would not have had any words. So she slipped from her chair for the first time, and, going to Lamont, she stood beside him, looking up into his face with trembling lips and never daring to venture a second glance toward The Duster.

Lamont put his arm around her and pressed her

closely to him, as though he were saying farewell to her forever. And, in a sense, I suppose he really was.

He started to say—"Duster . . ."—but caught himself, and instead began: "John, I have to ask a guarantee from you?"

"Yes," said The Duster.

"You can give it or not," Lamont advised. "Certainly I haven't any right or power to demand it from you. But I think we all three must try to forget that black sheep that had been wandering on the hills, as you were saying a little while ago. We ought to forget him and consider that this fellow who walked into Christmas town is a new man. He has no past. His name is John P. Thurlow. He does not talk about the things that he has been . . . but he tells me that he will not spend on my daughter a single penny that he has . . . won . . . before today. And in the future, he will keep his hands clean. No stolen money out of the past, Duster," he broke out with a great voice, "for both your sakes, dress her cleanly, even if it has to be in rags."

The Duster made a start and drew himself up. He raised his hand, but Lamont rudely knocked it down.

"Don't swear," he said.

The Duster gasped—even The Duster!

"Don't swear," repeated the minister. And he added his one really bitter speech that day: "You'll have to prove yourself worthy by time before your oaths are worth considering. But give me your hand on it, as one gentleman to another."

You could abash a mountain sheep on a high rock almost as soon as The Duster, but he was abashed now. All he could do was silently to take the hand of Lamont.

That poor man took his daughter in his arms and

kissed her in a muttering voice: "My darling, my darling. Oh, my darling."

Then he gave her to The Duster with his own hands.

V

When The Duster came home, it was late in the day. The sun had gone down, coolness had fallen on us out of the sky, the stars began to step out thin and small in the east, and a good fresh wind came and blew the smoke and steam of the cookery out of my face.

I was making a mulligan stew. That may make you think of gristle, lean shoulder meat, and a few rib bones with strips of fat sticking to them, a scattering of stale vegetables with the life cooked out of them, and all the moldy old bread in the bread can dropped in to give the thing substance. But I mean real mulligan, than which there's nothing better. I mean a good young chicken that's fat to the ridge of the back and larded with fat; a chunk of pork with the salt soaked and then parboiled out of it; and these two cooked together, while you cook quickly in separate pans, your carrots, and tinned beans, and tomatoes, and a smell of garlic, say, to make the taste all stick together.

Now, I had just put all the vegetables into the main pot, telling myself that, if The Duster came home late, he could have cold stew and go hang, because I was ready to eat just then, but, as I was lifting the pot off the fire to the back of the stove, I heard the hammering hoofs of his horse rush in under the trees and slide to a stop in front of the house.

"Good news," I said to myself, "good news . . . for The Duster."

For thinking of the pretty, kind face of the girl suddenly wiped the smile off my face.

He came striding in, throwing his hat into one corner and his quirt in another, and looking, as usual, three inches and thirty pounds bigger than the truth about him, which I once had carried senseless in my arms across that same room and laid on the bunk.

"It's done, Baldy," he announced.

"It is," I said, "and it's chicken mulligan, and a lot of good for the likes of you. Smell it?"

He sniffed. Mostly he always did what I told him to about little things that didn't count.

"It's done," he said again.

I looked at him. His face was shining like the face of a boy on Christmas morning.

"Aye, and not overdone," I said, "which is lucky for you that you came home just now. Pull up a couple of chairs to the table and cut a coupla slices of bread from that loaf. Homemade, mind you. I baked it this morning at three hundred in the shade. Which I ain't training for high temperatures, either, like you ought to."

The Duster slashed off a couple of slices from the loaf absent-mindedly. But instead of sitting, he began to perambulate up and down the room. He picked up the quirt and hung it on a nail. He took it down again and slashed the air.

"How fast are you going, Duster?" I said. "I hope you get there in time for supper. Did you hear me say that this is chicken mulligan?"

"Baldy," he said for the third time, "it's done, I tell you."

"Aye," I said, "and that's just what I'm trying to get off my mind, and put the mulligan on. Sit down."

Still he didn't sit down. He came and leaned over, his hands gripping the back of the chair opposite me, low down, so that his eyes were not high above mine. "Do you think that it won't pan out, Baldy?" he asked me.

I stopped eating, although the mulligan was prime. The Duster, the great Duster, was talking to me like any young fool in love. He was asking my advice.

"Hey?" I said, fighting for time.

"Do you think it won't go?" he asked.

"By the soft eyes of her," I said, "I knew it was a marriage the first time she seen you."

He frowned a little, but his mind slid over my mean remark and went back to his subject. "You think that we have a chance, Baldy? You sent me to her, you remember?"

"The sheriff done that," I reminded him. "Because he figured you had to get punished outside of jail."

"You don't really mean what you say," The Duster said with a sigh. "I wish you'd talk seriously to me, Baldy. You think we have a chance for happiness together?"

"Sure," I said. "Part of the time you'll have a fine time together, the pair of you."

"Part of the time?" he cried. "Which part?"

"The part when you're out of the prison," I said.

He tried to laugh, but only squawked.

"Sit down," I said, "before the grease gets up to the top of the stew."

He poured out a cup of coffee, burned himself with it, and went on pacing the room without swearing, merely licking his blistered lips.

"I love her," The Duster said, like a man running under double wraps and speaking softly. "I love her."

"I love the mulligan," I said, "and thank my stars I didn't forget to put in the garlic. Sit down, Duster, and don't act like a crazy man."

Of course, he paid no attention to me. He didn't even get angry, which I would have liked, but, at any rate, I'd stopped him talking if I couldn't stop him pacing, and I went moodily on with supper.

At last he cut in again with: "I'll be able to do it. I'll get work. I'll stick to it. I'll never go back."

That made me mad. He was praying out loud, as you might say. "Sure," I said, "you'd be all right if things were a little changed."

He came hurrying over once more and planted himself where he could watch my eyes when I answered. "Changed in what way?" he asked.

"If all the week was made up of Mondays, I mean," I said.

"You think that I'll weaken, and quit work, and slide back to the easy ways of making money," he said. "But you're wrong, Baldy. You know me only in part. I don't know myself. This day something is added to me."

"Sure," I said. "You'll soon have a new cook that'll work without wages, but you'll still have to buy the mulligan for two. Have you got the makings?"

He gave them to me with a sigh, still looking hard ahead into his future.

I built myself a cigarette, and, although I felt pretty hard, I managed to keep from tearing the paper. "Have you told her about the three hundred thousand that you start on for capital, and the field where it grew, and the color of the flowers when it bloomed?" I asked him.

"It's gone," he said. "I'll give it all away. Not to that cur of a Muncie, perhaps. But to some worthy charity and . . ." His voice trailed away, as though he were trying to find the right spot to drop that lump of money.

I had forgotten my lighted match, by this time, and it burned the tips of my fingers before I was able to drop it and say: "Give it away . . . Worthy cha . . . Listen to me, Duster. Do I look worthy to you?"

He smiled down at me in a sort of quiet, fond way. "Ah, Baldy," he said, "as if you'd take the stuff . . . the stolen stuff, I mean. Old man, I'd trade everything I have for the sake of your honesty. Then I'd know that our home was founded on rock."

"If you were like me," I said, "your home wouldn't be much more than a rock, for sure. And if . . ."

Now, as I said this, I saw The Duster straighten with a twitch back of his shoulders, and I knew that he was looking at someone who had silently entered the room. I turned my head and there I saw a thing I wish never had dawned upon my eyes.

He had stepped lightly in, and instantly to the side, so that he would have solid wall behind him, and not space through which gun muzzles could be poked into his spinal column. His face was the same as I remembered it—muddy white, like the belly of a catfish. A face that did you no good to see.

When I saw him now, I let out a sort of a choked screech that hurt my throat, for I was looking at the ashes that The Duster had buried so carefully up there on Christmas Hill. I mean, I was looking at the man whose ashes those were supposed to be, for there in the room with us, casting his shadow on the wall, was Hector Manness!

VI

"Choke that old fool," Manness snapped, "before he wakes up the entire town crowing as if the day were here."

"No," said The Duster, "as a matter of fact, the night seems a little darker than usual."

Manness merely smiled, and replied: "There's the same old light touch. I'm glad to see that you haven't lost it, Duster. Cuts a man's throat so that he hardly knows he's lost his life until he tries to draw the next breath. Shall I sit down?"

"Not in here," The Duster said. "If you sit down in here, think how much you'd be in the lamplight, Hector. The limelight, as one might say. And so many people anxious to see you . . . dead or alive."

Once more Manness smiled, and I never saw a smile that failed to improve any face as completely as that failed with Manness. I had heard so much about this man, and had seen him before, that I couldn't help knowing about his loathsome career in the past, but I didn't have to know about it. I could see it printed in the brain and the flesh of that sick-looking scoundrel. He was a little frightened now, by what The Duster had said. And he didn't make any effort to cover up his fear, but let it glisten in his eyes and jerk at his lips. Still, he was also pleased, as though by having been called the chief monster.

"They don't love me, Duster," he said, "and it

looks as though your friend, there, didn't love me, either. That's a grief to me."

"Aye," said The Duster. "When they catch you, they won't acquit you. They'll take your nine lives all at once. They'd take ninety, if you had 'em."

"Are you proud," Manness said, "because the fools have let you off five times when they should have hanged you? Or are you trying to frighten me? And to wind up with, are we going to keep on talking in the presence of that superannuated eavesdropper there?"

Now, a man can take so much, but no more, and although I had no more chance with that magical hand of Manness than I did with The Duster, still, I felt that I had to take a stand here and now. So I said to him: "Manness, you've spoken of me twice as though I were a dog. The next time, I'll have my teeth in you."

Manness looked me up and down. "Do you know who you're talking to, Wye?" he asked.

"I know fairly well," I answered. "I don't know all about you, but I know some samples of the sneaking murders, and stabbings in the back, and throats cut at night, and suchlike things that you've done. They ought to hunt you with a snake charmer."

Somewhere it had been floating around in my mind that Manness had one vulnerable spot and that he went almost crazy when he was insulted by being compared to a snake. I think there was a story of a fellow in Butte who had made that mistake, and the yarn went on that, in revenge, Manness had actually got hold of him and dumped him into a snake cave, and then stood by while the poor wretch came lurching out, squirted full of venom from fifty bites, and watched him yell and twist and die there in the Montana sun. That's pretty horrible, but I've heard it vouched for by honest men; certainly when you looked at Manness, and his sinuous leanness, and his unearthly, bright, unwinking little eyes, you could see why he'd resent the comparison. When he heard me speak now, he fairly turned blue around the lips, and his right hand flicked inside his coat so fast that I couldn't have brought my gun out of the holster in time to stop him.

The Duster could, however, and with a flash of his hand, he covered Manness there by the door.

"I'll let a streak of light clean through you, Manness," he said, "if you shove a gun at Wye."

Manness kept his hand inside his coat for an instant while he rolled his look from me toward my protector. I thought that he would take a chance with both of us, but that idea couldn't have lasted a tenth of a second with him. He brought out his hand with a sack of tobacco and a package of brown papers between the tips of the slim fingers.

"You talk like a fool, Duster," he declared. "You never had any real sense of humor. I wanted to see what sort of nerve your crook had . . . and I see that he hasn't got much."

I might as well be frank. I was scared into the shakes, true enough, but The Duster was kind enough not to look at me.

"You'd give anybody the horrors," Duster said. "Nobody feels at home with a Gila monster."

It made my hair rise to hear that—for two reasons. The Duster had put his gun away, so that he stood on even terms with Manness at that moment, and this meant that a fight was as likely as not. It meant, furthermore, that The Duster was inviting trouble, and, whatever else men said about Manness, no one ever had doubted his courage, any more than they doubt that of a lion.

But whether it was policy or fear of his master, he did not choose to accept the challenge at this moment, but merely smiled—which was no more than a flash of white teeth. "You've never grown out of your school days," said Manness. "Forever drawing a line and putting a chip on your shoulder. Stop being a child, because I want to talk with you."

"Fire away," The Duster said coldly.

"Alone," said Manness.

"But that's the point. I don't know that I care to talk to you alone."

"Are you afraid to?" Manness asked, leering at him.

"I'm busy," said The Duster.

"Thinking of Marguerite, I suppose?"

I thought The Duster would strike a slug into him at that. He hung on the trembling verge of it at least, but then controlled himself with a big effort. I wonder how Manness could have learned of that affair so soon? For he seemed to know everything.

"As a matter of fact," said Manness, "that's what brought me here. I wanted to make that marriage more possible for you, Duster, if you'll believe me."

"I believe that you never wanted to do anything to any man's advantage," declared The Duster. "I'm not going to talk to you, Manness. You've broken a promise in coming back here."

"Ah, yes," Manness said. "But you know that man only proposes, Duster. The luck was horribly against me. However, I'll prove that you ought to send that gray-headed old man out of the place while we have a chat. I want to suggest that before you can safely marry her, you'll have to remove a few obstacles. You'll surely see that."

"Obstacles?" The Duster repeated, lifting his eyebrows.

"The worst kind."

"Such as what?"

"Why, obstacles that may come up in her own mind, d'you see?"

"I don't know what you mean, Manness."

"You'd better, though."

"You're lying, as usual," The Duster said in final decision. "You know nothing about the affair at all."

"Don't I? No, you know that I'm telling you the truth."

"How could you know about her? No more than the night could know about the day, Manness."

He said it with open disgust and scorn, but Manness answered: "You have to remember that the devil has more ears than anyone else. But make your choice. One way or the other, I'm offering you your chance, Duster." He stepped a little toward the door, full of anger and hate—the only two emotions that could be natural to the beast.

I saw The Duster waver and then fall from his high ground.

"Baldy," he said to me, "let me have a minute alone with Manness, will you? You haven't watered the horses this evening, anyway."

Manness sneered at me as he won his first victory, but I said to The Duster: "Good luck, old man. Remember that if he so much as scratches you, you're finished, because he's sure to have poison on the end of his knife."

I thought that idea made some impression on The

Duster; it certainly made Manness jerk as though I'd hit him with a whip. But then I had to leave the room, mighty unwillingly, because the things that Manness couldn't talk about in front of me were not likely to be the things that would do The Duster any good hearing them alone.

I went out, but I didn't water the horses. I wouldn't have missed that conversation for any price.

All I did was to walk straight out in the path of the lamplight toward the barn, and then, stepping out of the light, I yanked off my boots and came back like a flash to the house and slid in under it. I mean, the old shack was raised on stilts from the ground to keep it from molding floors in the rainy season. It was boarded up with a skirting originally, but this skirting had rotted or been torn away, and the result was that there were big gaps through which I could easily work.

I got under, therefore, and lay down close beneath a big knothole through which the dim lamplight fell down and showed me a beetle struggling along with some sort of a burden.

After I got there, I heard Manness say that he would take a look to see whether I'd really gone, and heard footfalls cross the floor. They stepped out onto the ground in front of the door, and I actually saw that pale wretch crouch and look under the house. He remained there for ten seconds. The only reason I didn't pull a gun and shoot him in self-defense was that I was actually too frightened to move a hand. I thought I saw him spot me and reach for a gun, but in another moment he straightened up and stepped inside the house again.

"That's the trouble with good men, Duster," he said. "No matter how honest they may be, they haven't the courage to do what they want to do. Look at this fellow, Baldy Wye. He wanted to protect you from me, but he didn't love you as much as he feared me, and he's slipped off to get rid of the trouble and wash his hands of you while he waters the horses."

He laughed, and I hated him, and was shamed, and then foolishly proud as a boy to realize that even old Baldy Wye had slipped one over on Hector Manness.

Just after that there was a pause, in which I heard the rattle of voices of young fellows, bawling out to one another as they went. I was afraid that noise had blotted out some of the conversation from above me, but it hadn't. The first thing that The Duster said I heard as plainly as though I had been in the room.

He said: "I don't need the help of Baldy Wye or any other man. I can take care of myself with you . . . I always could, and I always can."

"On the contrary," said Manness, "you're absolutely in my hands."

VII

When I was a boy, I remember that my mother told me there was no fool as great as the man who ever believed a proved liar, but still, as I lay there under the floor, I couldn't help believing Manness. For there was a ring and a thrill in his tone. Acting sometimes passes for the truth, but this sounded like the dropping of a pure golden coin.

"In your hands?" said The Duster. "No, no, Hector, I'm not one of them for the first time in these years. I'm out of them, and I'll never come into them again."

"We'll see. We're going to talk the thing out, aren't we?"

"I suppose so, but let's be quick about it, Hector. You're as pleasant a sight to my eyes as . . ."

"As that Gila monster you were speaking of a moment ago?" suggested Manness briskly.

"Put it however you please. Let's be ended. I told you that the Muncie bank was the last job I'd work with you on. I meant it. The job is finished. I had your solemn word of honor that you'd never trouble me again when the work was done. And you know, Manness, that I didn't want to tackle that affair. The fact is that I was through before it started. You begged me to come in. You swore it was the last time you'd borrow my help. Like a fool I believed you."

He stopped for an answer, and, to my surprise, Manness did not attempt to make one. He allowed The Duster to begin again, and the latter immediately continued: "I was sick of you and your ways and your works a long time before, and I told you so. Is that true?"

"It's true, Duster," answered Manness—not submissively, but as though he had to admit the truth.

"I would have broken with you then," said The Duster, "but I didn't want to leave you in the lurch. They were cornering you. The whole country hated you like a plague. You had no friends, and no place where you could turn. You knew you were done for. Once caught, there was no chance for you. They would hang you with joy. No juryman would dare to vote in your favor for fear of being lynched after the trial was over. I had made up my mind to quit you and, therefore, I wanted to see you safe first of all. So I proposed that I should try this huge hoax that I've worked in Christmas. I'd come here and try to bury your ashes in the churchyard . . . the ashes of Hector Manness. That would prove that you were dead. And when luck brought us on the old Apache Trail to that thigh bone with the imbedded bullet, like your own, of course you remember that it clinched the purpose in my mind. I would come up here and prove to the world that you were dead by fighting to bury your ashes in consecrated earth. So I did it, didn't I?"

"You certainly did," Manness said, as before giving away every chance to dispute.

"And the scheme worked, didn't it?"

"It did. Every paper in the country carried articles about my demise." He laughed snarlingly as he said this.

"Yes," went on The Duster, "they carried the articles. Up to that time the police along every border, and at every shipping port, had been on the lookout for you. But now they know that you're dead, and the way is open. You can get out anywhere, with hardly a chance of them finding you. People don't recognize dead men in living ones. A change of complexion would have been enough disguise for you."

"That's still true," said Manness.

"Aye," The Duster agreed, "but before I did this, I made you swear that we were done as partners. Heaven knows why I ever worked with you at all . . . unless it was as Baldy Wye suggested just now, that I wanted to see if I could be a snake charmer."

It was as bad an insult as you could imagine, but

still that fellow Manness swallowed it without a murmur.

"And after I had done the work, you came back and begged me to help you to one last stake. You'd gambled the other stuff away. If I would help you on the Muncie haul, you'd clear out and never bother me again. Well, I agreed to that. To rob Muncie was simply stealing from a thief . . . that wouldn't be on my conscience hardly. So I did it. Again you swore, when we parted . . . I with a slash along my ribs that might someday send me to the penitentiary . . . that you wouldn't dare show yourself over the edge of my skyline so long as you lived. Is that correct?"

"All perfectly correct."

"Then what under the sky gives you the brassy nerve to come here tonight and trouble me again?"

"Luck," Manness answered with an odd quietness. "Bad luck. I've been cleaned out again, Duster."

"Bah! What's that to me?"

"You were always a charitable fellow. You never turned down an old partner."

"I'll stake you to a ticket out, if that's what you mean."

"I do. A half-million-dollar ticket out."

"Explain, Hector."

"It's the simplest game I ever saw. After Muncie's safe was cracked, every last one of his depositors . . . and you know he had some big ones . . . has transferred to the First National right here in the town of Christmas."

The Duster stamped on the floor, and I saw a thin shower of dust fall down through the knothole above my face.

"You want me to help you crack that job?" he asked. "Why, man, you know my principles! I don't mind relieving some fellow with a fat purse of some of the stuff that lines it. But the First National here has the accounts of all the little one-horse farmers . . . and the old broken-down cowpunchers and prospectors have loaded their last savings into it. The old-timers have planted in that bank their funeral funds. You want me to lift money like that?" He changed his tone: "Manness, how did you lose what you got on the Muncie split?"

"The yellow crooks in the stock market," snarled Manness. "The sly, sneaking, back-stabbing crooks in the stock market. I had a sure thing outlined. I would have turned that three hundred thousand into three million sure . . . ten million in three months, if I had my breaks in the game at all. I had something surer than wiretapping. But the yellow dogs gave me away, and the three hundred thousand slipped with that chance. Curse them! I'll have some of them for it. I'll have some of them, Duster, in a way they'll remember."

"Snakes?" The Duster said.

I heard a gasp of rage and controlled fury from Manness. "Will you listen to this job I have lined up?" he asked.

"Not to a word of it."

"I've got Pemberton willing to work with us and let us in on the ground floor. He asks fifty thousand flat, and that's every penny we'd have to put out."

I remembered Pemberton's round, rosy face, and honest smile, and kind, dim gray eyes. Well, I could hardly believe that he had sold out his employers in that bank. We'd been saying for years what an asset an honest man like Pemberton was to the Christmas First National. Men used to put their accounts in that bank simply because they liked to see the good fat smile of Pemberton, fat as a walrus' cheek.

"Not if he'd sell out for five cents. It doesn't interest me, Manness, and there's an end. I'd rather rob my grandmother then such a bank as the First National here."

"Well, Duster, you have no choice," Manness said. "I've got to have you in. And you belong to me for this last job."

I waited.

Then The Duster said: "Tell me how I'm in your hand, Hector?"

"This way. Before I came to see you today, I wrote a letter to the editor of the little paper here in Christmas. I told 'em frankly . . . for their own good, you know . . . that their sheriff was a simpleton and that the whole town was fat-witted. I pointed out how you have come here, buried some random bones and wood ashes that you called my remains, got yourself the confidence of the town, and, after robbing the Muncie bank with me, you've become engaged to the nicest girl in the town and intend to live on the coin you've stolen."

"You didn't mail that letter, Hector?"

"Of course not. I left it in the hands of a friend, to be mailed within three days, unless I return. I had in mind that you might murder me, of course, if you were not feeling logical minded this evening."

"Interesting idea," The Duster said, and even I could tell that he was shaken to the ground. "Not a scrap of proof for either of the things you say."

"My signature will prove that I'm alive. That signature's pretty well known, Duster. For second proof, they can find a brand-new, half-healed scar of a bullet wound raking across your left side."

No one spoke for some time, and my aching ears could hear the voice of the little alarm clock begin to break out into the silence, making a sort of irregular pulse, as though it were slowing to a stop, and seeming to falter on with a greater and greater difficulty.

At last I heard The Duster say: "I'll tell you, Manness, I have my share of the Muncie split without a penny gone from it. You can have that."

"You fool!" cried Manness, really breaking out for the first time. "There's a million and a half for the taking in the First National. It's got deposit boxes bulging, to say nothing of cash, besides! Damn your share of the Muncie split! I want you in this with me!"

I heard The Duster breathing like a broken-winded horse.

"Hector," he said, "you've got the thing all lined out safely. Why not go ahead? Then you won't have to make any split with me."

"I had the Muncie business all lined out, too," said Manness. "But what happened? The double-crossing cur of a cashier sold me, and I would be under the sod right now if I hadn't had your fancy gun work to blow a hole in the trap for me. No, no, Duster, when I walk into the First National vault, I'll have you beside me in the good old way."

"Why don't I kill you?" The Duster asked softly, thoughtfully.

That villain Manness answered as quick as you please. "Because the girl's worth murder or perjury. I looked in on her the other night. I wondered how she could have you so paralyzed. But even I could understand. She even made me, Duster, want to settle down. Do the job with me, Duster. Then ride ten miles across country to the place where I've left that letter to the paper. Take it into your own hands. Read it. Burn it. And then I'm gone out of your life for good. You marry the girl. You're rich, and can lead a beautiful life. . . ."

I didn't want to hear any more argument, or the answer, but started to crawl out from under the house, because I knew that The Duster was a gone goose.

VIII

After I got out into the night, safely away from the wickedness that was in that little shack of a house, I remembered that the horses were to be watered, and I went slowly out to the barn. Dolly threw up her head and nickered at me as I shoved back the sliding door, and somehow the sight of her fine head thrown up so high and the faint flash of her big eyes made me feel worse than ever, because it made me think of the difference between men and horses— horses that will run for you till they die, and men that you never can trust. I went to Dolly and untied her halter rope and that of the gelding and led them out to the watering trough. I had pumped it brimful that same evening, so that it took a good bright section of the stars on its face, and even when it had been ruffled by the thrust of the muzzles of the horses—Dolly always gets in above the nose—there were still little specks of fire in the far corners.

I watched those horses drink until a coyote sang off a hilltop behind the town, and the two big heads jerked up, and the ears pricked, and they stamped as if they were frightened to death. They were only playing a game of pretend, because they knew they were as safe as could be, but when I spoke to them— being between the pair—they turned their heads over and drooled water confidingly all over me. Then they drank again, and I wondered over them a little, and wished that the way of a man in life could be as simple and straight as the way of a horse. But when I raised my head, I could look through the trees to the light that shone out of the window of the house toward me, and inside that room I knew that Manness was completing his plan with The Duster.

A fine sight, that light through the night, turning around side of a big tree all faintly green, like a mist. But it made me feel worse still, because I knew that I really loved the poor Duster, and that most certainly I was going to betray him before the morning came. I didn't want to. I told myself that no matter what happened, I would never do it. But I knew all the time that I would have to, almost like the fellow who tells himself when he leaves the ranch that this time he won't touch a drop when he gets to town. Because that fellow never can get past the first swinging door!

I watered the horses and put them up and fiddled around, shoveling hay down in the manger. Then I waited a while at the door of the barn, but, no matter how much time I killed, I knew that I would have to go to the sheriff. Because when The Duster said that the First National was loaded with small accounts, I knew that he was only speaking the truest kind of truth. In fact, I knew twenty of the men and women who had these accounts, and the least of them was worth saving.

The Duster had no right to be considered. I argued that out in detail. It was true that I was fond of him. It might even be true that after this one job he would go straight. But his one happiness could not be balanced against the happiness of the scores of people who would be about ruined if the First National went bust. I thought of them and their faces. Then I thought of Marguerite Lamont and her face, and I can tell you that I felt sick and faint. However, just as I had known what I would do in the first place, I found that my feet were going down the street toward the sheriff's house, and pretty soon I arrived at it.

There was no more miserable little shanty in Christmas, where you could find plenty of the poorest in every section of the town, even on the top of the hill, near where Lamont's church stood. Well, I went up to the little house, and there was Renney sitting in the doorway, smoking away at his pipe. He must have had the eyes of a cat, because there was no light streaming out from the house, and yet he knew me at once.

"Hello, Baldy," he said.

"Hello, Renney," I replied. "How are things?"

"Pretty good with me, but kind of failing with the cabbages," the sheriff answered.

"What cabbages?" I asked.

"Them that I planted out behind the house."

"You got a patch?" I asked, feeling glad that the talk could float along for a while without coming to the point that I would have to make before very long.

"Yeah. I planted 'em out all according to directions. I got them started. I used to sit out there and watch those dog-gone cabbages growing. I used to tell myself how much they'd sell for, and they'd keep me in cabbage soup for half the year, and leave enough of them over for me to sell a right smart lot and get me a new bridle, which I sure been needing for a long spell. I used to wake up in the night and smell those cabbages out there. I used to get up and stand at the window and watch them waiting there all in line, looking silver in the moonlight. 'It's all right, Renney,' I used to tell myself. 'Those cabbages are sure doing fine.' Then I'd go back to sleep."

"Well, what happened, Sheriff?"

"There comes along an evening when I notice some white moths fluttering around out there. I didn't mind. If they liked the smell of those cabbages, they was free to inhale the bouquet of 'em, as far as I was concerned, because I believe in a liberal policy, even where it comes to moths. But the trouble was that the moths had other ideas than perfume. Pretty soon, I begin to notice that there is holes appearing in the big, broad, tender new leaves of the cabbages. Like they had been burned through with a sunglass. 'Too bad!' I'd say. 'And I must look into this.' But about that time I'm called away on a trip, and, when I come back here, those cabbages of mine look like they'd been used for transfers on a streetcar line, they were so punched full of holes. I knew that the moths and their younglings had turned the trick against me. So about all that's left of my cabbage patch is the smell, Baldy, as you can tell for yourself."

"Yes," I admitted, "I sure can smell it."

"But as for the sight," he said, "I hate to light a lamp in my house lately, because, when the light streams out the window, it shows me my new bridle all chewed to pieces, and my cabbage soup gone sour. Why don't you set down and have a smoke?"

"I ain't here for long," I explained. "I come to talk to you about something."

"Well," said Renney, "I've wanted to talk to you about something, too. How did The Duster come out with Marguerite Lamont? That's what I want to ask."

"I dunno. I should suspect pretty well."

"I'm glad of it," the sheriff said. "That man has been so bad that the other side of the leaf is pretty sure to be worth reading. I used to wonder that a straight shooter like you, Baldy, would work for such a thing as The Duster, but, since I've studied him some more and worked over his case, why it seems to me that in a lot of ways The Duster is a straight shooter himself."

"Does it?" I said, surprised.

"You bet. The Duster, now, is a fellow who never would double-cross a friend, no matter what the friend did."

That remark hit me pretty hard, and I stood mulling it over in my mind for a time. "Sheriff," I finally said, "the fact is that I want to talk to you about something that The Duster has in mind to do."

"Yes?" he said. "Did The Duster ask you to come down here and talk to me about it? Because," he added, "I figured that we were pretty near friends enough, now, for him to come and talk to me on his own hook."

"He's friendly enough to you," I agreed, "but the fact is that he's being dogged into a . . . a . . ."

The sheriff waited a second and then said: "Sometimes it's hard to get hold of the right word, ain't it? I remember that my father used to say that words that came hard sometimes weren't the right ones to speak, after all."

"What d'you mean?" I asked.

"Why, nothing," said the sheriff. "How did you leave The Duster?"

"I left him on a high place, walkin' a tightrope," I said.

"So you came for help?"

"In a way, yes."

"Well, a fellow like The Duster is best left alone, in a pinch."

"Sheriff," I said desperately. "The fact is that The Duster is going to . . ."

The sheriff was taken with a fit of coughing, and then sneezed, and then cleared his throat loudly. When he got through with that noise, he seemed to have forgotten that I was talking, and only remembered that The Duster was the theme of it.

"Poor old Duster," he said. "He's had his hard times . . . and his good ones. But he's going to have better luck in the long run, I figure, when he's married to Marguerite Lamont. He's a strong man, but she's a stronger woman."

"Stronger than The Duster?" I gasped.

"Aye. She'd die for the right . . . or for her brothers . . . or her father . . . to say nothin' of the man that she picks out to love. The Duster's brave. But she's fearless. He could face death, but she could laugh at it. Oh, yes, she'll be the stronger of the pair, and, when the end of the day comes, The Duster won't say . . . 'What have I been doing today?' . . . but simply . . . 'Have I pleased my wife?' " He finished off, chuckling.

"Does The Duster deserve her?" I asked.

"Who deserves to be followed by as much as a good dog?" said the sheriff, dodging me. "But then, The Duster has his points. As I was saying, he's a man that never would double-cross his friends."

I wondered at the way that Renney kept coming back to that point. And then it suddenly broke in on me. He knew perfectly well why I had come down there at that time of the night to see him. I had something to say that might wreck The Duster. I had something to say that might give Renney all the glory of capturing and showing up The Duster in the middle of a crime. It would make Renney a famous man—a great man all over the West. It would be the very first thing that he had given years of his life to accomplish. But here he was heading me off with all my information.

Then I remembered what I had heard him say, that he would rather turn one man straight than put twenty crooks in jail. At last I knew that he really meant it. He was simply a man above my head. I felt like a kid.

"Renney," I said, "I'd better go home to bed and sleep on it."

"I reckon it's getting late," he said very kindly. "Good night, Baldy."

And he shook hands with me, and I went off in a sort of a haze.

IX

When I got back to the Ridley house, feeling still pretty dizzy, I found the lights were out, and that relieved me a good deal, because I thought The Duster probably had gone to bed and to sleep as soon as I left. I stepped into the house lightly, for fear that I might waken him, and slipped over to my bed as quiet as a mouse, but when I got there, I knew that there was something behind me, and I was hardly surprised when I heard the voice of The Duster say: "Baldy!"

I turned around. Jumped around, I should say. There in the gloom near the outside door I saw The Duster. That man could move as quietly as a ghost, and it was no wonder that he had been able to get between me and the door, if he cared to.

"Baldy," he said, "where have you been?"

"I went out for a walk," I answered.

"Usually you don't walk as late as this," said The Duster.

"Usually," I answered, "I'm not kicked out to go and amuse myself watering the horses, and such things."

"Where do you go?" he repeated.

"I walked down the hill into the valley," I answered him. "Why'd you ask?"

I was beginning to be worried. Still, I could feel pretty sure that he hadn't been able to follow me to the sheriff's house. Just the same, I was worried, because the thing that you usually expected The Duster couldn't do was usually the thing that he was sure to manage.

He scratched a match and lighted a lamp.

"I'd like to talk to you a while," he said.

"Sure," I said, and sat down on the edge of my bunk, yawning a good deal, so as to cover up the scared look that I knew was on my face.

"I wanted to make sure," said The Duster, "that there was one man in the world so extremely honest that I could trust him, but I see that I have been wrong."

"Who?" I said. "You don't mean Manness, I expect?"

He did not laugh. He merely looked me coldly in the face. "There's no red dust down the hill to the valley," he pointed out.

I looked down at my trousers and saw the dust on them pretty clearly, although how he could tell the color by the lamplight beat me. "What of it?" I said.

"I took a little walk into the town on my way back home."

"You did?"

"Sure. Why not?"

"No good reason, I suppose."

"I guess not."

"Where did you go?"

"Why, just up the street."

He waited a moment. "You don't think that I'm asking for fun, do you?" he said.

"Why, I don't know. What's in your mind, Duster?"

"Where did you go when you first left the house?" asked The Duster.

"Why, out to the horses."

"What did you do before you went there?"

I stared at him. A real judge couldn't have made me feel more tied up and helpless than The Duster did as he asked all these questions. Was he bluffing, I wondered, or did he really know something? I stared past him, and saw the green gloom of the light that passed the door and fell on the face of the nearest tree.

"I don't know what you're driving at, Duster," I said.

"Don't you, Baldy?"

"No, I don't. What's in your mind?"

"That you've been crooked with me," he answered slowly. "Even you, Baldy Wye."

It was a shameful thing to hear him talk to me like this, and with such an air. All at once I knew that I wasn't in any physical danger from him, but as a matter of fact I was in a worse danger than that—the danger of losing his respect. This idea made me turn things over a couple of times in my head before I could speak again, and then I said: "What do you think that I've done, Duster?"

"Double-crossed me," he said.

"So?" I said. "Double-crossed you how?"

"That's what I hoped you would tell me," he replied. He sat down in the chair nearest to the door and faced toward me, making a smoke. He had been getting ready for bed, and his shirt was unbuttoned at the neck, and his boots were off, and I saw his feet, just the mates of his slender, sinewy, blue-veined hands. But still he didn't look rough or out of place. The Duster was the sort of fellow who would have been at home anywhere. It was a pleasure to watch him, always.

I stared again at the dust on the trousers I was wearing and for the second time I wondered how he could tell the color of that dust from the color of the dust down the valley side of the Christmas River. However, I said nothing for a minute, but simply turned the idea over in my mind. I liked The Duster. I more than liked him. It was something like the love that a father might have for a son, I think, and partly admiration of his smartness, and pity for his wasted life, and fear for his future, and disgust at his crookedness, and belief in his courage—but all these things began to boil in me, so that at last I had to speak out things that I hadn't intended to say.

"When I left the house," I said, "I crawled under it and listened to the talk."

The Duster licked his cigarette with the tip of his tongue and whipped the wet edge over the dry leaf with a swift, sure stroke. Then he placed the end of it in his mouth and raised his eyes to me. "Was it fair to do that?" he asked.

"Was it fair to make me think that Manness was going to lead you to the dickens?" I asked him right back.

"That's my business."

"The blowing of a bank is everybody's business," I answered. "You know it. But I could name twenty poor wretches who would go bust if that bank were broken."

"The little men could be bought off," said The Duster. "I mean to say I could pay my conscience and them, afterward, what they had lost."

"Manness would never consent to that."

"Manness couldn't control my half of the loot."

"You've told the minister that you're going straight, Duster."

"I've told him that," argued The Duster. "And I shall. What does one slip make? When a night has lasted ten hours, what does one more dark minute mean to anybody? Why, after this job is finished, I'll never look at a burglar kit again."

"You'd better," I said. "Because sooner or later Manness will be sure to land you in trouble up to the neck, and then you may have to steal yourself away."

He grinned a little. He was young, The Duster. But somehow I never had realized how young until that moment as I watched him. For suddenly it appeared to me that he was actually enjoying this whole affair. Enjoying the danger, the mischief, the threat of continual blackmail from Manness, of course, and the scorn and contempt of the minister, and, above all, the love of Marguerite Lamont. She could love a criminal as she had proved, but neither of us had much doubt that she would never be able to waste her time on a liar. Take women by and large, and it's the little sins that count with them, not the fine big ones that slam you down to the fire and the red torment for the rest of existence. She could more easily forgive The Duster a hundred sins of bloodshed than a single misstatement to her about himself. I realized this. The Duster did, too, beyond a doubt.

"Manness never could handle me," he declared. "And I'll see no more of the face of him. He'll take care of the others. He'll make my way smooth for me. But, Baldy, no matter what was in your mind, where did you go this evening?"

"I saw Renney," I said.

"Renney?" cried The Duster. "The sheriff?"

"Yes."

He bit his lip, and then looked up at the ceiling. I expected to see him fly into a rage. But he merely nodded his head a couple of times and said no more. He was waiting.

"I wanted to tell Renney what was happening, and I would have let him know the danger that the bank was in. But he wouldn't listen. He seemed to guess that I had something up my sleeve, and he dodged me. He began to talk about loyalty and men who never betrayed their friends."

That stirred The Duster to the quick, for he got up and stepped to me with a gleam in his eye. "Did Renney do that?" he asked me.

"He did."

The Duster made a turn through the room, then flung down his cigarette and ground out the lighted end beneath his heel.

"How many men like Renney are there in the world?" he asked me.

"Not one," I said, and I think I told the truth.

"He trusts me," said The Duster. "Baldy, I thought he was simply playing a game with me, but I was wrong. He trusts me. Manness . . . Marguerite . . . Renney . . ."

Imagine The Duster throwing up his hands above his head in surrender to the complexity of his problem. But I didn't wonder. I couldn't advise him. If he failed to do what Manness wanted, that rascal would expose him in such a light that Marguerite would loathe him as much as she had loved him, the town of Christmas would detest him, and he would have to step out of this chapter of his life. But if he accepted the demand of Manness and helped him in the crime, he became perjured to Lamont, and untrue to the girl, and—I think it bore with him as much as weight as anything else—he would be failing the trust that the sheriff imposed in him.

Now, as I looked at The Duster in his trouble, feeling perfectly certain that what he could not solve would be a problem too great for me to touch, I suddenly saw a way out, or thought I did, so that I cried out: "Duster, I've got it!"

X

The moment I spoke, I felt that my idea wouldn't do, but still it was the only way to get out of this trouble. The Duster came over and laid a hand on my shoulder, waiting for the word.

"Go on, Baldy," he said.

"There's two things to do," I said, tying my forehead in a knot. "To get hold of the letter that Manness has written. . . ."

"Ah," said The Duster, "are there papers to be found?"

I saw him smiling a little.

"Aye," I said, "it's exactly like one of those yarns. You get the papers, and then. . . ."

"And then Manness simply writes another letter and undoes all my work?"

"And when you get the papers," I continued, "you land Manness and kill him before he can write again." I had followed out my own thought, although now I went into a panic as I saw the outcome of my idea.

The Duster stared at me as though I were wearing a new face. "Here's a good, gentle idea for an honest man who lives inside the law," he said. "Do you mean it, Baldy?"

"How else?" I said. "Is there any other way out for you, Duster?"

"There's no other way," he said, "and this way is impossible. I never could follow the back trail of Manness. Why, Baldy, that fellow leaves no more track upon the ground than a bird leaves in the air."

"Has he always been that way?"

"Aye, he was always the one to manage the retreats and the marches when we were together. A grizzly bear couldn't have solved some of the trail problems that he used to construct. No, no. I'd never be able to backtrack him. Especially since I don't know when the track was laid."

"Then couldn't you cast around and find some other way of striking at his hiding place for that letter? Who's the man around Christmas that would let Manness confide in him?"

"You can buy ninety out of a hundred people to do anything you want," said The Duster.

"But a thing like this is pretty important. Everything depends for him on his ability to trust the man that holds that letter. Suppose that the gent, instead of playing square, read the letter, and found out what was in it, and then either went directly to the police, or else came and sold the thing to you?"

The Duster nodded. He walked suddenly to the door and stood there with his head thrown back, breathing the night. When he turned back to me, he said: "My brain's in a muddle. Total muddle, Baldy. Love is like overeating. It leaves you fit for nothing but sleep. Now I'm going to tackle this business with a clear mind. Of course you're right. Manness would either trust that letter to a simpleton who had received nothing, or else to a crook like himself who had been well bought. If he's given the letter to an honest man, we're lost and can't do a thing about it. But if he's given it to a crook, then I may be able to spot the man, because I know most of the people he's familiar with. Who's in Christmas?"

"There's Willie Dunstan," I said to help along. "He's been in prison."

"Dunstan," said The Duster, "is a coward who got his sister's money by forgery. He's not a crook . . . he's a yellow low cur. Manness is not a fool, and nobody but a fool would trust a coward."

I was silent after this. The criminal world was apparently something that a person had to view from the inside, if he wished to know anything about it. So I said no more.

The Duster went on, reckoning over the list of the people he knew in Christmas who had done shady things. It was wonderful how well he knew them. Once I asked him how he could remember faces so well, and he said: "For eight years there's been a rope ready to hang me, and every man I meet may be the fellow who wants to tie it around my neck. That teaches you to watch faces, Baldy."

A pretty good answer, and the result was surprising. He ran off twenty names of people he had seen in Christmas who had some sort of a strong-arm record as criminals behind them. He went through a list of green-goods men, and all sorts of yeggs, and gunmen, and rustlers, and thieves of all kinds, and even down to sheer murderers. Most of those names he muttered to himself, and part of the list made my hair stand on end. The Duster knew things that the police didn't dream of.

"Chuck Partridge," he said—that wasn't the real name, of course. "There's a good chance. Chuck knew Manness back in Chicago, several years ago."

"Why," I said, "Partridge is just a plain grocer and the straightest man in town, everybody says."

"Sure they do," said The Duster. "Sometimes people ride so fast that they scare themselves into getting out of the saddle. And sometimes crooks commit crimes that scare them into going straight. It's that way with Chuck Partridge."

"I don't believe it, Duster," I said.

"Partridge did this," said The Duster. "I'm talking to you in confidence, mind you, but you ought to have an idea of what sort Partridge is, anyway. Partridge, about twelve years ago, was a second-story man back East. I won't tell you his real name, because you don't need to know it for this story's sake. But at any rate, he was a good, prosperous, steady, second-story man."

"What do you mean by good, steady, and prosperous second-story man?" I asked.

The Duster frowned a little, as though I were asking to have a perfectly obvious thing defined. "He was good," he said, "because he didn't use a lead pipe or carry a gun. He used to think that it would be better to be pinched than to shoot his way to liberty. The one thing he dreaded most was getting into a corner and killing anyone. He was steady, because he kept at the business year after year. He was prosperous, because although he never did anything really beautiful and big, like Harry Kline or Hal Dikkon, still he made plenty of hauls, and he didn't spend more than half his life in prison. You see?"

"I see," I said. I really didn't, but I did see how far Duster was from the world and the people I'd lived with.

"And one day while Partridge was going through an upstairs room, picking up some small loot, here and there, a man blundered into the room where he was. He was an old man with a white beard, and the crook saw his image in the mirror. Ordinarily Chuck would have paid no attention. But this time it was different. He had just got engaged to be married. He had been up so many times that the next job would take him ten years up the river. Suddenly these things all jumped through his mind. He turned and shot and put a bullet through the old man's heart.

"Afterward, it came out that the old fellow was blind, and the shock of knowing that he had done a murder, and a useless murder, was pretty tough on Chuck. So he married the girl, and took his savings, and moved out here to Christmas, where he's gone straight ever since."

It nearly paralyzed me to hear this. "If Chuck is a murderer, then anybody can be a murderer," I said.

"Of course," said The Duster. "You never said a truer thing than that."

I wonder if he was right. At any rate, it stumped me. I suppose it's an old idea that we're all crooked, except by luck. And that case of Partridge hammered the thought home in my brain.

"But Chuck has gone straight now," I said. "It may be one of the other crooks that Manness has used, but it's not likely to be Chuck."

"Because he's gone straight?"

"Yes. Exactly."

"Don't you see that because Chuck is straight, he's open to blackmail? And blackmail is the style of Manness. It's cheap. As for the danger, if he's willing to risk it with me, don't you think that he'd risk it with Chuck?"

I thought that over. Yes, if a man would venture on threatening The Duster, as Manness had done in my own hearing, then he was brave enough to attempt anything.

The Duster began to pace the floor again.

It was an odd thing that I could stand seeing him do almost anything, but it was hard for me to watch him walk the floor. I'd proved over and over again that, in spite of his crimes, The Duster was kind, good-natured, generous, and never the fellow to take advantage of such a man as I. Yet whenever I saw him pacing up and down, it gave me a chill, because there never was so much of the hunting cat in his manner. That long, gliding, noiseless step used to make me feel that he was about to turn around and start hunting me.

He had a way of pausing, when an idea struck him, and raising his head, and looking at you the way that a tiger in the zoo will sometimes turn its big yellow eyes on you. Altogether, I never was a comfortable man when The Duster was walking to and fro.

At last he said to me: "Baldy, it may be that I've argued myself into the idea, but it appears to me that, after I've talked him over, Chuck Partridge is the man with whom Manness must have left the letter."

"Go on," I urged. "It's only because we've been talking about him so much."

"Of course," admitted The Duster. "That may be what's put the thought so suddenly and firmly into my mind, but I really think that I can't get it out now. At any rate, Chuck may as well be our beginning."

"You have to begin somewhere," I said.

"Will you help me, Baldy?" he said.

"Of course," I said. "If I can."

"I think you can. Come along with me, and we'll start for his house now."

"You mean right now? Tonight?"

"How long do you think I have before me?" asked The Duster without impatience. "I'm due to join Manness tomorrow evening at the First National. Will you come, Baldy?"

All answers were scared out of me. At last I saw myself dragged into The Duster's net, but I couldn't very well let him down now. So I stood up and went with him into the darkness.

XI

We made no particular preparation. Someone had said that a good horse is always ready to run, and I suppose that The Duster was in the same class—always ready to fight; he had fought so many times before and had done so many terrible things that all

I wondered at was to find myself heading with him for what was sure to be a storm.

I remember that he was whistling softly as we went down the path while I was saying to myself that before long I was sure to be involved in an explosion that was apt to blow the top off my head.

As we came out from the path through the trees and to the roadside, we had a good view of Christmas lights rolling up the hill, looking as though everyone were awake, although we knew for sure that was not the case. Most people were getting ready for bed by this hour, but there was a cart coming down the road close to us, so close that we could hear the jounce and squeak of its innards as it pounded along, and the bump of the wheels on the ruts, and the rattle of loose spokes in the wheels.

This cart pulled up close to us, where we could see the shapes of a man and a woman in the seat, with the darkness drawn over them like masks and great coats.

"Is that you, John?" said the voice of Lamont.

It took my breath. I mean, the idea of the minister coming on us just as we were starting off on an errand that we hoped would end in the death of a man.

"Here I am," said The Duster, and went up close to the cart.

I held back a little, but I knew it was Lamont and his daughter.

"Marguerite couldn't sleep without seeing you again," said Lamont. "So here, I've brought her over. I couldn't sleep very well without seeing you again myself, Duster. Though I don't want you to think that you're marrying a family when you take my girl."

I heard The Duster laugh, high and light-hearted,

as though he had no more cares than a boy. Suddenly I was sure that his head was light. That is to say, he could not make himself groan and worry over things the way other people did, but could separate each instant from all that came before and after. If he were on his deathbed, he would have been able to criticize and enjoy a glass of wine ten seconds before he was gripped by the last agony. I never knew anybody else like that, able to keep the present unshadowed by the past and unpoisoned by the future.

I mused on that idea and didn't pay close heed to the first words of the talking, except that I heard Marguerite laughing after a while, and that was as sweet and happy a sound as ever came bubbling out of a girl's throat.

Then I made out that they were discussing what The Duster would be able to do in order to make a living and support a family. It was the minister's suggestion that they start this discussion. He was just the opposite of The Duster, and believed "in facing every difficulty before it became an actual menace."

"But that sort of thing never shortened a bridge in the history of the world," said The Duster.

"It's kept many a pantry filled, however," replied the minister. "You'd better do a little charting of the future before you and Marguerite actually start out."

"I could break broncos," said The Duster.

"Ah, John," the girl muttered—not audibly enough to make a real protest, but enough to show what she thought of her darling risking his neck that way.

"The Duster is made of whalebone," said the minister in answer to that soft cry. "But, as a matter of fact, there are other objections to that sort of a job."

"Yes," said The Duster. "It wears out a lot of trousers, for one thing."

"Of course it does," said the minister, "but it would never bring in the amount of money that you need to live on, John."

"I can live as cheaply as the next man," said The Duster. "I haven't any larger appetite than most, and three yards of cloth will make me a suit."

"You're used to having what you want," replied Lamont. "You ought to realize that about yourself, and, if you start playing poor and living poor, you'll soon be in torment."

"Listen to me," said The Duster. "I'll pull my share with most men. I know it won't all be a sweet song."

"It won't," said the minister, "and I know that you'll not give up easily. But I don't believe in pain, Duster. If you start in as a day laborer . . . well, it may not work out except to starve you of every pleasure in life and callous the heart of Margie, here."

"You don't know," the girl burst out. "Oh, but I can work."

"Of course you can," Lamont affirmed, "for otherwise we wouldn't have done much eating in my house the last few years. However, I must say that you ought to try an easier line than mere manual labor, Duster."

"I might open a hardware store," said The Duster, "and specialize in burglar tools."

I thought that was a little too much to say right in front of the girl, but that hard streak in The Duster had to come out in some way every now and then. She would have to take him with it, or leave him without it.

"I don't think that you'd need to specialize in burglars' tools," the minister said. "However, there's no doubt that the quality of your knives and guns would be trusted by everyone, Duster."

That set me back on my heels, you had better

believe—I mean, to hear the minister meet Thurlow on his own ground in such a rough and careless way. You might have thought that he didn't care a rap who his daughter married.

"Or there's insurance," said The Duster.

"A harder line than breaking broncos," said the minister, who seemed to know a good deal about life, after all.

"I think it is," agreed The Duster. "Then what do you say about circus work . . . like trick shooting?"

After this a little pause followed.

"You don't take this very seriously," said the minister.

"No, I don't," admitted The Duster. "When the time comes, I'll have my hands filled with honest work. I'm sure of that. There's always a gamble, but it's the honest man who plays the sure thing."

"How do you make that out?"

"He's sure that the police will leave him alone, and that's a piece of mind that I've never known."

Suddenly they all laughed together.

I was glad to hear that laughter, for it seemed to me that The Duster was carrying things along with a pretty high hand. However, Lamont almost immediately said that he realized it was foolish to offer advice to young people, and told The Duster to go his own way. The Duster had enough grace to thank him. Afterward, however, he stepped close to the cart and I saw him take the hands of Marguerite.

"Are you worried about the future?" he asked her.

"Not the least in the world," she said, and kissed him. "You're in the safe hands of Mister Wye, and he'll show the right road out."

That was pretty good of her, ringing me in that way, and sort of making me part of the family circle. They said good night in another moment, and the cart went off down the road, with Lamont clucking to the horse.

"Good man," said The Duster, looking after them, "but he's got the hen instinct. Has to have people under his wings and shelter them from the world. I'll tell you what, Baldy. Good men do almost as much harm as the bad ones. You can corrupt a young man by teaching him crooked cards, but you can also corrupt his life and make it turn rotten under his hands by making him too self-conscious and too afraid of the future. Take most of these moralists and virtuous men . . . they're apt to spend most of their time praising heaven . . . because they've been saved. No sailor would be glad to get the ship to port if there were no cargo aboard. And wherever I land, I'll bring something ashore, or sink the ship in trying."

I knew what he meant—which was that he meant to lead a full life and a rich one, even if it were not rich in money.

We walked on down the street together. The Duster whistling, as carefree as ever. Finally he said to me: "But about keeping in the hands of Baldy . . . that's a grand idea that I intend to follow."

"Bah," I said, "you're no more in my hands than in the hands of the wind."

He took on a troubled voice, just as though he really were bothered. "Don't say that, Baldy," he said. "Look at me tonight, about to commit robbery and murder just because you've advised me to do it."

Well, what could you say to a fellow like that? He would be laughing on his deathbed and groaning on his wedding day, without a doubt.

As we went along, I pointed out a house bigger than the rest—the Gardiner place, with a lot of old trees around it. It was one of the first places built in

Christmas, out of the money that old man Steve Gardiner made by shortchanging his customers out in Goldfield.

"Muncie has come to stay there," I said.

"I know it," answered The Duster, "and that's why I wanted to go this way."

"Why? To look at the house?"

"I want to call on him. Come along," he said.

I went along with him, of course, but a good deal puzzled by this idea of his. It would about give Muncie a fit, I thought, to see The Duster again, because no matter what others thought, I knew that Muncie still clung to the idea that The Duster was the guilty man in that Emmet robbery that had taken $600,000 out of the Muncie vault, and damaged his banking business more than you could reckon up in a day. However, so long as The Duster wanted to see the man, I had no objection.

He had brought a saddlebag along with him when he left the Ridley house, and this he slung over his shoulder as we went up to the Gardiner place and let the old wooden gate swing back with a creak on the weight of its pulley. So we walked up the path, and into one of the strangest interviews that I ever witnessed.

XII

A servant opened the door to us. He was as straight as an arrow, but he was so old that he looked sort of moldy. I mean his skin seemed covered with gray dust, and his hair was thin, and there was even a film over his eyes. Those eyes floated past me and settled on The Duster. It was plain that he knew him—everybody in Christmas did, for that matter, by this time.

He took us into the parlor. Parlors are bad anywhere, but they're worse in the West. Old Gardiner came from New England, and this was a regular transplanted New England parlor, all carpeted in blue, with red flowers, and enlarged photographs on the wall of hard-faced men wearing goat's beards, and women not even trying to smile, their clothes were so tight. There was a horsehair sofa, and some chairs with plush-covered seats, and, when we sat down on them, the springs inside creaked, all in a different key.

The man went out of the room and came back in another moment with Gardiner and Muncie.

You could see why they were friends. Solder them together and get all their blood running under one hide, and they'd about have made one man. They looked as though one square meal could last the two of them together for a month. Their eyes were always narrowed, like a prize fighter's, watching for an opening, and their mouths were tightly shut, with the muscles at the base of the jaw working softly in and out. These old men were childless, and looked it. They appeared light—like hawks that are fast on the wing and have strong claws for striking. As they came gliding through the door on their long, thin legs, they looked as though they were hunting for something on the floor.

The Duster chose to be glad and hearty at seeing them. "Hello, Mister Muncie," he said, and stepped forward with his hand out.

"Humph!" Muncie said, and put his hand behind his back. But he brought it out again, by jerks, as

though he were afraid that something would happen to him if he refused The Duster's greeting; he acted as though he were giving a signature on a blank check, the old skinflint.

"Well, Mister Muncie," said The Duster, "I just dropped in to find out if you have any possible trace of the two scoundrels who robbed you there in Emmet?"

"I know the name of one of them," Muncie declared, wrinkling his face.

"Do you?" The Duster said. "Then I suppose he'll soon be in jail."

"He should be," answered Muncie, "but he's a slippery young fox."

"What's his name?"

"John Thurlow, commonly called The Duster."

The Duster laughed. "Do you still pin that job on me, sir?" he asked.

"No other man in the world could have done what I saw done that night," said Muncie.

"But that robber was wounded in the side," The Duster reminded.

"There are tricks in every trade," replied Muncie, "and I don't pretend to understand the tricks of yours. Why did you come here, Thurlow?"

"To prove that I'm an honest man," said The Duster.

Old Muncie grinned, and so did Gardiner in the background. They looked like a pair of hawks, more than ever. But I was surprised that Muncie didn't rage and fume. Instead, he appeared like a fellow playing a hard game of cards, and trying to guess what lay in his opponent's hand. I began to admire him a little, for an old, tough sport.

"I'd like to hear the proof," said Muncie.

"I'll tell you what it is," said The Duster. "I'm willing to go to work for you."

Muncie nodded and smiled again. "Go on," he said. "I like the sound of your voice, Duster."

"You have a ranch down in the Big Bend," said The Duster.

"Well?"

"If you'll pay me a share of the profit, I'll run that ranch for you."

Muncie turned a little and looked at Gardiner, and then the two old cronies laughed silently together. But Muncie did not refuse The Duster's strange offer all at once. He seemed pleased to play with the idea for a while. He said: "You know cows, Duster?"

"No," said The Duster, "but I'm a good hand with a Colt."

"You know how to keep a herd clean of disease, and such things?"

"Not a bit," said The Duster, "but I'm handy with a rifle."

"You've had some experience on a ranch?"

"Not a whit of experience."

"Then why do you come here and ask me to hire you?"

"I'll tell you why," said The Duster. "But you'll have to stop asking questions and answer a few."

"Go on, my boy."

"How much ought that ranch to be worth, with the stock on it?"

"Three or four hundred thousand dollars, at least."

"How long have you had the land and the stock?"

"Twelve years."

"How much have you made on it?"

"Why . . . ," said Muncie, "I make a . . ."

"I'll answer for you. That land you've never made a penny on, and now you tell me why."

"The rascally Mexican robbers join hands with the white rustlers, and my cows are sluiced away through the mountains and never see the markets I fatten them for."

"Why do you hang onto the land?"

"I won't be beaten, not it if costs me a hundred thousand a year. I won't throw up my hands and quit." His teeth clicked. He was a fighter, that old bird of prey.

"You see how I fit in?" The Duster asked.

"I'm sorry," said Muncie, "but I'm getting old, and I don't see things as quickly as I used to."

"I'll explain. If you could get a return of fifteen thousand a year on that land, you'd be one of the happiest men in the world."

"Fifteen thousand? It isn't much for the investment."

"I know how much you spent to get the place," said The Duster.

Muncie blinked and failed to pursue the subject. "Fifteen thousand would be worth considering," he said. "Do you know of someone who wants to rent at that price?"

"I'll take it," said The Duster, "and you give me what I clear up above that sum."

"Go on," said Muncie. "Explain why I should trust you with such a place."

"Of course I'll explain. In the first place, I can stop the gaps in those mountains, and close the sluices that have been carrying your cows away."

"Very well," Muncie said, his eyes sharper and brighter than ever.

"And in the second place, my ignorance about cows doesn't really matter."

"No?"

"No, because Baldy Wye, here, knows cows from A to Z. He would be foreman of the place for me."

Muncie turned his head and gave me ten seconds of concentrated attention that made me red.

"Yes," he said. "I know about Wye, and he could run a place of that size, I think, with strong backing."

"Very well," said The Duster, "I've brought along a little contract here, and I'll be glad to take your signature on it. You can glance over the paper. It's very simple, and yet it includes all the points of importance."

He handed over the slip, but Muncie did not look at it. He stared at The Duster, instead. "Do you think that I'm a madman, my son?" he asked.

"Not at all. I think that you're a sensible man," The Duster assured him, "and that, therefore, you'll see your advantage."

"Or else see all my cattle cleaned off the place in a week?"

The Duster looked up to the ceiling for an idea— and found one. "I've been accused of killing, of crooked gambling, of robbery. But never accused of lying, Mister Muncie."

"Do you really expect that I'll take you on?"

"Yes."

"Will you tell me why?"

"Because you know that three days after I get to the ranch, there won't be a rustler on this side of the Río Grande."

Muncie turned again in his chair, slowly, and looked in silence at Gardiner, who broke out testily: "Don't be a fool, man. Are you getting childish in your old age?"

"You think that I ought to throw the paper away?"

"And the man after it," said Gardiner. "The scoundrel has helped to rob you of six hundred thousand dollars, and probably has half of the spoils in that same saddlebag he's carrying with him now."

Muncie started a little. He had taken out a pen and now turned it back and forth in his fingers. "I've generally taken your advice all my life long," he said. "Now, old fellow, I'm going against it. Duster, there's your contract." He slashed a signature on it and passed it back.

I was never more astonished in my life, and Gardiner groaned out loud.

"You haven't read the terms," said The Duster.

"I'm taking a blind chance," said Muncie, "and why should I strain my eyes to see in the dark?"

"You've dropped half a million to this man already!" raged Gardiner.

"Gardiner," said the old banker, "why throw in your shoes after your coat? Duster, you have the contract. When do you start south?"

"In a week . . . as soon as I'm safely married."

Muncie nodded, and then stood up. "Duster," he said, "you have a front of brass. You are going to make money for me . . . perhaps more than you've stolen from me."

"About that Emmet affair," said The Duster. "A friend of mine had a hand in that. He wanted me to assure you that the only reward he wanted out of that evening was the fun he had marching you across the street at the muzzle of his gun."

"Suppose I had jumped . . . would he have fired?" asked Muncie.

"He would have blown your backbone in two with all the pleasure in the world."

"I believe he would," Muncie concurred with a faint sigh.

"He had so much fun that he asked me to return the cash he brought away from the bank," said The Duster. "So I've carted it over in the saddlebag, and there you are. Good night, Muncie."

Away he went, with me staggering behind him, and in our wake a pair of the most astonished and silent men in the world.

XIII

What's the quality of every great man? Ease, I'd say. Even in athletics it's that way. The fellow who ties himself in knots of effort never arrives, but the sleek-moving man wins the race. The fighter with big cushions and pads of muscle all over him is knocked out by the thin armed slugger, who throws a wallop like a chunk of lead on the end of a rope. Your great pitcher has a soft action that won't wear out; I've seen them on the mound making the ball look as though it were a bird that had to go where the master sent it. It's the same way with men of brains. The easy-going fellow is the one who counts in the long run. He's the chap who does his thinking without getting dyspepsia, and the result is that he can keep on thinking all the year long, without fatigue, while your fellow with the knotted brow goes to sleep in the critical moment and loses a million in a minute.

Here was The Duster, lazying along the street, with a third of a million in a saddlebag, and taking it to return it to the hands of the man he'd stolen it from. But not bribing him with the hard cash—making his point first, and landing his job on a big scale by sheer effrontery. Then letting Muncie have his reward, so to speak, afterward.

Reporting the words of the conversation doesn't give the picture, but I remember that at the time I wasn't at all surprised that Muncie gave The Duster the job. He had placed me, too, with a single word, and given me a better chance than I'd ever dreamed of getting at my time in life, when the big new jobs are hard to come at.

Suddenly I had a great confidence that he would win out all down the line.

There was still the letter to get from Partridge, and there was still the meeting with Manness to accomplish before the morning should come, but I was certain that he would not fail. Which didn't keep the gooseflesh from running over me in shudders as I thought of the work that lay ahead.

We went up the street toward the Partridge house with no more hurry than when we had started.

The Duster said: "Where would Partridge keep a letter like that?"

"In a safe along with his store cash," I ventured.

"You forget what his business used to be," said The Duster. "He's seen too many little safes cracked with a can opener to want to take chances now with such things."

"In the attic, then, or the cellar."

"Simply because there are a lot of things to be searched through? Boxes, old trunks, *etcetera*? No, because every robber knows that time will cover that difficulty . . . time and patience."

"Are you going to find out where the letter is by simply talking about it?" I asked The Duster.

He stopped a moment, with his hand on the top of a picket fence, and his head lifted, as he often did when he was thinking hard. There were no clouds in the sky this night, except the mist of the Milky Way, but there was so much dust in the air that the stars were dim points. He didn't answer my question directly, but after a moment he thoughtfully said: "There's Chuck's house before us, and Chuck's in the garden."

"You mean to say that you can see Chuck there?" I said, because all I could make out was a blue of the heads of vines over the top of the fence.

"I can see the head of the spray from the sprinkler, however," said The Duster.

Now that I strained my eyes, I could make that out myself, faintly shining like a thin mist, or a ghost.

"Does that mean Chuck has to be in the garden?" I asked.

"You're going to make a mystery out of everything," said The Duster, chuckling a little, "like one of the sleuths in detective stories. But Chuck's wife is too fat and lazy to be in the garden at this time of night. Besides, Chuck loves gardens, and that's why he has about the only one in Christmas."

That made his reasoning seem simple enough. For certainly Chuck had the only lawn and almost the only lawn sprinkler in that town.

"If you'll go first and talk to him," said The Duster, "I'll take a look through his house and examine his desk, because it's just possible that he has put the letter there."

"And if you miss it?"

"Then I come out and take it from Partridge with a gun."

"He wouldn't be carrying it himself," I said.

"I think he would."

"At any rate," I said, "I'm not going to mix myself up in this affair, Duster. I'll do what I can to help you clean up the mess. As for Manness, I'd fight that cur any time for you. But, otherwise, you'll have to count me out of the thing. That's fair enough, isn't it?"

"Fair?" The Duster said in that voice of his which was halfway between a sneer and a laugh. "It's as fair as shining gold, and it'll get you into heaven. Will you go ahead and talk to Chuck?"

"While you sneak up behind and hold him up?" I asked, because I was getting angry by this time.

"Go on, then," he said, "and heaven help all good men to do something outside of their own salvation."

"Duster," I said, "there's not even any surety in you that Chuck Partridge so much as has the letter. And you want me to have a hand in robbing him of something?"

"Do this, then," said The Duster. "Go ahead and you'll find Chuck cooling himself in his shirt sleeves and singing to the water as it spills on the garden. Go up to him and say good evening, and ask him in the next breath where I can find Hector Manness. Will you do that for me? Then, when you leave, you can walk up the street and pay no more attention to what happens."

"And give you a signal about what I've heard?"

"I'll be close enough to hear that," said The Duster.

That made me a little angry again, because The Duster's assumption of omniscience and ubiquity would have made anyone grow hot for a flash.

"Let me think that over for a moment," I said.

He wanted my help, and yet he chose that moment to mock me again. "Ah, amaranthine thoughts of Baldy Wye," he declared, and walked slowly on.

I set my teeth when I heard this, but I controlled myself until I knew that my voice would be steady. "Duster," I said, "I can't work with you in this job." He did not answer, and then I added: "Perhaps you'd do Chuck no harm. But I simply don't feel like trusting you, or helping to put another man's life into your hands. . . ."

Still he did not answer. We had been strolling along for the last few seconds, and he seemed to have fallen behind, but, when I turned around, The Duster was gone!

It startled me, and then angered me again. We were walking along near a battered, seedy, time-worn fir hedge, as transparent as the naked ribs of a ship. Even at noon it would hardly have cast a shade on its own roots. I had no doubt that The Duster had slipped through a hole in this.

"Duster, Duster!" I called as loudly as I dared. "I tell you, I'm not going ahead in this job."

Still he did not answer. There was such trickiness and cheapness in this disappearance of his that I grew hotter than ever and really yearned to see him so that I could say what I thought of such cheapness. However, still he did not come, and all at once I knew that he would not come, but he had gone ahead of me and would soon be at his work in or near the house of the grocer of the two lives, Chuck Partridge.

"You can wait there forever, so far as I'm concerned," I muttered to myself, and turned on my heel.

Straightway, I turned back again, for once more the picture came into my mind of The Duster crouched there in the shadow, or stealing from one half-lighted place to another, waiting for me, and the power of his expectancy was more than I could endure.

I began to walk forward, telling myself that I would soon stop, but that I must think out the proper procedure. Then I told myself that I was simply hypnotized and that I must use my will against this young man, like a bird against a snake.

But still I walked forward. I remember looking down the long slope of the hill expecting to see the dim, star-struck blackness of the Christmas River in the hollow, but the valley was thick with a rising land mist that clouded the cool of the night in all the low places. Christmas Hill was surrounded by thin fog on all sides, and made me feel like a man walking out of the sea onto an island.

But still I went on against my will, until I came to the garden gate of Chuck Partridge, and I told myself that at least it would do no harm to see if that fake prophet, the young Duster, really was right about Chuck himself being out there at that time of night, watching the watering of his ground.

A whirl of wind came at me just then and filled my eyes and my nostrils with choking blow-sand, so that I was still choking and crying when I looked over the gate and down the path. There, sure enough, I saw the figure of Chuck in silhouette against the white face of his house. When I say that I recognized him by the silhouette, you'll be surprised, but I may say that the silhouette of Chuck was as personal and characteristic as the face of another man in the full light of the moon.

The curves in Chuck went all the wrong way. His chest was hollow, and his stomach flowed out magnificently, and he had a great hump behind his shoulders that thrust his head out in front at a downward angle. His neck, which ought to have been huge to match the big, flabby hanging jowls of his face, instead was quite thin and very long, and it looked always rigid, as if with the weight that it was carrying around, and red as sunburn, or the chafing of his coat collar.

He was standing there, as The Duster said, watching the rising of the spray that went upward from the patent lawn sprinkler and was known rather by its whispering sound than its sight as it first arose against the shadow of the hedge, stood up silver and thin against the sky above, and fell showering back. There was a sound of hushing as the water swept out, and there was also the pattering of a very light rain. I hardly wondered that Chuck should stand there to get cool, as late as this, with all his house black and sleeping behind him.

Now, out of the hills beyond Christmas, in the direction of the mines, I heard a tremor of sound that, at that distance, I knew must be a great charge of powder, detonated at this late hour. But that did not surprise me so much as the fulfillment of The Duster's little prophecy. Because it made me feel that he must be absolutely right in every respect in his judgments.

XIV

A man can grow tired of mystery. When I was a kid, I've lain alone at night in camp or in a house listening to sounds until I got bored with being frightened, and simply got up and yawned, or else turned over and fell asleep like a stone. I was tired of this mystery about The Duster's foreknowledge in the same way, and I said: "Hello, Chuck! That you up so late?"

He came over to me with a fat man's waddle, and, when he spoke, there was a taste of salt sea in his voice—I mean it was hoarse as a sea storm blowing. As a matter of fact, he was an old bluenose. He came so close that he could put a hand on the top of the gate post and he spoke in a confiding way, which he nearly always had, as though he were inviting you into the most private chamber of his mind.

"I like to come out here, Baldy," he said, "and listen to the ground drinking, and let the wind blow a couple or three puffs of the spray against my face. Because, afterward, I'm sure of a cool sleep, and it satisfies my thirst more'n a half dozen bottles of ice-cold beer, if you foller along what I mean?"

I said that I did. "You ought've been a farmer, Chuck," I said, "liking the ground this much, and the things that it grows."

"The ground is honest, Baldy," he said. "It gives you back what you put into it. It ain't a bank. It gives you back a tree for an acorn, and is plumb ashamed of itself if it can't return you a thousand percent. This here garden of mine, it's got a big heart, which means something. And when it's willing to do so much for me! . . . Look at that wisteria, will you? I planted that just five years back, and look where it's growed all over the whole dog-gone' face of the house, will you? In five years! I say, when the ground will do that much for me, why shouldn't I do something back for it . . . which it's only asking for water? So I come out along here in the evening and turn the sprinkler loose. Sometimes my old woman, she sets there in the rocking chair . . . you can see it by the pillar . . . and she rattles the newspaper and pretends to read by the light that comes out through the window, but really it's the same as me . . . listening to the water falling, and the roots drinking, and the whole dog-gone' place saying thank you under its breath. I tell you, I listen, like that, and it's far better than any conversation."

It made me feel good to hear him talk like this. It made me feel warm around the heart and pity him a little, the way you always pity children that are not smart, the way you always pity simplicity wherever you meet it, even when you make use of it.

I remembered what The Duster had said about this man, and, although I couldn't think that he actually would lie about Chuck, still I had an idea that he was as wrong as could be about him now. If Chuck was not a good man and an honest citizen now, I would eat any man's hat.

I almost laughed, but I let the question pop out, anyway. "The Duster wants me to ask you where he can find Manness, Chuck," I said.

The grocer didn't answer. His slanting neck, and his hanging, big head on the end of it, made him look as though he was a buzzard standing there and thinking it over, with his fat hand still on the gate post. But then he sort of slipped and slid and wrapped his thick, soft arms around the top of his post, and laid his head on those arms.

I couldn't make out what he was saying, except that he was whispering something softly to himself. I was so amazed and disgusted that you wouldn't believe me.

I poked my finger at him. It went into his shoulder like into the stomach of another man. "Chuck," I said, "brace yourself up, will you?"

He made a big effort, I could see the wave of it go up through his body. "I'll brace up," he said. "But it took me aback. It . . . it pretty near sunk me." He reached out, and, over my hand, he put one of his, wet and soft as a warm sponge. "Baldy," he said with a dreadful quavering in his voice, "I always wanted . . . my wife, too . . . my wife and me . . . always wanted to have you in to dinner, Baldy . . . which I mean to say . . . well, old friends . . ."

I couldn't listen to this. It made me so terrible sick and dizzy. The Duster was right. I knew that. I suddenly could see this man shoot down the old blind fellow. The same man who would do that would now be here muttering and trembling and begging at this garden gate—but probably willing to murder me, too, if he thought that would preserve the quiet of his life and of his house.

I loathed him. But, somehow, my heart swelled up with pity and sorrow so that it almost broke. He might be a toad, but he had made a woman happy, and he had built this house, and he had made the only garden that ever grew in Christmas, this ex-second-story man.

"I only want to know, Chuck," I said, "just that, and I'm gone. I'm not talking. Besides, I don't know anything. I'm only told to come here and ask you this question."

He seemed to be shaking his head, but I knew that this was only the result of the horrible uncertainty of his nerves. He was so close now that I could see the quivering of his fat, pendulous cheeks, and the loose gaping of his mouth.

Mind you, there was no man in Christmas so much loved as Chuck Partridge that knew the first name of every mother's son and daughter in the town, and that used to have his pockets filled with store candy for the children, and that used to be Santa Claus on the big day of the year, the day that gave the town its name. One of the little kids had called him Mr. Christmas, and we all thought that it was a pretty good name for him.

Yet, one touch from The Duster, and this poor wretch was a shaking pulp. It disgusted me. But it also made me almost hate The Duster.

"It's a sudden question, Baldy," he said, "even from an old friend like you . . . which, as I was saying, we ain't had a chance to see you as much as we would like . . . only, Baldy . . . oh, heaven help me now. . . ."

Do you think that sometimes fat men are like women? Only strong on the outside, but going to bits under a pinch. At any rate, poor Chuck began to clasp his thick hands together and gasp out his words. Then I remembered that The Duster had asked me only to put the question, not to insist upon any answer to it.

So I said: "It's all right, old-timer. I don't know anything. I've asked a question. You couldn't answer it. Good night, and don't let this spoil your sleep."

I started to back away, but he almost broke the gate down, throwing his arms out and dragging me back as if he loved me. "Don't go, Baldy!" he said over and over. "Don't go!"

"I won't," I told him. "Damn it, don't you hear me? I won't go, Chuck, poor fellow. I'm staying here as long as you want me to. Now, what's the matter?"

He could only keep on clinging to me and begging like a woman. He began to cry. I never felt so sick and embarrassed and hot in my life as I did that moment with Mr. Christmas, the best-loved man in the town.

"If you go, The Duster himself will come for me," he said. "And if Manness is a ghost, The Duster is a monster . . . I beg your pardon . . . he's your friend . . . you know a little joke, Baldy, and . . ." He actually tried to laugh, the poor disintegrated fat rat.

"I'm here," said a soft voice at the side of the hedge, "but not to do you any harm, Chuck."

It was The Duster himself.

I grabbed Chuck under the pit of the arm, for I really expected him to drop down to the ground when The Duster appeared. If I had upset him with a question, what would the great Duster do? But I was wrong. Imagination was stronger than fact with Chuck Partridge, it appeared, for now he stiffened up and stopped his whimpering and whispering.

"Duster," he announced. "I don't know why you should have sent to me to find out about a dead man."

"Hush," The Duster said kindly and gently. "Don't bother with lies and deceptions, Chuck, and tell me at once where to find Manness."

Partridge made a gargling sound, but then he added: "Duster, whether he's in heaven or . . . No, Duster, I really don't know where he is. . . ."

"Give me your wallet," said The Duster.

"Aye, willingly," said the grocer. "You could have more money than there is in that, if you needed it, Duster. I'm your friend. I mean to say, I believe in you, and I've always admired you, and . . ." He brought out his wallet and was handing it to The Duster, but The Duster, instead of taking the wallet, caught at the thick arm of the grocer and then pulled a letter out of the sleeve. "You still have a fast hand, Chuck," he said.

Partridge fell loosely back against the gate post, but he didn't say a word. I could listen to his breathing, distinctly, and even that was shaky, like the beating of a fibrillating heart.

The Duster put the envelope into his pocket.

"Now . . . Manness," he said. "Tell me quickly, Chuck, where Manness can be found."

"Manness . . . Manness . . . ," said Chuck. "I . . . I . . . what do you want with him, Duster?" He kept wetting his lips with his tongue. He couldn't speak at all without doing that repeatedly. Yet he never got his voice above the hoarse whisper.

"I'm going to kill him," said The Duster, "so tell me where he is, Chuck, and I'll guarantee that he'll never bother you again."

I expected Chuck to answer at once. But he didn't. No, sir, paralyzed with fear as he was, still he wouldn't betray what he knew of Manness. It was the strangest contrast of terror and shame and pride and decency that I ever saw or heard of. Poor Chuck.

The Duster didn't press the question at all. In fact, he stepped back a trifle from the fat man, and then he said softly, with real wonder in his voice: "I didn't guess that, but I might have. Manness is actually in this house, Chuck."

XV

So that was the explanation of Chuck's reticence. Ex-crook, and broken in spirit as he was, still he had enough of the West in him to want to be true to the duties of a host, even though the guest had foisted himself into his house. Well, that was one of the strangest things that I ever heard of. It gave me a chill up the spine, like impossible, brave things that you read of in books, or hear some grand liar tell.

I had another chill that was worth two of anything that Chuck gave me, and that was to think that The Duster might be right in his guess, for there he was, turning on his heel and walking back down the path toward the front door of the house.

That great billowy monster of a man, Partridge, lurched after him, but I had sense and strength enough to grab him and haul him back.

"I've got to stop him," whispered big Chuck. "I've got to save . . ."

"D'you have to save one killer from another?" I asked him sharply, and somehow that way of putting it enabled him to pull himself together.

We stood there—with me feeling wonderfully glad that I was outside the gate instead of inside, on the same property where a fine tragedy might occur at any moment. I was in a better position to run, I mean, and yet I was so excited that I wouldn't have been any farther away.

So we watched The Duster go down the path, even on the noisy gravel of it, his footfall making no more than a whisper. He went up the porch and disappeared in the steep shadow of the verandah roof. Then, although we didn't hear or see another thing of him, somehow I knew that he had opened the screen door and entered the house. Then the suspense grew terrible. I've had the feeling that comes when a fighting man pulls a gun on you and aims down the barrel—that the time of waiting was very much like this.

I still wondered how he would go to work in the dark of that house. There were a lot of places that would possibly have to be searched if he wanted to find the sleeping chamber of the great Manness.

We waited there, holding each other up, as you might say, on opposite sides of the gate.

All at once, fat Partridge said to me: "Look here, Baldy. I only planted those roses two years ago, and look at them now."

Yes, that was what he actually said as we stood there waiting for the noise of the battle. Right on the heels of this strange speech of his, there was the loud, hollow report of a revolver inside the house—the sound of a revolver and not of a rifle, because one can recognize a rifle shot by the metallic clangor of it. There was that one shot, which made the hair lift on my head, and then a form slid out of a window in front of the house and slithered down the verandah roof and toppled over the edge.

The shadow might be The Duster. It ought to be Manness. But it hung there with both hands from the echinus of one of the pillars, and then dropped to the path beneath. It slumped down to the ground, and then fled around a corner of the house.

"Manness!" I said the Partridge. "It's Manness, and he's left The Duster dead in your house!"

Mrs. Partridge began to scream then, inside the house, and both Partridge and I went on the run. We let her shout, while we started searching for The Duster, and failed to find him, but in the door of one of the front bedrooms, now standing open, we found a little half-inch hole such as .45-caliber slug would bore.

"The Duster isn't here," Partridge stated calmly enough. "Manness shot this bullet through the door and then ran for it, and, between now and the morning, they're going to meet somewhere, and have the thing out. I hope they kill each other . . . and be hanged to them both!"

He was pretty much himself again, and I said to him: "Partridge, whatever happens, when your neighbors come spilling in here in another moment, all you know is that you heard a shot, and a man came out through that front window, and dropped to the ground and ran. A burglar, you think, that had had a fight with his partner while they were actually about to loot the place. Is that straight? Or d'you want people to know that you've had Manness in your house?"

He turned a blinking, hostile eye on me, and then nodded. "You're right," he said. He looked as though he wanted to say still more. It was plain to see that, now he had recovered his nerve in the midst of some hot action, he hated me because of what I knew about him—or what he guessed that I knew. At any rate, I know that I had an uncomfortable feeling in the small of my back when I turned away from him and started down the stairs, where Mrs. Partridge was still squawking foolishly.

From the head of the stairs her husband said one word, not overloud, and she shut up as though a hand had been clapped over her mouth.

As I went out from the house, I was amazed because all the neighbors were not pouring in up the path, but, as a matter of fact, I suppose the noise of that shot, muffled inside the walls of the house, was not a quarter as loud as it had seemed to our straining ears at the garden gate.

I went down the path, with the water spray whispering like a ghost in the air and standing like a ghost against the stars, and out through that gate, and so down the street and straight for home. That is, if I could call the Ridley house home, but the days I had spent there with The Duster had been so exciting and so crowded, that I felt about half my life had been heaped into that short space of time.

Going up that path through the trees, I had a new idea, and, turning aside, I went out to look at the horses in the barn. There was only one of the bays beside the shed, and the one that was missing was my Dolly mare.

So I could guess that the great Hector Manness, running for his life with the threat of Thurlow behind him, had got out of the town on horseback, and The Duster had followed him, making a detour long enough to put himself in possession of the mare. He knew her speed and her heart and her wise footing in bad going—no better horse than Dolly for a manhunt.

They were gone, the two of them. It made me think of the world as a small place, and two giants galloping across the black, rough curve of it on the skyline.

Then I went to bed. Well, there was no use in sitting up. I lit the lamp and put it by my bed, and smoked a cigarette, and tried to read, but that was no good, for I still had to look up from the page. So at last I blew the lamp out and fell asleep, dreaming of a battle between a cat and a snake in which the snake had its coils around the body of the cat and the latter had its teeth in the throat of the viper.

Then I woke up and saw a silhouette standing in the doorway. It slid aside into the shadow beside that door, and I thought that I recognized that side-step.

Had Manness come back there? Yes, to murder me, and so wipe out the other man who knew that he was alive. The great Duster lay dead somewhere, and his body, perhaps, would never be found or buried. I thought of those things, and all at once the fear left me, because, to tell you the truth, I felt so much grief that there was no room at all for fear left in me.

I got my gun with one sweep of the hand and slid

out of the bed, when I heard a voice saying quietly: "Don't shoot, Baldy."

It was The Duster, after all.

"Duster!" I said. "Duster!"

"Well?" he said very dryly.

That withered up my foolishness and made a man of me again.

"Maybe you'd like some coffee?" I suggested.

"Sure . . . if there's any around."

I went and built up a fire in the kitchen stove— and I remember that there was still a red coal among the ashes—and I soon had a big pot of coffee boiling.

The Duster stayed in the next room, and I could hear him moving about and humming, but I didn't go in there, and he didn't come in to me.

Only when the coffee was ready, I carried the pot back in, and I had a couple of big tin mugs to drink it out of, because I guessed that we both needed it a good deal.

When I came in, the first thing I noticed was a black smudge on the forehead of The Duster. I gave it a good look, and knew that it was a powder burn.

"You must've had a backfire when you were out hunting squirrels with your shotgun," I said.

"As a matter of fact," The Duster replied, "that's exactly what happened." And he smiled at me.

Yah! That sent a shudder through me—his smile, I mean, and something sort of sleek and contented about him, like a cat that's been fed on fish all it can eat. I knew that he'd killed Hector Manness. I knew it so well that I didn't have to ask, and that Manness had come so near to killing him that the powder smudge on his face might have marked a bullet's passage through his brain, instead.

He drank two cups of scalding coffee, one after another.

"Chuck's place shows what can be done with water," he commented.

"Aye," I said, "it certainly is wonderful how he's made the things grow and cover up that sandy ground."

"Yes," The Duster said, "water's a great thing to cover up, or to carry away."

And that, believe it or not, is the only word that he ever said to me about the death of Manness, or just how it came about. Although I've eaten out my heart many a time to know, still I guess that my dream was just about right.

What The Duster wanted me to know by his words was that the Christmas River was rolling the body of Hector Manness toward its cataracts and waterfalls.

XVI

How to wind up, I hardly can tell. But I suppose that it would be more logical to carry along down to the time when we came to the ranch in the Big Bend.

There is plenty to tell about that life, and especially about that day when Muncie wired that The Duster was discharged on the spot, and how The Duster wired back saying: **Do you really prefer to have me join you in the north?**

Muncie did not prefer to have The Duster join him in the north, and a mighty wise man he was not to, because there would have been a gun on The

Duster's hip when he made the trip. He was wise for other reasons as well, because, although we had the big pinch all right, and felt it to the bone, still we managed to pull through. The Duster's ignorance about cattle was a big handicap, but he was right in what he told Muncie—and a good hand with a revolver and a rifle was about what the ranch needed in that country, and in those days.

Well, I suppose that there is no use in talking about things in the Big Bend, although that's where the really interesting yarn begins, and where I can show you today as fine a gang of Herefords as ever clacked hoof or mooed at the calf pen. But the way that people are raised and the way that they read books, they've got into the habit of thinking that a marriage is the end of things and not the beginning. Although every day we can see that marriages start a lot of stuff—stuff that can't be finished by those that begin the fight, as you might say. However, I can't tell about the days in the Big Bend, because you wouldn't like to carry on that far, and you want to know how The Duster married Marguerite Lamont.

Well, you know already.

Of course, the whole town was there, but the big sensation was not the real wedding, I think. The Duster had had a talk with his father-in-law before the wedding, and, when he marched down that church aisle, who was behind him as his best man? Why, it shocked people breathless, but, of course, you've guessed already. Yes, it was Renney. But even that wasn't the biggest shock.

For just before the ceremony began, somebody noticed a youngish, tallish boy, mighty brown in the face, standing in a corner.

"By the jumping Lord Harry," said the man next to me. "If that ain't Tommy Lamont."

Yes, it was Tommy, and not back in defiance of the law, either. He'd come there to Christmas because that same Sheriff Renney had seen the governor, and because the governor was a white man, and understood that Renney knew best. So back came Tommy Lamont with a grave, brown, young face, and stood there in the corner, worshiping his pretty sister, but loving The Duster even more.

Well, I don't see why I should spread myself on account of the wedding, and the flowers, and the talk of the town, and all the sort of things that newspapers write on such occasions. The Christmas paper has that account, and you can read it there.

The really amazing thing was the way that The Duster softened up when the pinch came, and hardly played the man at all.

"Stay close to me, Baldy," he said.

"Why," I returned, "you're turning yellow."

"I need a drink," he said.

"You better have one, then," I advised.

He gave me a look. "And meet her with a dizzy head? No, no, Baldy, from this minute I need all my wits . . . in order," he said, "to walk straight."

I knew what he meant. It was a neat way to put it. Well, he was as white as a sheet when he went down the aisle, and everybody noticed it.

"How noble he looks," I heard a goose of a woman say as we went by.

He did, though, and, when he had put on the ring, and they were tied firmly and tightly by the words of Lamont, and he had given the girl to The Duster with his own hands, why, sir, The Duster was so shaking that he could hardly manage to face her.

"Kiss her, you loon," I whispered.

Which he finally done, but Marguerite, while she was as cool as you please, and like a child playing a game and mighty happy at it, she heard what I had said, and over the shoulder of The Duster she gave me her sweetest smile.

"Thank you, Baldy," she said.

Now the church business was finished, and we all got out and went by the big, loose, smiling face of Chuck Partridge, who had cleaned his garden plumb out of flowers in honor of that day. And we got home to Lamont's shack, and there we had supper together. I mean, the boys and Lamont and me, because The Duster and Margie didn't count much, except to one another.

It was a good meal, although the venison had been a mite too long in the Dutch oven. It was good, though.

I remember toward the end, I was telling a story about my first job as a straw boss, and, as I made a pause before coming to the main point, I heard The Duster saying softly to Marguerite: "Darling, when did you first care for me?"

Well, it sickened me. I mean, the idea of a man like The Duster making such a plumb fool of himself, like any young jackass who didn't know how to act.

I took a quick look over at the girl, expecting to see her laugh at him, and tell him to be his age, but not at all. No, sir, her head was raised and tilted back a little, and she was looking at the moon, you might say, and her eyes were like a soft, blue mist.

"I know when it was," she said. "Oh, always from the first moment I saw you, dear, but most of all, finally, when I saw you standing with your head bent at the grave of your poor friend, Hector Manness. That made me love you, John, because I knew from that moment how gentle and kind you were at heart."

NIGHT HAWK

STEPHEN OVERHOLSER

He came to the ranch with a mile-wide chip on his shoulder and no experience whatsoever. But it was either work on the Circle L or rot in jail, and he figured even the toughest labor was better than a life behind bars. He's got a lot to learn though, and he'd better learn it fast because he's about to face one of the toughest cattle drives in the country. They've got an ornery herd, not much water and danger everywhere they look. The greenhorn the cowboys call Night Hawk may not know much, but he does know this: The smallest mistake could cost him his life.

ISBN 10: 0-8439-5840-5
ISBN 13: 978-0-8439-5840-9 $5.99 US/$7.99 CAN

MEDICINE ROAD

WILL HENRY

Mountain man Jim Bridger is counting on Jesse Callahan. He knows that Callahan is the best man to lead the wagon train that's delivering guns and ammunition to Bridger's trading post at Green River. But Brigham Young has sworn to wipe out Bridger's posts, and he's hired Arapahoe warrior Watonga to capture those weapons at any cost. Bridger, Young and Watonga all have big plans for those guns, but it's all going to come down to just how tough Callahan can be. He's going to have to be tougher than leather if he hopes to make it to the post...alive.

ISBN 10: 0-8439-5814-6
ISBN 13: 978-0-8439-5814-0 $5.99 US/$7.99 CAN